a HUNT of BLOOD & IRON

A HUNT of BLOOD & IRON

THE WILD HUNT
BOOK ONE

CARA NOX

STELLA CHARTA PRESS

A HUNT OF BLOOD & IRON

Copyright © 2024 by Cara Nox
Cover and interior design by Stella Charta Press, LLC

Published by Stella Charta Press, LLC.
stellachartapress.com

ISBN 978-1-960379-08-5 (hardcover)
ISBN 978-1-960379-07-8 (paperback)
ISBN 978-1-960379-06-1 (e-book)

For more information on the publisher, including upcoming releases, preorder bonuses, giveaways, and more, visit stellachartapress.com.
For more details on the author and their works, visit caranox.com.

For those struggling with themselves.

CONTENT WARNINGS

I've attempted to compile a list of prominent warning keywords to the best of my ability. However, since I'm only human, it's very possible I've glossed over something that could be sensitive to you. Please use your own discretion when reading and only continue if you feel safe to do so.

This story contains: Alcohol, anxiety, blood, childhood trauma and abuse, death, depression, discrimination, emotional abuse, gore, grief, implications of suicidal thoughts, manipulation, murder, physical abuse, post-traumatic stress episodes, self-harm, stalking, torture, violence, and vomiting.

a HUNT *of* BLOOD & IRON

GREY

"Nothing comes without sacrifice."

The words drifted up to the loft, shackling themselves around Grey's wrists, lightly stained with charcoal. He ran the stick over the paper, shadows dancing with each movement in the orange glow of the setting sun. Flittering, torn sheets of off-black fabric hung over his little nest, framing crumbling buildings slowly sparking to life with candlelight.

"We *know*," whined one of the children clustered past the dilapidated railing.

"What's that got to do with the story?" piped up another.

The husky chuckle of the older man soothingly clung to Grey's soul, like smoke on his clothes from the clove cigars the man enjoyed every morning. "Tonight's tale begins with a brave knight from all the way back when the world first fell to the Wild Hunt."

Silence descended, save the creak of the older man's wooden chair and Grey's pale hand dragging against parchment. Soft blades of grass climbed upward with each flick, filling in his imaginary landscape of someplace far from here where midnight hues wrapped themselves around stones and trees circling this clearing —the one from his dreams.

"She was a fledgling macharomancer—"

Grey quietly scoffed, shaking his head while he began smudging the shadows of his work. A bitter tang welled up from the back of his throat, and he swiped away a phantom twitch under his left eye.

"And her lover was a skilled austromancer princess, trapped by her own father, the king of their young little kingdom. Every few nights, the princess would travel via dreams to her dear knight, but every time she did this, it would leave her body weak and unrested. Eventually, the king became suspicious, and called upon his captive sciomancer to force his daughter into a deep, dreamless sleep."

A little hand shot up, and Grey peered over the railing again.

"Yes?"

"Don't sciomancers feed on dreams?"

"Ah, that they do." He wagged a finger at the boy, a twinkle in his dark eyes. "And that was the king's first mistake. He didn't yet understand the true scope of his enemies' powers, so he sat back, pleased he had solved his problem without realizing that he'd given his captive a wellspring of it."

Grey wiped his hand on the knee of his pants and stood, wandering over to the large, metal lever. The crisscrossing bulbs drooping from the ceiling brightened in the wake of the fading sun, but the children were still glued to their storyteller like they were every night. He leaned over the railing, shaggy black hair dipping over his eyes as he let himself fall into the story as well.

"The princess, realizing something had gone horribly

wrong, had suspected that the captive had been made to consume her dreams, and snuck down to the dungeons to bargain with him. She said that if he could allow her half of a night's dream, he could have the other, and then they could both benefit. He agreed, and they plotted their escape with the aid of the knight.

"Every night, the princess taught the knight the layout of the castle, pointing out its weak spots when it came to enemy magic. And the knight gathered up a small army of mancers, who helped train her in exchange for a shot at looting the palace or taking revenge on the king from a past transgression."

A shrill little voice cut in. "What kind of loot?"

"Yeah! Was it faerie treasure? Soul glass?"

"A sacrificial ruby? Oh! Oh! What about—"

The man laughed and brought his hands down in a placating gesture. "That's not really important, but let's say it was a lot of alchemist gold."

The children broke into excited whispers, and Grey hummed a gentle sigh, his fingers curling around the lacquered wood. All anticipation was ripped away with the squeal of a door and an older woman stepped inside, dropping a bag in the entry with a clatter of goods tucked within. Every eye snapped to her and her prominent scowl.

"Atticus, shouldn't these children be home by now? The sun's gone down."

A chorus of tiny pleas cried out, and Atticus softly clapped his palms together. "I suppose this tale will have to conclude tomorrow. Aunt Ingrid is right. I guess I let time get away from me." He rose, and his audience of pouting children clamored to their feet, trying their hands at one last attempt to convince him otherwise before Ingrid nudged them out the door.

"Honestly, Atti, you really shouldn't be filling the neighborhood kids' heads with fluffy stories—"

"They're not just *fluffy stories*," he said, mirth creeping into his tone.

Ingrid's eyes scaled the ladder, finally narrowing on Grey. "Is he lying?" Her tone flat.

Grey hesitated, pushing his hair to the side with a grimace. "I'm not sure, but... I don't think it's a great idea to be romanticizing other mancers..."

She shot Atticus a scowl, but the man simply rolled his eyes.

"I think you two are being too overly critical—"

"Overly critical?" Ingrid folded her arms over her chest. "Grey, come down here."

He swallowed, pushing off the railing and sliding down the metal ladder's frame. Dust stirred up at his feet the moment his shoes hit the floorboards, each following step a complaint on his way to stand next to them both.

Ingrid gripped his arm, shoving his hair away from his left eye for Atticus, who turned his head away like he'd been slapped—all lightheartedness gone from his expression, traded for a wince of pain. Pain because of the milky iris staring back at him, even though Grey couldn't see through it. He felt his hair fall back into place, mostly obscuring it from view again.

"Do you really want to lure those kids into a false sense of security?" she asked, her forehead wrinkling. "Think about how so many of us have died at the hands of other mancers or tortured because they despise our abilities—*us*. This boy shouldn't have had some sick, twisted individual cheer over beating his magic and robbing him of part of his sight."

Grey's head dipped, and he tugged his sleeves down over his hands, feeling awkwardly embarrassed about the entire situation.

Ingrid sighed, Grey's ear perking at the scrape of her boots against the floor just outside of his periphery. Her steps dampened as she moved further into the hovel of an apartment.

"Grey," Atticus breathed. "You know I didn't mean any harm—"

"I know." He lifted his chin, locking gazes with those twinkling, hopeful eyes set into such a rugged frame of a face—rugged with spots from age and sun exposure instead of the many fights he used to tell Grey stories about.

A small smirk returned, and he reached for Grey's shoulder. The warm, strong weight that followed anchored him in the midst of that deep, haunting ache. "I'm honestly surprised you haven't up and left us by now. A bright young thing like you shouldn't be hold up with a couple of old maids."

Grey huffed a short laugh. "Forty-something isn't that old—"

"Please, forty-nine is practically fifty. I've lived well over two of your lives." His fingers pressed into his muscle. "When I was twenty-one, I was itching to see the world, and you're just sitting up there night and day with your drawings and journaled musings."

He pushed Atticus's hand away, shaking his head. "And I'm fine with that."

"What are you going to do when you finally feel your Calling?"

He snorted. "Ingrid said not everyone has a Calling. I think I would've run into it by now."

"There's still time, and I don't want you to be afraid when it keeps you up at night and tries to drag you outside this wreck of a town." Atticus waved his finger in front of Grey's nose.

He bit back a bemused smirk. "I'm not nearly as adventurous as you, Uncle Atti."

"You never know, my boy. You never know."

Warmth settled in Grey's belly as he sank into his mattress after dinner, curled up with his journal and a chewed-up pen. His drawing from earlier puffed up the prior pages from where he pasted it inside like a captured memory, where it pushed back with each word pressed into its conjoined piece.

Every inked letter soothed him closer toward sleep, along with the soft humming drifting from the neighbor's window. He yawned and stretched as he set his flimsy, leather-bound notebook to the side and huddled into the blankets. His eyes closed, and the world vanished for a fraction of a second.

In a blink, the apartment was dark, the melodic notes climbing through the window had ceased, and pale light spilled over the floorboards, licking at the railing. He turned over, half-sitting up to bask in the presence of the moon's waxing state. Grey's head dropped back down to the pillow before he rolled over to his back, sucking in a deep, calming breath and closing his eyes.

But this time, sleep didn't take him.

Instead, the image of his drawing seared into his eyelids, taunting him. Grimacing, he threw back the covers and sat up, rubbing at his face. Each movement turned into a jolt, demanding he keep going, like some restless creature had slunk under his skin. He pulled on his worn, faded hoodie over his rumpled black shirt. Muddied boots were tugged over slim, ripped, dark jeans. His hands absently shoved item after item into his bag—a lantern, a compass, a knife, a small collection of coins he'd saved from the artwork he'd been commissioned for. Then his fingers twitched as he reached for his journal, resting next to his small heap of art supplies.

That alarm pulsed through him, snapping at him to hurry like a rabid dog on his heels. Grey scooped it up, dumped it into his bag, and bundled up his supplies to tuck them inside as well. He scurried over to the ladder, quietly crawling down until a creak sounded at the bottom.

"No Calling, hm?"

Grey spun around, eyes wide as he caught Atticus lingering at the edge of the hall, leaning against the corner. A soft, tired smile tipped up the corner of his mouth. Grey swallowed.

But Atticus started for the kitchen, plucking open the cabinets and wrapping homemade protein bars and dried fruit in cheesecloth. "You should probably take some food with you just in case you're traveling out of the way for a few days." He slid the care package across the counter in offering as Grey finally moved from the other end of the small living room. The padded, quiet tap of cabinets closing again gave him pause with his bag dipping off his shoulder.

"I don't want to inconvenience you two—"

"Please, Grey, like you've ever done that." Atticus turned back around and rested his forearms against the smooth granite. "We had the choice to dump you in the arms of someone else, and we chose to keep you. You'll always be our son—nephew, whatever you want to call it. Blood or no blood, you're always welcome here. We will always take care of you."

Grey fought against the pressure pricking at the backs of his eyes, opting for a nod instead of a thank you for fear of his voice cracking. He collected the dry goods as Atticus rounded the counter and pulled him into a hug. The faint notes of cloves made his heart squeeze before anticipating that final pat on the back.

And then Grey was out in the hallway of the complex, half the windows boarded up with the other half blown out and cleared away. He jogged down the stairs, goosebumps running up and down his arms the further he traveled alongside the cool night air. The propped open door at the end of the candle-lit lobby gave way to car-cluttered streets. Each one positioned to be a rusted, moss-covered, makeshift barricade to deter any mischievous fair folk from the nearby forest. He made his way through to the huddled group of insomniacs posted at the edge of town, always on watch like guards.

"Grey?" one of them asked, a trail of smoke pouring from his lips as his cigarette wafted to his side. "Going somewhere?"

"Yeah," he breathed, slowing at the rim of rubble and rebar.

A couple of them shared hesitant glances and frowns. "Where?"

"Don't know yet."

"Ah," the first replied with a knowing smirk. "Enjoy the ride then. We'll look forward to the party once you get back. Safe Calling."

A clap on the back, then another with a call for good luck, and Grey weaved his way past the makeshift wall into the sea of charred houses. Straight into the undulating shadows within the untamed woods in the early hours of the morning.

⚘ 2 ⚘

GREY

A warm, orange hue spilled over the clearing before Grey, framing a decaying city basking in the last light of day before it was snuffed out by impending night. He gripped his bag strap as he stumbled closer to the iron-link fence on aching legs. The steel sheets reinforcing it barely held off the vines weaving through the diamonds.

His heart leapt into his throat when he glimpsed the two guards starting to push the gates shut. "Wait!" he called, waving his hand as he sprinted across the last stretch.

One paused and reached for something at his hip. "State your business."

Grey stopped short, skidding against the mix of gravel and asphalt underfoot the second the guard's weapon glinted—darkened steel and rounded muzzle. He threw up his hands and swallowed. "I-I'm just a traveler."

The gun still dangled at the guard's side while the other put his hand on the one at his own belt, quietly waiting for a signal to back up his partner. Guard number one frowned and jerked his chin toward him. "Mark or no entry."

Grey hesitated, sweat breaking out along his spine, especially once he saw the unadorned triangle inked on his opponent's uncovered forearm. He slowly reached for his sleeve, his heart racing as he pulled it up. His own reversed triangle with two lines —the upper bar just short of touching the edges while the lower struck cleanly through.

The halomancer guard scowled, but he beckoned for Grey to come forward. He slunk toward him, ducking his head before he was directed to stand just inside the gate. A resounding *clang* of the two bumping together and latching into place sent chills through Grey.

"Follow me," the halomancer guard snapped, mid-stride on his way past.

Grey jogged behind and worried at the ends of his sleeves as he noted the additional ring of barrier between him and the inner wards. He peered past the vertical bars to the dilapidated cinderblock, brick, and corrugated, rusted metal all obscuring his view of anyone dwelling within. A heavy door squealed open, and he tensed up, jerking to a stop before the halomancer nodded for him to step inside.

"Bren will get you checked into the city," he grumbled. "Don't cause any trouble for him, or you can spend the night in a cell."

Grey jumped as the door slammed shut behind him, the guard leaving him in a room where he could touch both walls with his fingertips if he stretched his arms out into a T. A single, dim, exposed lightbulb hung above a small square table and folding chairs with another door lingering behind it.

He shifted and readjusted his bag before wiping his palms on his pants. From the sweat starting to slide down the back of his neck, it had to be at least several degrees warmer in this box of a room, especially with the lack of wind he'd enjoyed outside. Grey jolted as the far door opened to a man in crisp, white button-up with the sleeves rolled to his elbows—his black-inked sliced-through triangle mark on full display.

Austromancer.

The man—Bren, Grey supposed—nudged up his round wire glasses with a knuckle. "Please, have a seat."

Grey absently nodded and pulled back the chair in time with Bren, settling into the ripped padding with a teeth-gritting *squeak*.

"So..." Bren began, unfolding a piece of paper and flattening it out against the table. "I'll need your name, approximate age, and your reason for admittance."

Grey's fingers dug into his knees. "Um, my name is Grey—with an E." He watched him quickly scribble it down. "I'm twenty."

"And you're a hemomancer?" Bren glanced up with a raised brow.

"Y-yes," Grey whispered, noting the man's pursed lips and subtle nod as he recreated his hemomancer mark. "I-is that a problem?"

Bren hesitated. "No, however, we do have the requirement that hemomancers wear gloves while in public. If you're caught without them, that's grounds for a night in the cells."

"O-oh." He swallowed. "I-I don't have any gloves." Grey reached for his bag with the bizarre hope that there would be a pair in there.

"We have spares," Bren said with the wave of a hand. "I can collect a set for you after we're done with the paperwork. Onto the reason for admittance first."

"I'm just traveling," Grey said, rubbing his hands together under the table.

"So you're passing through?"

"Um, I might need to stay for a couple nights, but I don't know yet."

Bren scowled. "You don't know?"

He squirmed in his seat. "Well, um, I'm in the middle of a Calling—"

His eyes lit up with a sudden understanding. "Ah. Understood." He quickly jotted something else down before smoothly drawing what had to be his signature at the bottom of the page. "All right, assuming you're telling the truth, I'll be giving you a temporary pass and gloves. Should you be caught without either of these..." He motioned for Grey to finish for him.

"Cells?" Grey said quietly.

"Cells. Same goes for if we discover you're lying about any of the information you've given me, including the reason for being here. We don't take kindly to hemomancers that take advantage of the system to continue serial killing."

Grey's eyes widened, and he shook his head. "I wouldn't—"

"Yes, yes, I'm sure." He snapped the paper in the air. "I'll be right back with your things, and then you'll be released into the city." His chair scraped against the cement floor, followed by the rush of a small breeze with the door swinging open and closed again.

Grey fidgeted with the loose threads of his bag while he waited. The Calling didn't nag him in any way he'd expected, despite still being unsure of where he was meant to be going, let alone what he should be *doing*. He straightened again when the door popped open and Bren waved him through.

He scrambled out of his seat and slammed his hip into the

corner of the table on his way out. Wincing, he hobbled through the caged hallway to an open window with a small shelf bearing a thick-banded, neon-green, nylon bracelet and a pair of gloves with that same violent green color stitched into the backs in the pattern of hemomancer marks.

Bren handed them over, careful not to make any skin-to-skin contact, which made Grey's heart drop. He should've expected it, but the action stung worse than he cared to admit, especially after dwelling solely among other hemomancers that trusted each other. Those who pulled blood from other mancers were an anomaly—something Uncle Atticus depicted in tales as unhinged monsters, corrupted by the fair folk.

But Grey tugged on the bracelet and the gloves, trying to ignore the sting of rejection that came with them. Bren turned his key in the gate's lock and pushed it open.

"You're free to go. Behave, and you'll be fine."

Grey ducked through the doorway with the *clang* of the gate sounding behind him. He stared up at the half-exposed stairways climbing upward in the shells of once-magnificent buildings towering over the walkways below. Awe overtook him as he slowly spun around to soak it all in: the people kicking their legs off the balconies missing railings, nature breaking through patches of broken cement and hunks of metal to cling to walls and spread roots underfoot, and the individuals enjoying the last gasp of the evening sunlight while they snapped on electric lamps and lit candles in storefront windows and bars.

He stared forward, folding his gloved, marked hands under his crossed arms like he was fighting off a non-existent chill on his way to find a hot meal and a bed. The clusters of mancers dipping in and out of crowded venues made his stomach clench—no way to tell who was what with the blur of sleeves, bandanas, and jewelry obscuring their marks as they passed.

The double doors to a pub with a hand-carved sign greeted him, drawing him in like a moth to a flame, despite having to side-step the patrons walking out with thermoses in hand. Quiet jokes about heading off to work drifted between them as Grey slipped past and inhaled the homey scent of roasting potatoes. He walked past the booths, gripping his bag strap on his way to the bar to claim a seat.

Grey hoisted himself onto a wood-topped stool and gently dropped his bag at his feet with a brief glance around at the other customers chatting amongst themselves, not paying him any attention until a bartender stopped in front of him. His head swiveled around to a kind-eyed woman with tight curls. "What can I do for you, sweetheart?"

He wrung his hands under the bar counter. "Could I get a glass of water?"

"Sure thing," she said, tapping the countertop before she spun around and plucked up a glass. A moment later it scraped against the wood countertop in front of him. "Can I get you something to eat too?"

"Yeah, actually… What's today's special?"

"Grilled chicken with a side of roasted, cheesy potatoes. Does that work?"

He nodded, and she beamed before trotting off to the kitchen. Grey reached for the glass, knocking some of it back until he caught a man glowering in his direction from the corner of his good eye. He quickly set the glass back down and hid his gloved hands under the counter again. Unfortunately, the whispers had already started with the guy leaning over to talk to the other person he was with, who then, in turn, glanced over his shoulder at Grey. They got up from their bar seats and moved down to the other end, earning confused looks from the other patrons.

The scrape of a chair at one of the tables a little further down made Grey squeeze his hands together in shame. Every stray eye moved from him, back to their dining companion and then occasionally slipped back, forcing his heart to pound in time with the demanding clap of soles against the plank flooring. When it stopped, a hand shot out and gripped the countertop next to him, followed by a body slinking into the stool in front of it. But Grey could only focus on the neon-green stitching of the glove until the fellow hemomancer leaned forward to disrupt his line of sight.

A wicked, feral grin and sharp, dark eyes barely visible behind a shaggy mop of dark hair just about stopped his heart. "Hey there, kid? I'm guessing you're new to town. Name's Hyde." He held out his hand to hover in the small gap between them.

Grey fidgeted with his gloves, glancing around the pub with that trickle of fear of other peoples' reactions to his magic.

"Hey—"

His head whipped around to the scowling bartender. She set the plate down with a little more force than Grey expected, making him jump. But her irritation wasn't aimed at Grey—it was at *Hyde*.

"Leave this boy alone," she snapped. "You're lucky I haven't kicked you out yet—"

"What?" he drawled, a self-satisfied smirk tugging at the corner of his mouth. "I can't talk to one of my own?"

Her lips parted in surprise as her eyes darted over to Grey, who instinctively reached for his hair to brush it over his face like it might hide him—and ripped his arm back down the second her face twisted in conflict. She'd seen that mark, but instead of commenting on it, she turned and moved onto the next patron.

Shame wormed through him, even more so when Hyde sighed and dropped his chin into his palm. "I'd get used to that sort of reaction if I were you," he mumbled as he watched her go. "Not many people around here care for hemomancers. They assume we're all one bad day away from snapping. We might as well be outcast as fair folk at this rate, so it's no wonder we have our own havens."

Grey hesitantly picked up his silverware and began cutting into his chicken, despite the sickening feeling that churned in his gut. "I'm Grey, by the way," he whispered.

A soft chuckle sounded in return. "I also take it you're new to the cold shoulder treatment?"

"A little. I've only ever lived around other hemomancers."

"Well, there's a small ward of us here in the city if you're looking for a place to stay."

Grey lifted his head, finally meeting his eyes again as he halted his cutting. "Really?"

That sharp, cutting smile surfaced again. "Of course. We got to take care of each other in a place like this."

<hr>

Hyde whistled as he led the way through the streets, though Grey stumbled every couple blocks on uneven pavement. A few heads turned to find the source of the noise before their gazes drifted to Grey. The worried and perturbed looks followed them from shadowed nooks in stairwells and overhangs as they passed, even with some starting for their doors to turn in for the night.

That is, until a commotion up ahead drew them away from their hovels. Heads poked out of dimly lit window frames and doorways while Hyde's tune faltered and cut short with his stroll.

Grey stopped alongside him, taking in the small crowd surging forward in front of another sector gate.

"They're coming!" cried a woman wobbling on a crate along a bisecting wall. "The fair folk will destroy this place and rip us all to pieces if we don't give them what they want. I've *seen it—*"

Hyde scoffed and grumbled, "Another damn lithomancer off their rocker."

Murmurs rippled through the crowd before a young man piped up: "But the last Wild Hunt was a decade ago, wasn't it? The fair folk shouldn't be asking for another just yet, should they?" His head swiveled around, as if to confirm with the rest of the gawkers.

"He's right," an older man chimed in, scratching his beard. "They're usually at least a quarter century apart."

The woman stomped on the crate, demanding the crowd's attention again. "Then how do you explain the increased aggression from the woods? Are you claiming not to hear the howls at night?"

She threw her arm out toward the wall obscuring the pinkish-purple gasp of evening. Right on cue, a shrill scream of a creature ripped through the air. Everyone jumped or tensed, their fear echoed by a baby's cry from a window.

Her arm fell back against her side with her chin held high. "It's never been this bad since before the last Wild Hunt," she ground out. "Believe my vision or not, but if we don't give them what they want soon, they'll bring the Hunt *here.*"

A sharp whistle cut her off, and Grey immediately recoiled, jerking his hands up to his ears as every eye turned to Hyde. He cleared his throat and loosely held out his arms in a slight shrug. "You act as if the Grand Capital's legion hasn't always taken care of this when it's time to ship off our little sacrifices for the fair folk's blood sport." They crowd shifted and glanced around at each other while the woman glared daggers at him.

"That's not—"

"Always the case?" Hyde growled. "It *is*. Those fuckers have tea with the damn fair folk from what I've heard. They're more than willing to collect a few mancers to appease them and continue living their cushy lives while they leave the rest of us to squabble over things we need to survive. So, if you don't mind" — he stepped forward, showing off the back of his gloves, instantly parting the sea of people with glimmers of fear in their eyes— "us hemomancers are just trying to head home for the night."

People shuffled back or dispersed as Hyde led the way past. Grey scurried behind him with his head down, only half-hiding his gloves in the folds of his sweatshirt or under his bag strap. The jingle of the chain-link fence signaled their freedom from scrutiny, followed by a sharp clang as it fell back in the frame.

"Fucking doomsayers," Hyde hissed. "They act like they don't know that the fair folk want entertainment more than anything. There's a reason why they agreed to not killing us forever ago in favor of just taking six to torment—a game to mess with each mancer in fun new ways." He wiggled his fingers like a street magician might after swindling their audience.

Grey shuffled alongside him as they passed an older man whittling a small piece of wood. He rocked back and forth in time with Hyde's footsteps on their way up to the building. An exchange of nods gave way to the man eyeing Grey, but he said nothing on his way inside, despite the curious glint to his gaze.

The door creaked open to a decrepit, propped-open oven, pumping heat into the crumbling duplex. Its main floor's adjoining wall was partially blown out with fae-crafted letters carved into the wood like an ominous threat. Hyde strode along them and started up the stairs, his voice echoing off the paneling: "The spare room's at the end of the hall. Marielle—the old guy's daughter—typically makes breakfast after her morning shopping. I'll ask her to make a little extra for you so you don't go hungry."

Grey sputtered. "You don't have to—"

Hyde waved a hand as they reached the landing. "Please, it's not a big deal. Us hemomancers got to stick together, right?" His smirk was far less sharp and menacing this time, traded for something softer and worn. He patted Grey on the shoulder and nudged him toward his room. "Get some rest. One of us will show you around in the morning."

GREY

Halfway through the night, Grey had jolted awake to a shrill, high-pitched cry somewhere beyond the city wall. His heart pumped in his chest as he scrambled to sit up in bed and claw at the thin blanket covering the window soaked in moonlight. City guards patrolled the grated catwalk just inside the wall and pointed into the depths of the woods.

Shimmering reds, yellows, oranges, and violets popped in and out in pairs like glowing gems. Streaks of light appeared and disappeared in zigzags through the brush until the wall obscured the view, the fae creatures prowling closer to the boundary.

The guards slung their rifles from their backs and ripped pistols from their holsters. Growls and screams from the predators rippled through the air, making Grey shiver as the crack of gunfire clashed against it.

He didn't sleep for the rest of the night after that.

The whimpers of wounded fae and guards' complaints kept him from drifting. His fingers curled into the blankets like they had so many years ago when he'd sat in the grass of a clearing and marveled at the flowers blooming in midday to recharge their nightly glow. The memory of his mother kneeling down beside him still remained seared into his mind, even if her face was hazy now.

This is what the fair folk have always sought to protect, so it's vital to remember to respect them for preserving these wonders.

He could practically feel her ruffling his hair before taking his hand and leading him to a quiet, shaded spot to enjoy a small picnic of tea and biscuits.

His cheek sank further into his pillow as the hours waned, pulling him into the first gasp of morning light. He swung his legs over the side of the bed and tugged on his boots before heading to the washroom to clean up. Grey's mouth watered at the scent of freshly-cooked bacon and bread wafting through the floorboards, beckoning him down the stairs and into a kitchen where Hyde lingered at the island with a coffee mug and watched a woman with curly, pinned-back hair maneuver through her work space.

"Did you talk to the city guards this morning?" Hyde asked her with his mug hovering near his lips.

"Yes," she replied, a sigh lacing that breath of a word before turning around. Two plates of warm, buttered bread, fried eggs, and crisp bacon scraped against the table after her eyes snapped to Grey, who still lingered in the kitchen doorway. A warm smile took over the flicker of surprise on her face, and Hyde shifted in his seat to follow her gaze.

"Ah, you're awake," he said, smirking and patting the countertop next to him. "Grey, this is Marielle. Marielle, Grey."

Grey gave a timid wave and scurried up to his spot, where she pushed one of the plates in front of him. When he opened his mouth to object and nudge it back toward her, she shook her head and turned to pull down another plate.

"So, what brings you out this way, Grey?" she asked through the clinks of silverware.

"Calling," he said, barely above a whisper before biting into the still-steaming hunk of bread—just the comfort he needed after the cold welcome of yesterday.

Marielle raised a brow as she slid her plate in front of theirs and started for the water pitcher. "I would say that's rather exciting if it weren't for the fair folk getting so aggressive lately. The city guard had to fend off a small pack of faerie beasts last night. They didn't really detail the damage, but it didn't sound particularly reassuring..."

The splash of water filling each glass cut through the yelps echoing through Grey's mind from earlier that morning. The fork's handle dug into his hand.

"If you feel the urge to leave," she said, turning and setting a cup down by his plate, "do let us know, all right? I'd hate for you to go wandering out into the night and get ripped apart by those things."

Hyde snorted. "You don't honestly think this is going to continue, do you? It's probably a weird season change or moon phase—"

"It's been over a month." Marielle shook her head with a grimace. "Not to mention I've heard talk about quarantining hemomancers because they think a blood moon is coming and we'll wipe out the town." She sighed into her glass, sending ripples through the water. "It always gets worse before it gets better."

Hyde waved his fork around. "You're right, you're right.

Enough doom and gloom for now. Why do *you* think you're here, Grey? Hm?" That smirk reappeared, and Marielle rolled her eyes.

Grey stiffened the second all attention shifted back to him.

"You don't have to answ—" she started, Hyde clicking his tongue at her.

"Um…" Grey began, pushing egg around his plate. "I'm not really all that sure."

"What are your strong suits?" Hyde pressed. "Marielle, here is an excellent chef, so her calling brought her to set up a small little restaurant here. And I'm here because I have a knack for story-telling. Even some of the other districts have me entertaining on the weekends." A glimmer of amusement danced in his eyes as he nursed his coffee again. "So? What do you tend to gravitate toward?"

Grey's chewing slowed as he locked onto the dirt under his fingernails—the graphite nearly uncleanable from nights upon nights of sketching. He swallowed. "Drawing."

"Oh ho? An artist?" Hyde grinned and nudged him with an elbow, nearly knocking the glass from Grey's hand. "You'll have to show us. Imagine all the commissions you could do around here. I could see some of these people paying handsomely for something like that."

The water shook as Grey forced out a nervous chuckle. "I had some people commission me back home, but I'm not so sure anyone would—I mean, there are a lot more people here, and they probably have a lot more talent—"

"Please," Hyde drawled. "How about a demonstration before lunch so Marielle and I can be the judge of that?" His razor-sharp grin told him he couldn't argue, so he nodded instead.

Hyde puffed out a draw of his cigarette beside Grey while they sat on the porch. The old man continued his carving and hummed a slight tune as pages flipped back and forth with scrutiny in Hyde's grasp.

Grey shifted and pinned his hands between his knees to keep from squirming as he waited for Hyde to say something—a torturous activity that was cut short by movement along the edge of the steps. An orange tabby stared back at him, creeping closer to sniff his boot.

His couldn't help but smile, his stress from Hyde's scrutiny melting away in favor of gaining the small creature's approval. He held out his gloved hand for the cat to sniff, hoping they wouldn't be offended that it might've smelled strange and musty from wherever the town had been storing these spares.

A thorough examination from the feline, and he was rewarded with a headbutt against the back of his hand. His heart squeezed as he reached to scratch under their chin, and the cat inched forward for more.

The turn of another page broke Grey from his trance, and he cleared his throat, still trying to focus his energy on the cat. "They're nothing really that spectacular..."

A huff of smoke slipped past Hyde's lips with a chuckle. "Nothing spectacular?" He shook his head. "You could certainly make a pretty penny from this sort of talent, hemomancer or not. Hell, some of these people might start thinking better of us if you offered this up to the wealthier folk in the center of the city." Hyde snapped the journal shut, took another long puff of his cigarette, and pushed himself to his feet. The cat gave him a perturbed look, flicking their tail with a growl before Hyde took a step down and the creature skittered off.

Grey's heart sank as he watched the cat dart down an alley. He scrambled to his feet, hopping forward to catch himself as Hyde started to wander off with the cloth-bound book in his grasp. "Can I have it ba—"

Hyde *tsked* and flicked ashes against the crumbling pavement. "Not until I sell someone a portrait to get your foot in the door."

Grey sputtered and grabbed Hyde's sleeve, the fabric slipping through his gloves with awkward grip. "W-wait—"

He spun around and held the journal above his shoulder in challenge. "What you have is something that can be used to bring us a little more respect. *This* is your Calling, Grey. And I feel like it's part of my duty to finesse the sale of your artistry to flip our reputation." His brows knit together in concern as Grey pulled on the strings of his hoodie. "You're nervous."

"I-I'm not exactly—" Grey forced out, starting to reach for his eye before he stopped himself, letting it hide behind his hair. "Not exactly comfortable sharing that with other people. It's sort of a personal sketch journal of sorts, so..." His arms snaked around his body in a self-hug.

Hyde's forearm wobbled and dipped before he held it back out for Grey. "Then why don't we find you a fresh sheet of paper and a place to sketch, hm?"

He spun on his heel and picked up his languid stride toward a side street. Grey hurried behind, ducking and weaving past refuse in the form of metal and plastic bins, mattresses bleeding stuffing, and glass bottles. Hyde made a sharp turn past a light pole and jogged through the propped-open door.

Grey skidded to a stop on the threshold and gaped. Neatly lined containers of bundled and single pencils and baskets of paper propped up notebooks on the bookshelves. It was more than Grey had ever encountered back home. Uncle Atticus had given him his journal as a gift shortly after taking him in and told him to take good care of it. Looking at the sad state it was in now with its chewed-up edges and warped paper, he supposed it'd at least been well-loved.

But, unlike Grey deciding to gawk in the door frame, Hyde pressed on to the back of the shop, dropping his gloved hands to the counter in front of another hemomancer tending to her ledger. "Yes, Hyde?" she asked, pushing up her glasses with an elongated sigh. "If you're here for another notebook—"

"I'm actually here for some thicker paper. Something with some smoother texture to it too, perhaps."

Her face scrunched up before her dark eyes flicked to Grey. Her choppy, dark hair fell over her eyes for a second before she brushed it away, and she moved to the other end of the counter. "Should I ask *why?*"

"Trying to help my friend here," he said, half-turning and motioning for Grey to creep a little closer past the various metal baskets and plastic storage bins in this nook of a supply store.

Friend. What a strange thing to call Grey, a boy who didn't really have *friends.* Friends—keepers of secrets, hopes, dreams, fears, and sorrows—were a luxury he couldn't afford because his heart was too fragile to share.

The shopkeeper hummed and flipped through a couple boxes. "How many pieces?"

"Two."

She slid them against the countertop and Hyde plucked a couple metal coins from his pocket when Grey reached into his bag.

It's on me, he mouthed as he dropped them into the woman's open palm.

The warble of the sheets flapping in Hyde's grip called Grey to follow him. Like a fawn following its mother, he chased after

Hyde through more streets to the hulking mass of an iron-laced wall. That emblem of safety and dread backdropped a patch of wildflowers and rogue weeds, drawing Grey toward it, despite Hyde stopping short. Grey dropped his bag and crouched at the edge of the field, letting his gloved fingertips tickle the dandelions and daisies.

"What do you think?" Hyde mused with a chuckle, nudging his knee with a boot. "Think you could show off your skills with a little slice of paradise like this?"

By the time Grey finished up, it was lunch, and Marielle welcomed them both back with sandwiches and lemonade. She gushed over the graphite sketches while his drink sloshed in the glass, pins and needles still biting as his legs, even though he thought it would've worn off during the walk back.

Hyde vanished shortly after the meal with a ragged notebook in hand, spouting off how he'd take Grey out in the morning to gather him some patrons. And the house descended into tranquility.

Itchy tranquility.

Grey's legs bounced as he flipped through his journal at the kitchen island until Marielle's clasped hands slid against the countertop into view. "Something wrong, Grey?"

His head jerked up, and he bit his lip with fingers pressing into paper. "Um... I..." He folded the journal shut. "I think the Calling wants me to leave." He hated saying that, but the restlessness that seeped into his soul pained him just as much. The people he'd found here were too nice, too helpful, too *perfect* for what he'd expected being dragged to. That had to be the explanation with how badly he wanted to refuse to give into the phantom force nagging at him.

Marielle frowned and her head dipped slightly to the side, tendrils of hair cascading past her cheek. "Are you sure?"

He scoffed. "No, but—"

"I've always said the Calling is a bit of a cruel faerie trick," she whispered. "It sends us out and away from the people we once knew to keep us uncertain and afraid." She pushed away and turned to the oven, popping it open to the fresh scent of warm cookies. "Why don't I pack some of these up for you for the road then?"

Grey slid off the stool. "You don't have to—"

But she was already bundling them up and shaking her head. "I know I don't have to." Marielle placed the cheesecloth of cookies in front of him. "Us hemomancers have to stick together."

He'd left the neon-green-stitched gloves behind for another hemomancer to take his place in the sanctuary of a house he'd dragged himself away from. Marielle's quick hug and whisper to stay safe lingered with him as the sun dropped in the sky, conjuring the shadows. The Calling didn't let him idle for more than five minutes, it's cry more and more urgent as dusk closed in, rolling over the sky like a blanket that made Grey long for sleep. He clapped his hand over his mouth as a yawn slipped out and half-stumbled over roots into the edge of a clearing.

Blue-green blades of grass reached for the waning sunlight, an eerie, ethereal glow coaxing him further inside. Grey rubbed his arms, biting down on his tongue as he slowly crept along. The crunch and snap of small stones and twigs under his boots made every nerve in his body jump. Finally, a shadow came into view, its shape pointing skyward like a beacon to the stars.

Grey stopped short, the purple glow of the horizon slipping away as he took in the monument from his dreams. Only this time, it bore a detail he hadn't seen before: a hemomancer mark chiseled into the top of the obelisk. He took a shuffling step to the right, tilting his head as he caught another faceted mark engraved in the stone.

A right-side-up triangle. The mark for halomancer.

His knees buckled, and his head whipped around at the sound of a pop several yards back. The shadowy figure with short, choppy hair poking out of a knit cap froze like a deer in headlights. They both jumped at the quiet rumble of a motorcycle, and Grey spun to a guy dismounting his bike on his left—a tilted arrow inked on his arm.

"Oh, shit," came a hiss from the other side of the obelisk just before high beams powered on behind them.

Grey threw up his arms in defense, the light forcing him to squint until the rev of a new engine jump-started his heart. They were all Called here.

To a six-sided obelisk.

Six mancers—one of each.

Six sacrifices for the Wild Hunt.

This time his instincts overrode his Calling.

Run.

He sprinted back across the clearing, fueled by pure adrenaline and the crazed, frenzied cries of the drivers and feral goons giving chase.

Faster.

Grey glanced over his shoulder before pitching forward and smacking against the grass. He scrambled back to his feet, ducking into the brush and slipped. A yelp escaped him in his tumble down a small hill. The wind pushed from his lungs when he collided with a tree, sending his head spinning as he shakily pulled himself up.

Tears sprang to his eyes as the voices grew closer, and he gulped down air the second his body would allow it during his pathetic half-jog, half-limp away from the obelisk, despite losing some of his bearings. He gasped, leaves curling and fluttering downward as his pain receded, like he was the bringer of autumn.

Keep running.

Breaking into a sprint again, he shot forward, his legs crying out just before a shock rippled through his body. He seized, falling backward with a scream tearing from his throat as small, dazzling sparks ran along the near-invisible mesh net. The crunch of newly dried, shriveled leaves turned his scream into a sob.

"Aw, come on, kid. You should be honored."

A gloved hand wrapped around his arm, dragging him away from the fence. Grey twisted, gritting his teeth as he flailed in his attempt to sink his fingertips into the guy's flesh.

"Careful," came another man's voice. "Think this one's our hemomancer."

Another sharp crunch reverberated through Grey's soul, chilling him to the core. "Let me *fucking go*—" He batted away a second glove reaching for his bag.

"Flip him over and pin him. This is too damn dangerous without him restrained."

Grey flailed as a tongue clicked in displeasure, but his body trembled too hard to resist the press into the grass. A knee dug into the small of his back as rough leather struggled to push his wrists together.

"Now, now, if you'd just cooperate, we wouldn't have to tie you u—"

A howl of a scream rang out eerily close by, his enthusiastic captor pausing while the other shifted just out of Grey's view. The spinning of rubber wheels trying to find traction on grass caught, and the skipping hum of a motor grew louder. Grey bucked, his captor cursed, and a single headlight spanned the small pathway before illuminating the forest to his right, painting the foliage in buttery yellow.

The *click* of a gun cocking sounded before his captor's guard sprawled out on the ground, his weapon misfiring as it collided with the dirt. His captor growled, seizing Grey's wrists in one hand and ripping something from his belt with the other, jostling him with the motion before it was accompanied by a blood-curdling scream.

Grey felt his grip loosen and shoved him off, stumbling to his feet and lurching forward toward the bike—toward the macharomancer from the clearing. His whole body recoiled, but he forced out, "Th-there's an electric barrier—"

The macharomancer's green eyes widened for a fraction of a second before hardening again, his hand going for a blade sticking out of his boot. "There are more coming. Get on."

Every fiber of his being screamed that this was a mistake—that he was better off slumping over in the grass until the wardens came to collect him than escaping with this guy on his motorcycle. The sharp, phantom pain returned to his left eye, subconsciously recounting the moment a twelve-year-old Grey screamed and sobbed into the cellar floor pooled with his blood and knew he'd be blind in a matter of days.

His pulse thundered in his ears as rallying calls echoed through the clearing beyond the woods, and Grey threw his leg over the back of the bike, wrapping his arms around his enemy and sole ally. He squeezed his eyes shut, gritted his teeth, and prayed to whatever might have mercy on his soul before the motorcycle shot forward. A tingle of electricity raised the hair on Grey's arms for a breath, and then it was gone, along with the hungry cries for sacrifices.

❀ 4 ❀

NOEL

"Stop the bike."

Noel almost didn't hear the muffled plea against his denim jacket over the roar of the engine. It'd been the vibration of his passenger's chest pulsing along his back that made his ears perk with the delayed message clicking in his mind to slow down. Before he knew it, the guy was bent over a bush, heaving until he collapsed against a tree.

He shut off the bike, the keys jingling in his grip as he kicked the stand into place and crept toward his new companion—his fellow *Hunt prey*, he supposed. "You okay?"

"Fuck no," he breathed, dragging his sleeve across his mouth.

Noel ran a hand through his sandy brown hair, glancing back down the trail of bent grass left from his motorcycle. "Hey, I know you're stressed, but we should probably keep moving since they've probably realized they're down at least two prey and there's a gaping hole in their fence."

"Why?" he croaked. "Why did you save me?"

"Well…" Noel forced out a breath. "For starters, we're all pretty much dead, right? I'm pretty sure none of us want that—"

He scoffed, muttering, "At least you have a fighting chance."

Noel frowned. "I don't think a win is really a win in this case if we're being honest, and I saved you because I figure two of us escaping has a better chance than one since they'll have to split their efforts at some point. If we're lucky, maybe someone else escaped too."

His arms wrapped around himself, continuing to stare down at his boots. Noel turned his keys over in his palm, waiting for him to say something—anything—until the guy's throat bobbed.

He held his hand. "I'm Noel, a macharomancer."

The guy's one dark, visible eye snapped to the tattoo on Noel's arm, sticking out from the edge of his rolled denim jacket sleeves. His fingertips dug further into the folds of his ratty sweatshirt.

"And you are…?" Noel prodded, hesitant to pull his hand back.

"Grey," he finally mumbled. "You don't want to shake my hand."

Noel's fingers slowly curled in question as Grey nudged up his own sleeve, still refusing to make eye contact with him.

Oh.

It felt rude to rip his hand away at the sight of a hemomancer mark, his blood curdling at the thought that he'd played roulette and ended up with the bullet. Any of the other people he could've grabbed would've been far less dangerous than the one who could weaken and drain him with a single touch. But he supposed Grey hadn't killed him to take his bike and bolt when he had the chance to try to find another way out.

Noel tucked his hands into his jacket pockets and fished out his gloves, holding them out in offering. Grey's nose wrinkled, and he jerked his chin up. "That's great and all, but what's going to protect me from *you?*"

He opened his mouth in shock. "Seriously? What could I possibly—"

Grey pushed away the hair obscuring his other eye, and Noel's heart dropped. That short curtain of black waves fell back into place.

"You don't have to wear the gloves," Noel said softly, folding them back into his pockets. "And I promise I won't hurt you. Whoever did that was a monster, but I know saying that won't change your mind about how you think of me, much like how I'm not exactly all that fond of teaming up with a hemomancer in this grand escape."

"Escape to *where?*" Grey puffed out, his shoulders dropping. "If any one of us goes back home, won't they just ransack the place? They're probably drafting up bounties for our heads right now—"

Noel stiffened at the distant snap of underbrush and held up a finger. "Quiet."

Blessedly, Grey paused, his gaze following Noel's to a point further down the untraveled path into the dark woods. The world fell eerily silent without the soft chirping of cicadas and rustling of small creatures underfoot. Noel heard Grey swallow just as the faint, haunting glow of red shone in the distance, sending a shiver up his spine.

"Get on the bike," he whispered, his tone sharp and urgent.

Grey didn't object to the order, the two of them climbing on with the fumbling jingle of keys being pulled from Noel's pocket. The engine revved as two angry, red dots pierced the darkness, accompanied by a low, guttural growl. Grey's hands found the opening of Noel's denim jacket and held tight to the metal zipper teeth.

Please don't try to use your magic here, he silently pleaded, imagining the blood he'd never get out of the fabric and a drained forest left in their wake.

The motorcycle shot forward, and Grey gasped out a yelp, squeezing his arms around Noel's body as a clearer, more horrifying outline of a hulking bear-like silhouette slunk into view.

"Turn, turn, turn—" Grey chanted, his voice climbing with each panicked syllable.

Instead, Noel ducked down, punching the bike forward.

"Are you crazy?" Grey yelled over the engine.

Maybe. Then again, he knew it was suicide to take any untraveled route out of these woods. The creatures dwelling deeper within might make an exception for their ritualistic prey, but that wasn't a chance Noel was willing to take.

He slid his blade out from his boot again, a comfort to feel the worn leather covering the hilt in his hand. But even more comforting was the knowledge that solid iron extended from it. A satisfying howl tore from the creature's lungs as they passed, dagger sliding through shadowy hide. And by the time it turned to give chase, Noel and Grey were long gone.

❧

Grey stayed glued to Noel's back, even after they left the woods and rolled along the dirt trail toward home. The wind teased his skin the further they went, taunting him to drive straight into the arms of the game wardens once again.

"Where are we going?" Grey's voice sounded small and worn, but it jolted Noel back to the task at hand.

"I don't know just yet," he mumbled, the bike slowing in answer.

Cold spread over him as Grey pulled away, his arms trembling in their brush against Noel's sides. "Do you need to stop for a bit? You used your blade back there—"

"Hm? Oh, that wasn't macharomancy. Just me slicing it with iron to keep it off us long enough to escape."

"What about the net?"

Noel opened his mouth and snapped it shut again. He supposed he had, and he'd been running off pure adrenaline since their escape—enough of it that he must've pushed down that gnawing sensation in the pit of his stomach from channeling his power. So, he guided the motorcycle off the path, bumping along the grassy hill with Grey's hands gripping his jacket.

Grey half-fell into the grass when they dismounted, and Noel scrambled to grab his arm, almost recoiling at the reaction when he reminded himself this boy wasn't just any mancer.

"Did *you* use your magic back there?"

"Yes." He winced, righting himself and—thankfully—shaking off Noel's support. "But I already traded. I think I'm just spent."

Was that a lie to get him to drop his guard? He'd heard of some hemomancers hitchhiking and brushing off any strange behaviors or scars. It was only later that the poor souls that became their victims learned that those were warning signs. Maybe Grey's eye was from a macharomancer defending themself?

Noel shifted awkwardly, brushing off his jacket before he took a seat in the grass, far enough away from him that he'd have time to react before succumbing to his trade: energy for energy. Meditation would have to suffice since he ate the last of his rations hours ago with the assumption he'd be able to hold off until he reached another town. His eyes closed, and his tensed at the subtle rustling from Grey dropping down next to him.

Grey made a noise like he was trying to clear his throat. "What do you use in your trade?"

"Food, usually," Noel mumbled. "I can manage some with—" The zip of nylon popped his eyes open again, narrowing on the shadowy bag he fumbled through before holding him a granola-bar-looking thing in offering. "Thanks..." He gingerly took it, sniffing it as Grey retrieved some dried fruit.

Okay, so maybe he was still stringing him along? Or he really meant what he said about Noel having a greater chance. Honestly, he didn't think that really mattered when the sole survivor of the Wild Hunt typically died in the confines of the Grand Capital within a week because they succumbed to fae madness.

He eyed Grey, watching him pick through his rations to nibble on. If he didn't eat anything from his bag, Noel certainly wouldn't risk it.

"I think I'm shaky because I didn't really eat anything since noon," Grey murmured. "Probably won't do us much good to be running on fumes." He fidgeted as he popped a couple clusters of granola in his mouth and hunched in on himself.

Noel slowly chewed, relishing the honey, oats, and other flavors he couldn't quite place. His magic greedily accepted the offering, dissolving it before it filled his stomach and demanded more. *That's it for now,* he silently scolded, rubbing the stickiness off his fingers.

A small paper bag crinkled in front of him. "Cookie? Might as well help me eat them just in case we don't get the chance to enjoy them tomorrow."

Noel's magic vibrated in anticipation, and he bit back a relieved sigh. God, that word sounded like magic to his ears. He barely even thought before his hand dipped into the bag. Noel wasn't going to turn down a treat after a nightmarish evening. "Is this thanks for saving you?"

"A little." Grey tugged one out for himself and folded the bag back down, setting it off to the side. He stared out into the distant tree line. "But it doesn't seem like you have much of a plan now that we're away from the obelisk."

Noel bit his cheek. "Yeah, well, there wasn't a ton of time to consider that when the goal was just to escape... Do you know of a place that would greatly oppose the Grand Capital? Some place far enough away from the Old Trail?"

Grey shook his head. "Isn't every surviving city on the Old Trail? Everything outside of it is dead land. No one can live out there without some sort of well-thought system in place. Even then, the fair folk at the Fringes won't let you get that far." His words shifted into a mutter as he took another bite of cookie.

Noel broke off another chunk, relieved when his magic didn't tear it to pieces. That trade was complete, so now he guessed he could run off a little sugar for the night. "We'll need to get fuel first, I think. Probably should stop by a compound before word spreads too far that we're loose out here." He chewed the rest of his treat, brushed his hands off on his pants, and stood. "Ready?"

Grey quickly bundled up his spread of goods, folded everything back into his bag, and struggled to his feet, still wobbly. Noel tried to shake off the twinge of concern needling in his chest as he got on the bike again. The key slid into the ignition, and he went rigid as arms encircled him.

It's fine. This is fine.

Noel shifted, ignoring the heat of a boy resting against his back. Hemomancer or not, of course *now* he was hyper aware of

Grey's pulse. Grey's presence. Grey's unnecessary generosity. Grey's terrified quiet in the midst of uncertainty.

And you're both destined to die.

Maybe that was why he was suddenly feeling a little boy-crazy. But his body surrendered to that bleak sentiment, anchoring him back to reality with his soles on the pedals and his head firmly on his shoulders, rather than lost in the clouds.

GREY

Light pricks of rain made Grey bury his face in the back of Noel's jacket. It took everything in him not to shiver in brief spasms with the chilled wind slipping past. His body ached for sleep, complaining with every shift of the motorcycle breaking his lull.

At least he wasn't riding with a heartless psychopath, as far as he could tell. He'd initially told himself the remorse reflected in his green eyes had been a sham—a trick of the forest's swimming shadows. But after he'd pried him from the jaws of danger for a second time and hadn't demanded anything when they stopped to rest, Grey decided that this was as close as he'd probably get to an ally in this sick, twisted Calling.

"It's funny," Grey mumbled, pulling his face away from the black denim. "The Calling kept pestering me to hurry and get to the obelisk and now it's dead silent."

Noel snorted. "It probably stopped because it knows we're fucked. If there's a way to escape it, it certainly doesn't give a shit. Just some twisted fair folk echo slowly squeezing us to death."

To death.

Grey swallowed and stared at the back of Noel's jacket. He didn't *want* to die—not like this. Not for some sick game, all for the fair folk's amusement.

It made him question where he'd gone wrong. He'd left trinkets and saucers out for the fair folk when he was younger—a habit that turned into him growing various wild plants on the outskirts of his town, even if Aunt Ingrid frowned whenever she found him tending to them. Guilt still gnawed at him from healing himself back in the obelisk clearing by unconsciously sucking the life from tree branches and their leaves. But Grey had always done his best to respect the fair folk with whatever he did because that's what he'd always been taught.

He peered over Noel's shoulder as a trailing wall came into view, not nearly as tall as the city he'd wandered through the streets of nearly half a day ago. That austromancer woman spouting doom and gloom surfaced to the front of his thoughts, where he recalled how some of the other townsfolk told her it was too early for another Wild Hunt.

There had to be a reason for it—something that could be mended or appeased to lull that bloodlust back to sleep for a little while longer. Something that could show the fair folk that he wasn't one of the mancers they wanted to hunt because he'd respected their wishes his whole life and kept to himself.

"You think maybe there's a way to break this thing?"

His eye flicked to Noel's working jaw. "Maybe... I'm not sure where that answer might be though. Well, outside of stored away in some book or something the Grand Capital."

Grey's face dipped toward jacket again, the world unfocusing, even as the motorcycle slowed near the compound's chain linked gate. There had to be a way to break it. There hadn't always been a Wild Hunt like this—not something this ritualistic and well-controlled from the old tales Atticus had told him.

"Hey." Noel's soothing tone snapped him out of his thoughts. "When we go in here, don't use your real name, and hide anything that might identify you, okay?"

"Yeah, okay," Grey forced out in a whisper, unsure if it would be appropriate to let go of him now or when Noel had to dismount. He awkwardly held on while a whistle sounded from Noel's lips.

The post guard that jogged over to the gate, mid-chuckle barely gave them a once-over before pushing it open and ushering them in. Noel guided them through, and the metal clanged behind them.

"Where's the fueling station located?"

Grey fought the urge to crane his neck around with the man lingering on his left, too far out of his vision.

"Two storefronts down. There's a sign posted out front—you can't miss it."

"Thanks."

"Sure thing."

The bike lurched forward again, gently rolling along the side of the wide dirt road, past corrugated metal roofs and grated iron over windows. Grey didn't realize he'd been holding on a little too tightly to Noel until he jolted at the gentle pat against his sleeve.

"You good?"

"Y-yeah, sorry," Grey ripped his arms away, pulling his sleeves down over his hands and scrambling off the bike.

Noel strode into the fueling storefront, bright electric lights spilling through the windows and iron-laced glass door. Grey rubbed his arms and stepped in front of the larger plaques by the door with maps of both the town and the Old Trail. He shivered as he tried to soak it all in, blinking back the urge to slump against the siding from pure exhaustion. His barely uncovered fingertip traced the marked pathway from the compound to the nearest town: Goldcrest.

The door swung open again, and he turned on his heel to find Noel with a fuel canister.

"There's an inn down the road. I didn't want to ask about it at the gate, just in case, but I think it's probably good to stop and sleep while we can." Noel placed the canister down next to the bike and uncapped the tank. "Find something?"

Grey nodded. "They have a couple maps up, so I was looking at some of the closest places we might be able to gather some information from."

Noel raised a brow. "You seriously want to try this? You know if we stick together, our odds of getting found are greater, right?"

His face scrunched up, and he shook his head. "Either we're eventually caught, or we at least try to break this—spell, curse, whatever it is," he hissed, glancing back at the shop door, to the woman rearranging the shelves behind the counter. "Plus, I don't exactly have a way to escape if they roll up in big trucks and cars again, so I'd rather take my chances with someone who's in the same shitty boat."

Noel emptied the canister in silence, undoubtedly mulling Grey's words over.

"You don't trust me," Grey whispered, his shoulders drooping. Of course he didn't trust him. Why trust a hemomancer when they were all viewed the same: unhinged bloodthirsty killers. It ultimately didn't matter if they were both fighting for their lives, did it?

He tensed in answer, quickly shaking his head. "It's not that —I just... I'm just not sure. I'm not sure about any of this, and I think we need rest before we make any big decisions." He screwed the cap back on the canister and strode back into the shop, leaving Grey alone again with his thoughts, even if only for a moment.

When Noel returned, he hopped back on the motorcycle, pausing with his key in the ignition to stare at Grey. He patted the back of the seat, and Grey hesitantly climbed on again before the engine sprang to life one more time for the night. The agonizing trip down the road was met with further discomfort in the form of late-night workers smoking outside storefronts. The inn's flickering, half-burnt-out neon sign turned into a shining beacon for Grey's exhausted body.

His feet dragged once Noel parked the bike in the small, crammed side lot, forcing them to walk the rest of the way through the creaky door and into the surprisingly plush lobby. A fireplace, overstuffed furniture, and hand-woven rugs were among some of the luxuries, giving way to doubt as to whether or not they'd be able to afford a night.

"How much you willing to part with?" the man at the counter drawled.

Noel pulled out a couple coins and set them against the repurposed bar top. Grey reached for Noel's arm to object, but the man shrugged, collected it, and plucked a key off the rack.

"Room 22. Breakfast is on the house."

The keychain dropped into Noel's palm, and he led the way up the stairs. Every creak made Grey tense with the dreaded thought that maybe all of the décor was a well-crafted façade. Serif-cut numbers were nailed to each door they passed, marked 28, 27, 26... 22 rested at the end of the hall, where Noel twisted the handle and turned on the flickering light.

Inside, the setup was just as inviting and cozy—even more lavish than he'd ever had the privilege of enjoying back at Atticus and Ingrid's. The bed beckoned him forward, and he fell into it, blacking out the second his head hit the pillow.

❦ 6 ❦

NOEL

oel immediately detoured to the small bathroom and pulled back the shower curtain to make sure there wasn't anything lurking in the shadows.

"Looks like everything's clear, but unfortunately there's only one—" He stepped out, flicking off the light and hesitating as he took in Grey sprawled out on the closest side of the mattress. "Bed."

Heat flooded his face like he was an awkward, crushing twelve-year-old again. He cleared his throat, shifting from foot-to-foot until he decided to barricade the room. Noel dragged the small writing desk's chair over to the door and propped it up under the handle. He rubbed his arms and shuffled back over to the bed, carefully crawling onto the other half and laid flat on his back.

Just don't think about it. Just pretend he's not there.

A monumental task, especially after the sudden, soft snore that seized up every muscle in Noel's body. He forced out a sigh and closed his eyes, the gentle patter of rain against the windows caressing the edge of his mind and pulling him into the depths of sleep.

❧

Noel's motorcycle was gone when he stood in front of the obelisk this time, staring into the smooth, black surface of that hulking monument with his macharomancer mark carved into one of its six faceted sides. No game wardens. No other prey. Just him, the obelisk, and the stars. He stepped forward and placed his hand on the smooth stone, slick to the touch as he dragged his fingers past the first corner in his clockwise walk to the other five sides. Triangle struck through the top: austromancy. Upside down triangle stuck through the bottom: lithomancy. Tilted line with a circle instead of his arrow: sciomancy. Normal triangle: halomancy.

He paused at the final facet, staring at the hemomancy symbol there, where his thumb traced the grooves like it might snag his skin and pool with his blood. After all, that's all this ritual wanted, right?

Blood.

Death.

Sacrifice.

Everything that'd poured into the ground over the years after the rise of the fair folk and their wild magic. Wild magic that seeped into people's bones, turning them into nothing more than subjects on the other side of a veil, incapable of refusing to bend to the will of their vengeful masters.

No-el.

He whipped around in search of the eerie, sing-song tune floating through the clearing. His hand fell away from the obelisk, reaching for the dagger in his boot, but no hilt stuck out for him to grasp.

No-e-l, it sang again, drawing out the L with a teasing giggle teetering on a cackle.

His hackles rose, despite feeling rooted to the spot. When he forced himself to take a step toward it, his legs moved like they were weighed down with bags of sand. His father's stern warning of never running after something without a weapon to channel his magic into stopped him again.

"What do you want?" he called, hoping the faux-courage in his voice carried past the trees and into the dark.

Seconds wore on without answer, save the pounding of his pulse in his ears.

We would like to propose a trade.

Noel would've scoffed if he wasn't so terrified that his heart was about to burst from his chest. "Trade *what?*"

Give us the hemomancer, and you can walk free at the end of the Hunt.

His fingers turned to ice, spreading through his arms and pushing straight to the bone. So *this* was how they determined who would live. He hadn't missed the convenient omission of what sort of state he'd be in once he walked free.

After all, there was always one "survivor" that the fair folk so graciously returned, even though they'd shattered their mind beyond repair.

Noel's hands curled into fists. "Fuck off." He wasn't stupid enough to hand them both over to the wardens and hope for the best. "You're scared we'll find a way out, aren't you?"

Raucous laughter welled up from the creature—or creatures —amusement layered in a dizzying chorus of clashing voices. Then it fell into a deep, husky tone that made Noel shrink back.

Go ahead and try, little boy. Sooner or later, we will have what we want.

❦

Noel's eyes flew open to the thumping of rain against the window, sounding in time with his heart. The mattress complained as he pushed himself up and paused when it continued to tremble. He glanced over to Grey, curled up and shivering where he'd left him. Noel slid off the bed and untucked his side of the comforter to drape it over his shaking form in a cocoon. The trembling lessened after a minute, and Noel perched on the end of the bed, rubbing his face.

Give us the hemomancer.

His eyes drifted back to Grey's bundled body again.

You don't trust me.

Noel folded in on himself, his stomach twisting from the line he was riding. He should've agreed the second Grey suggested *anything* because, honestly, what did they have to lose? The fair folk were already taking over for the Calling, trying to pit him against the person he saved in the midst of the chaos.

Because he knew he wouldn't survive the Hunt. The only way he'd manage is if he'd make a deal—he was almost certain. The fair folk knew how to pry into his mind and poke until they got a reaction. They always had, especially when he'd encountered them as a child.

Pixies had lured him into the woods near his home when he was eight, the light tugging at his clothes growing more aggressive the further he journeyed inside. They'd led him onto winding paths with the promise of adventure and treasure until he was lost and afraid. And yet, they still tried to force him toward the faerie portal somewhere deeper within.

Noel had clapped his hands over his ears and huddled in the dirt with his eyes squeezed shut and knees drawn to his chest, where he waited for the pixies to abandon him. They didn't—not until his father found him, scooped him up, and carried him home. His mother had fussed over every little cut and bruise, tears shimmering in her eyes. It wasn't until later that he discovered she'd been terrified that her Noel was still in the woods while she cleaned up her new changeling, never to see her real son again.

He stared down at the floor, slowly shaking his head and running his hands through his hair until the rain's pattering shifted its rhythm. Stretching, he stood, and freed the chair from the door, taking one more look back at Grey before he picked up the room key and crept out into the hall. The *click* of the lock behind him and a small jiggle of the handle gave him a little bit of peace before he descended to the lobby.

The night clerk sat back at the front desk, a book in hand and a glass of amber-tinted liquid resting on the counter, his eyes flicking up to Noel. "Need something?"

Noel hesitated, stopping himself from shaking his head and escaping out into the compound—like it'd do him much good to wander around when he could simply *ask*. "Do you have a map?"

The clerk's chair creaked, and the book folded between his fingers as he slid it on the counter. He rustled through a drawer for a moment before holding out a worn, crinkled paper, folded in half.

"Thank—"

"You running from something?"

Noel's blood ran cold, despite the immediate instinct to furrow his brows and shake his head. "Why would you think—"

"I've had enough people walk in and out of this place that I can tell," he grumbled into his glass. "They always show up in the dead of night, taking their chances with the fair folk wandering the hills, and ask for a map."

Noel bit back a cringe. "I—"

The clerk held up his hand. "Take the map. Whatever you're running from, I won't tell a soul you stayed here, got it? You paid for the night and left your key on the counter in the morning. Never saw you check in with a friend. Never saw you in the middle of the night. Never handed you a map. Never fed you breakfast. And my lithomancy has been unreliable since the day I was born, so I couldn't possibly produce any reasons, even if I wanted to."

Noel's shoulders relaxed as he tugged the paper from the clerk's hand. "I appreciate it."

He nodded and dismissed him with a flick of his wrist. "Map's yours. I always make a few extras." The clerk settled back into his chair, reclaiming his book like the entire conversation had never happened, and nursed his drink as Noel turned to leave.

When he returned to the room, he spread the map out over the desk and traced the path to Goldcrest. It was almost *too* close to their current location for his liking, but it was one of the few they'd at least be able to stop into without being questioned for their names or brands, especially if they were able to make it before nightfall.

Woodhurst and Ivywood were the only two viable options, but they were much further out. *We'd be lucky to make it there in a night.* He worried his lip, tapping his finger against Ivywood. It sounded familiar, like he'd heard it from someone a while ago, but he couldn't remember in what context. He drew a little circle around it with the inn's small, worn pencil before his eyes snapped to the Grand Capital.

The further they traveled away from it, the better, but... He pressed his palms into the desk, letting his full weight bare down on it while he thought. *How likely will we find answers that far out?*

He supposed there was only one way to find out.

❧ 7 ❧

GREY

Grey opened his eyes to the glow of pinkish orange splashed across the room's entry with a comforter weighing him down. The mattress complained as he pushed himself up and took in Noel's body stretched out in the desk's chair, his head resting on his knuckles with his eyes closed. Grey immediately shot up out of bed.

You idiot, he snapped at himself. He smoothed out his wrinkled clothes as he crept toward Noel, guilt sinking in before his fingers grazed his shoulder. "Noel."

He stirred, breathing out a quiet mumble—moan—Grey couldn't tell which, and idled again.

"Noel," Grey said a little louder, relieved when Noel's lids cracked open. His hand pulled back, and Noel's eyes met his.

That sleepy gaze immediately swapped to alarm, and he jumped, his face falling into his hands. "Shit. I fell asleep," he murmured, scrubbing at his forehead.

"No, I'm sorry," Grey quickly blurted. "I didn't realize about the bed, and—You probably should've just stolen the comforter before I did—"

"N-no, it's fine. Really." Noel scraped a piece of paper off the desk, sending a small pencil rolling to the edge which he scrambled to catch. "I couldn't sleep, so I got us a map." The sheet drooped in his hand as he held it out to Grey, and he hesitantly took it. Pencil lead drew up paths, circled cities, and scratched out notes along each potential destination.

It crinkled in his grip as confusion burrowed its way into him.

Noel's hand dragged along the back of his neck. "I had some time to think last night, and I think you're right. We can either delay the inevitable or trust each other and try to break it."

Grey's eyes flicked up to those clam, green irises boring into him.

"So... how about some breakfast, and then we head out to Goldcrest?" An inviting smile tugged at his lips and relief spread through Grey in answer.

❧❦❧

Warmth consumed Grey after a meal of fresh baked rolls, cooked bacon, and fried eggs. Bags packed, and inn key left on the counter, he followed Noel to the supply shop for rations before they mounted the bike again.

Overcast skies darkened the bleak horizon, like an omen of worse things to come as Noel shot out of the compound and down the road before veering off the path. Grey tried to settle in for every bump, bounce, twist, and turn through the worn-down, beaten trails.

"Grey?"

He tore his gaze from the fields of tall grass and far-off trees. "Hm?"

"Did you dream about anything last night?"

Noel's zipper track dug into his palms. "Um... Yeah, actually..."

"Was the obelisk in it?"

Grey huffed out a short, joyless laugh. "Yep. Did you?"

A sigh. "Unfortunately. What happened in it?"

He sank down a little further, his arms pressing against Noel's sides like he might fall off. "Not much. The fair folk started whispering to me while I stood in front of my mark, and—" Grey bit off his explanation, recalling the quiet wails turning into urgent pleas for help as leaves crunched underfoot.

"And?"

Grey shook his head. "I heard my own voice crying for help," he mumbled. "Like, a younger version of myself, I guess. By the time I got to it—me—I was in front of a sealed-off faerie portal at the base of a tree, and other me was sobbing on the other side..."

Noel cleared his throat, shifting his weight slightly. "Was there... anything else?"

"No," he whispered. "It ended with me trying to dig child-me out with this horrible feeling that I was being watched."

Silence pooled between them, hovering like they were passing through fog until Noel spoke. "The fair folk asked me to give you to them in exchange for letting me go after the Hunt."

Grey's stomach dropped. "What?"

"I told them to fuck off." He brushed aside wisps of fringe. "But I figured you might've gotten the same offer too since it seemed like a way for them to make us turn on each other and let them have their fun." Noel sucked in a breath as Grey stared down at the worn patches of his denim jacket. "And I do trust you. So, I hope you'll trust me, even after this admission."

"Is that why you decided to go find a map?"

"Mm hm."

"Thank you for telling me." Grey released his grasp on Noel's jacket zipper and clasped his own wrists as he leaned forward. "Hopefully we can find a way out of this, so all this running isn't in vain."

◈

Goldcrest was the polar opposite of its name. Grimy, tattered papers and sheets hung over the shipping container walls stacked three high, spanning out for kilometers in the depths of the valley it was confined to. Gates were left open, rather than closed, allowing them to simply roll on inside, not that anyone questioned them potentially being fair folk while riding a machine the creatures despised.

Other bikes rode past, their drivers readjusting goggles and jackets before they left or parking by porches of bars like they were hitching up horses. Grey shrank down against Noel as a man watched them from a second-story apartment balcony on the main street, tapping a cigarette against the railing.

"Relax," Noel mumbled. "Act natural."

They ventured a little further in, weaving through streets and alleyways laced with utter despair or exhaustion. Dread coursed through him when Noel began to tense, his head panning to take in his surroundings like he was on high alert.

"Where do you think we'll be able to find anything here?" Grey whispered.

Noel hummed and sped forward. Grey smacked into his back

in his overcorrection not to fall off. The motorcycle jerked to a halt outside another bar, and Noel nudged his kickstand into place. "Best place to ask around is the watering hole, right?"

He dismounted and Grey scrambled off. "I thought you wanted to avoid talking to people?"

"Yeah, but we have to in this case, or else we'll be awkwardly wandering around for hours and earn weird, suspicious looks in return. Come on." He jogged up the steps, striding through the propped open doors to dim lighting of the sparsely hung bulbs overhead. Mismatching wood and metal tables and chairs were crammed in as much space as possible, even crowding the bar before more patrons filled in within a couple more hours.

Noel scraped a coin against the bar top, tapping it with a finger as he ordered a drink. Grey stepped up next to him and rested his arms against the counter, eyeing the patrons watching them from the table tucked into the corner. He swallowed and tore his gaze away.

"Question," Noel began, already trying to strike up that casual conversation with the barkeep. "Is there anyone around here that specializes in faerie shit?"

Grey refrained from flinching, but the barkeep bit her lip and drummed her fingernails on the countertop for a minute. "There's a guy a few blocks from here. He's sort of an archivist and doctor with an oddities shop. I think that's probably the closest you'll get if you're trying to identify or sell off something faerie-related."

"Thanks," Noel said, holding his bottle up with a smirk. "Trying to offload some stuff, so hopefully he can help or point me in the right direction."

She nodded. "Sure thing, sugar. Is there anything I can get for you, sweetie?" Her head turned to Grey.

"N-no, thanks." Something told him she wouldn't be calling him 'sweetie' if she saw the mark under his sleeve.

She patted the bar top. "Just call if you need anything." And she strode down to the other side of the bar to help another patron.

"Faerie shit?" Grey hissed. "Aren't people going to ask questions if—"

"Nope," Noel breathed, tipping the bottle back against his lips. "Treasure hunters are a big thing the further you get from the Grand Capital. Don't worry about it. This is normal out here."

"You're sure?"

"A hundred percent." He downed a little more and waved to the barkeep before he turned to leave. Grey stuck next to him on their way out, back onto the bike, and down the street to their next destination.

Cavan's Oddities spanned the width of the first-floor window in silver-trimmed white painted letters. Noel pushed the door open, jingling the bell hung along the frame as they wandered into an eclectic collection of boxed crystals, carved stones, and mirrors hanging from floor-to-ceiling of one of the walls. An entire library sat undisturbed in the next room over, the archway caged off by an old-fashioned elevator shutter.

"Lithomancer," Noel muttered, tracing the tables with boxes of loose rocks with a finger on his way to the gated doorway.

Grey picked up one of the crystals and ran his thumb over the buffed edges. "I'm not sure we're going to find what we're looking for here if this is it..."

"Looking for what?"

He jumped, juggling the crystal and squeezing it in his grip as he spun with Noel to a man in a black, long-sleeved tee-shirt rolled up to his elbows and faded, brown leather gloves. He was tall and lanky with disheveled, coffee-colored hair and a five-o-clock shadow that only furthered to emphasize his sickly pallor. His dark eyes slid from Noel to Grey as he took a step forward, the crystal digging into Grey's palm when the man's vision stuck to him before dropping to where one of his supposed oddities was being held. Grey held back a grimace from the mere thought that it was probably slick with sweat by now.

"Some text related to faerie rituals," Noel said with a shrug, like he was tossing the idea out there. "We found some weird markings and stuff, so we're just trying to make sure we're not being followed or anything creepy like that."

Grey went to put the crystal back, and the man plucked it from his hands, turning it over. "Amethyst is quite good for protection," he said, tapping it against his other palm with a gleam in his eyes. "I'm Doctor Cavan, by the way. I'd be happy to assist if you'd like access to my books or anything else. It's quite rare to have someone pop in with an interesting request like this."

Biting his tongue, Grey put on a tight smile to match Noel's on their guided tour to the mini library. Doctor Cavan slid the amethyst in his pocket, trading it for a key he twisted in the lock and pushed the gate back.

"Come in, come in. Take a look around." He hovered by the entry, holding his arm out in invitation to step onto the large, woven rug. Dust puffed up with each step, drifting through the air as they proceeded toward the hulking bookcases. Noel tugged a tome off the shelf, and Doctor Cavan pushed off the frame, humming and peeling off his gloves on his way back to the front of the shop.

Pages fell open in Noel's hands, sounding with the creaking of the book's spine. "Try not to go for anything directly connected to the Hunt right away," he breathed.

"S-sure," Grey forced out, peering at the shelves. Creature names and fair folk encyclopedia volumes spanned the first one at his eye-level. His fingers trembled as he reached for one, the weight buckling his arms for a moment.

"Are you okay?"

"F-fine." Well, he'd felt fine when he walked into the shop, but now he wanted nothing more than to collapse into a chair and take a nap.

Noel scowled and pulled the tome from his grasp. "You look a little worse for wear, maybe you should stick to the lighter—"

"There's some more books upstairs if you two aren't finding what you're looking for." Footsteps sounded behind them again, spinning Grey around. Doctor Cavan stopped short of the threshold, hands tucked into his pockets with a wistful smirk that made Grey's stomach twist. "They're considerably thinner since they're specially bound scholar notes. Would you be interested?"

Grey hesitated, sharing a questioning look with Noel before he pushed down that unease and started forward. "I'd like to take a look if that's all right."

Doctor Cavan beamed. "Right this way."

The second Grey moved to follow, and the doctor slipped from view, Noel grabbed his sleeve. "Are you sure you're okay?"

Grey nodded. "Yeah. I'm fine. I'll check upstairs."

Noel frowned, but he let go, and Grey jogged after the doctor.

Doctor Cavan pushed back the curtain to the stairwell he must've manifested from when he and Noel first entered the shop, and they ascended a flight of steps to a small office, complete with a desk and patched-up office chair with a loveseat sitting on the other side of it for an audience. Sure enough, along the far wall were a small collection of journals and specially bound books.

"Is this your office?" Grey asked, looking around in admiration, somewhat reminded of his loft's secluded recess away from the chaos.

"Indeed, it is." His boots softly thumped against the creaking floorboards as he pulled a journal from the collection. The thin, leather cords strung into a bow unraveled at his deft touch, and he bent it open to a well-creased page. "I don't suppose you could give me more details about what you found, hm?"

"Um…" Grey rubbed his arms, trying to force back the chills pricking at his skin. "It's sort of difficult to explain."

The bell rang out downstairs, and Grey jolted, his stomach dropping with the added sound of the journal snapping shut and Doctor Cavan's sigh. "Interesting history of amethyst: It used to be more commonly utilized to protect people against faerie wine and apples back when the veil originally collapsed, but that's needed less and less now since vendors employ lithomancers to test goods before they're distributed. Grand Capital law and all…" Leather rubbed against other leather covers as he pushed the journal back into its nook. "Now, it's more often used for absorbing a small fraction of energy—typically negative—in exchange for proper rest and rejuvenation, making it a rather good trade stone for someone like me."

Grey's fingers started to turn icy, and he found it hard to swallow, a dry *click* answering instead.

"The downside is that it's not very good at emulating images. However, it does a *very* good job at emulating certain magical frequencies."

"Like?" The word almost came out in a squeak—half cut off by a crash downstairs. Grey jumped, his heart leaping as he whirled around to the stairwell. A bulky man loomed in the doorway, his macharomancer mark on full display and jagged, bleached scars marring tanned flesh. Grey stumbled back with the man's menacing step forward, Noel's name now stuck in his throat.

The guy lunged, and Grey tried to dart around him, ducking under his outstretched arm. A gasp tore from his lungs as his hoodie collar choked him in a sudden, backward lurch. The world upended and pain rippled through him as he collided with the floor.

"Be *careful* with him," Doctor Cavan ground out, his lighter steps growing louder.

Those four words renewed Grey's punch of adrenaline as his attacker pinned his arms to his chest, snapping something at Doctor Cavan he didn't catch. His sole thought became: *he knows about the Wild Hunt.* Grey struggled to push himself along the floor and twist from his grip, but when a third shadow emerged from the stairway, his body slackened. And the room faded to black.

"*Grey.*"

Grey grimaced as he blinked awake to blurred concrete, fighting against the pounding in his skull. His wrists screamed as they rubbed against sharp plastic digging into his skin, panic welling up in turn.

"Grey, look at me," Noel hissed, his green eyes roaming over his face when he jerked his head up. His legs were bound by zip-ties to a chair pressed up against a wooden beam, his arms pulled back around it. With a quick attempt to move his legs, Grey realized he mirrored him, backed up against another beam in the rectangular basement. And he'd been brought here by a macharo-mancer. Grey jerked his wrists against the zip-tie.

"Grey—" Noel's voice climbed with alarm. Like a panicked bird in a cage, Grey snapped the restraints against the pole again, gritting his teeth as it bit into flesh, threatening to spill blood—until Noel's rustling ripped him back to reality. His body would forcibly trade with whatever living thing was around: Noel. He stopped, panting as his vision blurred over.

"Calm down for a second and look at me, okay?"

Grey shook his head, the first drops of tears dotting his pants.

"Hey, it's going to be all right, but you got to work with me—"

A shuddering swing of a door opening at the other end of the cellar made Grey tense, his chin lifted to watch Noel's growing unease tugging at his features. The bob of his throat and downward tug of his lips fueled Grey's anxiety, his skin jumping with every shuffle of shoes.

"No, no, no, *no, no*—" Grey's voice pitched higher with each whispered plea.

One of the figures twisted into the form of a woman for a flickering second, the basement's phantom chill ripping Grey to a moment in time he never wanted to revisit. But the mirage instantly broke with Doctor Cavan's smooth cadence. "Good, you're awake."

His cordial, casual smile sent chills through Grey, even more so when he didn't bother sparing Noel a glance. Grey shrank down in his chair, suppressing a whimper as Doctor Cavan seized his jaw and forced him back up. That terrified child buried deep inside him screamed again and pounded on that faerie door in his dreams like how he'd bruised his fists beating against the frosted windows in that basement long ago.

"Leave him alone," Noel growled.

The doctor paused, his head turning to finally acknowledge Noel from over his shoulder while one of his entourages—the macharomancer—stepped forward and backhanded him. "Shut your mouth," the man spat.

Doctor Cavan clicked his tongue, his grip on Grey's jaw tightening like a vice when he tried to turn his head a little more to take in the third, shadowy accomplice just out of his view. "Gag him if you have to," the doctor said, somewhat dryly as he returned to Grey.

All the little thoughts in his head scrambled to collect a list of things he should do: scream, yell, fight back, demand why he was there, beg to let them go, bargain—*anything*. The only one that silenced them all was the one that told him none of that would get him anywhere. So, he kept his mouth shut as Doctor Cavan gently brushed back Grey's hair and his lips pinched like he'd tasted something sour.

Another dose of fear slid through Grey's veins again, making him bite down on his tongue during those horrible seconds of pressure running along the edge of his unseeing eye. When the doctor's other gloved hand was in sight again, the sour expression morphed into one of pity. "Already damaged... That's rather unfortunate. But perhaps still salvageable."

He let go of Grey's jaw, leaving his head spinning with the short, shallow breaths he hadn't realized he'd been sucking down, and the doctor opened the tall cabinet doors pushed against the wall. Inside, the glint of the nearby bulb illuminated a peg board of tools and magnetic strip of knives.

Grey's body locked up, but Noel immediately jumped to the opposite reaction: "What the fuck do you want with us?"

The macharomancer pulled a knife from his belt. "Quiet, you little shi—"

"Relax, Daz," came Doctor Cavan's even command. A low, eerie hum crept through the basement as his gloved hand ran over the hilts of his instruments. When he turned around, he flipped one over in his palm, examining the sharp edge in his slow stroll back over to his captives. He pointed it toward Noel, his wrist limp and casual in his grip on the hilt. "*You* are simply fodder at this point. Trade bait, assuming this one really is a hemomancer."

The blood drained from Grey's face. *No.* Panic seized him with the idea that he'd be forced to endure whatever pain they chose to inflict on him with the horrible addition of siphoning away Noel's life force. "Please—"

"Oh, shh," Doctor Cavan cooed, grabbing a chair. He dragged it over, straddling it to sit in it backward and resting his arms along the back. "If you'd like to make this easier on me, I'd be more than happy to skip a few steps. So, let's start with your name."

Noel jerked against his restraints. "Fuck off." Daz slugged him in the stomach.

"Grey! It's Grey—Please stop—" he pleaded, his wrists burning with the instinctive twist to jump up and help.

"Grey," Doctor Cavan repeated, drawing out the name with a velvety touch that made his skin crawl. "What are you?"

Grey pressed his back up against the beam, looking from the knife to the doctor's tilted head. Malicious curiosity tingled behind the man's dark eyes.

"A h-hemomancer..."

He frowned and shook his head. "I suppose we'll do this the hard way then."

The chair complained as he stood, and Grey's heart dropped. "W-wait—I don't understand—"

"He answered the question!" Noel yelled, coming to his aid and yet again bringing down the wrath of Daz upon him. In a flash, Daz's fist plunged down toward Noel's leg, and a scream tore from his throat. Blood welled up when the thug ripped his blade out, crimson licking at his faded jeans.

"*Stop!*" Grey begged. "I'm a hemomancer. Please just leave him alone. I'll tell you whatever you want to know—"

Doctor Cavan started behind the beam, vanishing from

Grey's line of sight before he felt his hoodie sleeve pushed up to his elbow. Cold iron bit into his arm, and then a questioning hum echoed through the basement. "Interesting…"

Grey's arms relaxed against the beam again, stunned as Noel panted through gritted teeth and the doctor casually walked back to his chair, frowning down at the thin line of blood on his knife.

"What did you do to him?" Noel asked.

"Nothing," the doctor answered, holding up a hand before Daz could retaliate. "Just a little test. Trin, would you prepare a room for our guest?" He swiped away a red bead dripping from his nose, narrowing his eyes at Grey.

But Grey was too preoccupied with the blood seeping from Noel's leg until Trin's fingers trailed his forehead, and the world disappeared again.

❧

The *click* of a lock pulled Grey from one dark abyss into another. He blinked away sleep to the low light seeping through news papered windows shadowed by grated iron bars. Plastic zip-ties still held his wrists together, but at least this time they were in front of him with his body cradled by a thin mattress—the sole piece of furniture in the small room.

"He's still sleeping, but he should wake up again soon." A quiet, calm voice that Grey guessed had to be Trin.

"As long as he's kept pacified and somewhat comfortable, do whatever you need to." Doctor Cavan.

Grey shifted, trying to peer under the door to find an outline of shoes.

"And what about the macharomancer? We can't just let him go."

"I'll have Daz keep him quiet until tomorrow night. I know how to dispose of him after we make our offering."

"You sound so confident they'll accept this one."

Doctor Cavan sighed. "I *hope* they'll accept this one. If not, I'll have to find another one, and there aren't all that many options, are there?"

Grey shivered as floorboards creaked under their shifting weight before the doctor continued, "I'll commune with the crystal first. If they reject, I'll try to figure out what to do with him until I can trade him with another. Just... keep him quiet."

The descending moan of footsteps on stairs made Grey push himself up, his heart hammering in his chest as he stood and crept over to one of the windows. The pinkish hue of dusk filtered through one of the tiny holes, the sun vanishing over the city's shipping containers in the distance. He moved to the other window, trying to orientate where he was in the building. Judging by the stories of neighboring buildings, he was on the third, towering just above the nearby shops.

Grey stepped back, closed his eyes, and took a deep calming breath. *Calm down. Think.*

They didn't want them for the Hunt—at least, that's what it seemed like since the doctor didn't give a shit about Noel and tried to use him as trade bait. And even then, Grey's focus had been so fixated on Doctor Cavan, he'd traded with him before it could reach Noel—and before Trin used his sciomancy to knock him out and drag him away.

He half-turned toward the door to find Trin's shadow lingering under the handle side. Grey slowly made his way over, wincing at every little sound he made. A gentle press downward on the handle, and Trin moved. Grey shuffled back.

"It's locked," Trin said quietly. "Lay back down."

Grey didn't move, twisting his bound wrists as he gathered up the courage to speak. "What do you want with me?" he rasped, immediately feeling like that was the wrong question as he recalled Doctor Cavan's question he supposedly didn't answer in the basement. "What did he mean when he asked what I was?"

Trin remained quiet for a moment, the frame complaining like he was leaning against it. "He was asking you if you're a changeling."

"Changeling?" The word tumbled out in surprise. "I-I'm not—"

"We know." A calm, gentle reply. "You wouldn't have been able to heal when Cavan used iron if you were."

"I don't understand. Why are you keeping me here? Please, I—"

"Keep your voice down," Trin said, his voice low and urgent. "If Cavan hears you, he'll have me put you back to sleep."

Grey's shoulder's fell, hope bleeding out of him as he stared at the door—a physical manifestation of the prison in his dream. His hands curled into fists, fed by that slow-building frustration that strained against his restraints. He yanked on the handle again, pushing down on it with all his weight.

"Grey," Trin warned, sternness lacing that even tone. "I already said it's locked."

Tears sprang to his eyes from the ever-increasing pressure. First the Calling, then the Hunt, now Doctor Cavan and his twisted ideas—whatever they were. He let go, his arms shaking as he collapsed to the floor.

"Would you like to go back to sleep?" The question sounded like his uncle asking if he wanted to be left alone for a while.

"No," Grey sobbed. "I want to leave. Where's—" He choked

back Noel's name, fearing they might try to use it against him in whatever way they planned on using Grey's.

"Your friend?"

"Where is he? Is he okay?"

Trin's boots scuffed against the floor. "He's fine for now. Bandaged and upset, but fine."

He sniffed, careful to brush his eyes against his hoodie sleeve. "You're going to kill him, aren't you? So why keep me?"

The lock clicked, and Grey's head jerked up in time to blink back light pouring in from the hallway. Trin's frame blocked it as he slid inside, pulling the door shut behind him and crouching in front of Grey. His gloved hands rested in his lap, his shadowed features a blur of blacks, dark browns, splashed on a bronze canvas in Grey's vision.

"The more questions I answer, the more noise you're going to make," he said softly. "So, you can either lay down on the mattress and be quiet, or I can put you under until tomorrow."

Warmth slipped down Grey's face, his stomach churning from the mere idea of digging his fingers into this man's flesh and letting his hemomancy take control. He wasn't even sure how far he'd get before Trin knocked him out anyway—his touch would likely win out in a matter of seconds.

So, Grey bowed his head and crawled back to the mattress, watching as Trin rose. His hand rested on the door handle for a good twenty seconds as they locked eyes, Trin's gaze filling with remorse.

And then Grey was alone again.

❊ 9 ❊
GREY

Mist obscured the creeping greenery of the forest, making the hairs on the back of Grey's neck stand on end. He rubbed his arms, the soft fabric of his hoodie not doing much to warm him. The light snapping of twigs underfoot echoed with each careful step forward.

Where are you going?

Grey spun on his heel, searching for the source of the voice—a lilting, husky tone filled with teasing bemusement. Fair folk.

Are you lost?

"N-no," Grey breathed, taking a step back.

Are you sure? A chuckle. *There's no need to be scared.*

"Please l-leave me alone," Grey forced out, his teeth starting to chatter.

Come here. Let me have a closer look.

Grey shook his head, unable to pinpoint where the voice was coming from. It might as well have been nowhere and everywhere at once. He turned into the fog, picking up his pace in the midst of clouded trees.

Then the voice was right next to him.

Hello, Grey.

He yelped and jerked to the side, covering his ear and shaking as he collapsed into a trunk. Bark snagged his sleeve and scraped his hands while he panted, searching for the person it'd come from.

Another chuckle sounded, radiating in from all sides. *What a frightened little thing you are...*

Grey shrank down, pressing himself into the small nook at the base of the tree, like the creature wouldn't be able to reach him there. Nothing lurked at the corners of his vision or silhouette itself in the churning mist.

"Go away—"

Now, now.

He flinched, covering his ears as the voice pressed in again.

Don't cause a fuss, my little finch.

A phantom touch caressed Grey's cheek, and his arms shot up, batting it away as he toppled over.

You'll be mine, soon enough.

❦

Grey woke up drenched in sweat and gulping down panicked breath after panicked breath. His anxiety was only suppressed by footfalls climbing up the steps. He shoved his hoodie sleeve in his mouth to keep quiet.

"Good news, they accepted." Doctor Cavan's cheery tone made his head spin. "I sent Daz out to get the van. We'll load them both up in an hour and head out."

"And payment?" Trin asked.

"Considerably more than giving them trinkets the past few

times. They're rather pleased, so I can't imagine them backing out once we offer him up."

"Do you want to have him cleaned up before we go? Wouldn't that—"

"No time. When they say as soon as possible, I plan on delivering as soon as possible. I'm sure if they want him cleaned up, they'll handle it. Not our problem, so long as he's in decent condition. I'm going to close up the shop and run out for supplies. If the macharomancer does anything stupid, kill him."

The chunk of his sleeve fell out of his mouth with the jogging footsteps back downstairs. Grey stayed perfectly still, counting down the seconds after the doctor left before he pushed himself up on shaky legs. "Trin," he rasped, hoping against all odds that he might be able to somehow talk his way out of this with the sole member of the group that appeared to have a shred of humanity.

"Quiet." A harsh snap he hadn't expected, especially with his calm demeanor earlier.

Grey recoiled. "Trin, please, I—"

"Be. Quiet." A growl this time.

He lowered himself back down to the mattress, staring down at the floor. That *creature* knew his name—pried into his dreams. Whatever Doctor Cavan showed them, they latched onto, but Grey didn't even know what the crystal might've leeched from him.

You'll be mine, soon enough.

Trin's shadow vanished from the door, his near-silent footsteps trailing away.

Grey shivered and buried his face into his arms, cradling them between his knees and his chest. Would they toss him straight into the Hunt once Doctor Cavan handed him over? Did this creature even *know* he was a part of the Hunt?

He'd heard stories of people wandering into faerie circles and being tortured for days before they were dumped on the outskirts of the forest. Nothing but toys to play with and discard. Imagining this monster ripping him apart and dropping him straight into the Hunt to fight for his life made bile creep up his throat.

The steps complained again, multiple footfalls making Grey tense. It was all happening too quick and incredibly slow as the key slid into the door and light poured in. Trin moved inside and dropped down to a knee in front of him. The glint of a knife flicking open made Grey jump.

"Grey, listen to me," he whispered, tucking the blade between his wrists and snapping the zip-tie free. "Run, and don't look back. Don't step foot into a single forest, and don't reply to anything you can't see, understood?"

"I-I don't—"

"Cavan will keep hunting you, just like the creature he communes with. The only way to break free is to find something greater to offer them."

"But... why are you letting me go?"

Trin pulled him to his feet. "My sister was taken by the fair folk. I didn't think Cavan would ever take it this far, but"—he shook his head—"I can't go through with this." He shoved Grey out into the hall, putting him face-to-face with Noel.

His face was smudged with blood and grime, but his shoulders fell in relief anyway. "You're okay," he breathed. An object flew past Grey's head, falling into Noel's hands. A key.

"Lock me in and get out of here," Trin said. "Hurry."

Grey spun around. "Won't Doctor Cavan—"

"Don't worry about me. I can tell him you tricked me into opening the door and weakened me before I could do anything.

Even if he doesn't believe me, I've dealt with him enough, I can manage. Go."

"Thank you," Noel said, reaching for the door handle. "We won't forget this."

Trin waved it away, taking a seat on the floor as the door clicked shut and Noel slid the key into the lock. Then Noel seized Grey's hand and tore down the stairs, dropping the key in Doctor Cavan's office when they ducked inside. Grey's bag sat slumped over in the corner and some of its contents scattered along the floor.

"Bastard," Noel hissed, dropping to his knees to help Grey scoop everything into it. "Did he actually show you anything useful when you were in here last?"

Grey shook his head. "No. Let's just get the hell out of here."

Noel ripped open a couple of desk drawers, fumbling with random notebooks and baubles as Grey slung his bag over his head. He held up his motorcycle key in victory and shoved his knife back into his boot. "Let's go."

He led the way again, bolting through the shop and kicking open the door. His bike still sat outside, undisturbed during the day they'd been held captive. Noel hopped on, revved the engine, and Grey scrambled to climb on behind him—right as a rusty, beat-up van rolled up.

"*Hey!*" Daz hung out of the driver's seat, rage burning behind his irises.

"Hold on," Noel ordered, punching the gas and shooting them straight through town.

Grey tensed, burying his face into Noel's back and squeezing his eyes shut. Shouts and cries carried out behind them as the bike tilted back and forth through turn after turn. He only opened his eyes again when a squeal and crash sounded behind them, and Grey looked over his shoulder to smoke spilling out of the van's hood just as they whipped around another corner.

The city gave way to countryside, and Noel dipped off the road, back on the winding, beaten trails once again.

10

NOEL

The ache in Noel's thigh worked its way into a tremble, his body straining to fight through the pain. Grey's weight against his back turned into his sole reason to continue, despite the nagging corner of his mind that he might be fighting back just as much pain from some hex or whatever that crazy doctor might've done to him. The embarrassing urge to cup his hand around one of Grey's grasping at his jacket was deterred by the sweat slicking his palms.

"How bad is it?"

Grey's tired question made him tense, his muscles struggling and screaming in protest.

"I can manage."

His face rubbed back and forth against Noel's jacket, like he was shaking his head. "Pull off in the tall grass for a few minutes so I can look."

Noel slowed, automatically accepting the command and gliding the bike through the grass. Gaps of shorter or pressed down blades gave him pause as he imagined fair folk creeping out and camping here at night. Or, perhaps this is where people camped out to hide from the fair folk. Wild lavender brushed against his pant leg as he hopped off, nearly toppling into the almost-hidden pocket haven before letting his knees buckle.

Grey pulled his bag over his head and abandoned it next to the bike in favor of dipping down next to him, his hands immediately going for his outstretched leg. Noel's neck heated, and he snapped his face to the sky, pretending to find the sparse collection of clouds more interesting than the boy tending to his wounds like a doting partner.

Lavender wilted as the pain subsided, and Noel's arms gave way for him to lie flat, giving in to exhaustion. "Thank you."

Grey stared down at the browning patch of grass next to them, slowly shaking his head. "Don't thank me. This is my fault."

Noel scrambled to push himself up. "What are you talking about? Grey, we *both* walked into that shop, knowing that something could go wrong—"

"Knowing that they might turn us in to the *Hunt*, not—" He motioned helplessly back toward where they came before running his hands through his hair. Even his unseeing eye appeared to be searching for answers in the dirt. "I shouldn't have touched that crystal."

"You didn't know." The words were firm and gentle, hoping Grey felt the full impact of his empathy. That renewed urge to grab his hand again was quickly deterred by Grey wrapping his arms around himself. Noel leaned forward, trying to catch his gaze. "Did they do anything to you? Are you hurt?"

"Doctor Cavan gave something my name. They clawed their way into my dream and started hunting me, but I couldn't see them. I could *hear* them though..." Grey swiped at his face, trying to hide the fearful tear that slipped out, cracking Noel's heart. "And feel them when they touched me. I don't know why they want *me*, but—"

Noel reached for him this time, cupping Grey's arms. "Did Trin say how to get rid of them? I heard something, but only bits and pieces."

"To offer them something greater." He loosed a bitter laugh. "I don't even know what that constitutes, but I'd imagine anything would be greater than me unless this thing is so twisted they just want someone to rip apart."

"Don't say that." Noel's fingertips pressed into the loose fabric, relishing Grey's warmth. "I said I'd help us escape the Hunt, and we'll get you out of this too. We'll find something to make them leave us alon—" He stopped, staring past Grey at the drooping, browned lavender. "Maybe that's how we get out of the Hunt."

Grey's head tilted ever-so-slightly, his face winkling in confusion.

"A trade. They want us for the Wild Hunt in exchange for not breaking the veil, but if we give them something they consider greater, they might let us go, right?"

"Noel, what could the fair folk possibly want more than fear and bloodshed?"

He bit his lip, letting his hands fall away from Grey's arms to rest on top of his own head. "Well... Didn't the Wild Hunt begin because the fair folk were upset with everything we'd built to destroy nature? Would giving them something to protect or heal it make up for that?" He plucked the now-brittle lavender from its stem, watching it crumble in his grasp.

"I'm pretty sure they already have that with us being under their rule."

"Yeah, but—" He groaned, rocking back again and throwing his hands into the grass. "There's got to be something... A book, a relic..."

Grey's brows knit together. "What would they do with either of those?"

"Well, do *you* have a better idea?"

He tore up a couple of the browning blades, his eyes unfocused, and Noel instantly regretted the jab. He leaned forward again, careful not to brush against Grey's hands as he picked through some of the grass with him.

"Sorry," Noel whispered. "I shouldn't have—"

"It's okay." He wiped his hands on his pants with a sigh. "Neither of us know enough about what the fair folk want, but you're at least trying. I'm just... drawing a blank."

Noel shifted, pulling his leg under him. "What did the fair folk say when they talked to you in your dream? Maybe that would give us an idea?"

Grey shook his head. "Nothing, outside of calling me their little finch and saying I'll be theirs soon." He shivered, and Noel's fingers dug into his leg before he glanced over to Grey's bag.

Like hell he'd let some fair folk rip his only ally away. Noel leaned over, dragging it next to them as he rummaged around for the map. The worn, crumpled paper fell open in his hands and his sights fell on Ivywood. He turned the name over his mind again and again, trying to recall where or why he remembered it. Pointing his finger at the spot on the map and holding it out toward Grey, he asked, "Do you know anything about Ivywood?"

The way he gently slid the map from Noel's grasp—their fingers brushing for a mere moment—made his heart race. He tucked his hand under his thigh as he watched Grey mull over it, as if pinning down the offending limb would suppress his ridiculous pining.

"Isn't Ivywood known for looting? I think I've heard about fair folk running wild there more than once because of thieves and how close it is to the woods."

Noel sat up straight, his father's recollection of his Calling's travels surfacing in his mind. "They've also recovered books from manmade ruins—history books. I think they store it all in an iron-laced bunker or something just in case the walls are breached."

The paper crinkled, buckling under Grey's grip. "Trin told me not to step foot in the woods."

Before Noel could process what he was doing, he grabbed Grey's arm again. "We won't go in the woods. And if we go near it, I'll make sure nothing gets you, okay?" He slowly let go, Grey's sleeve catching his thumb as he chided himself for continuously trying to touch him. "You keep us patched up and walking, and I'll keep the fair folk away. We're a team. That's the only way we're going to be able to make it through this, all right?"

Grey gave a hesitant nod, folding up the map again while Noel pushed himself to his feet. He held a hand down for Grey, his heart starting to sink at the way he paused. But he took it, restoring the hope of the little, greedy thing coiled inside Noel that didn't want to let Grey out of his sight anymore. Grey was his new comfort—his anchor. A constant in a new world of unknowns.

Which is exactly why he couldn't fight back a smile when Grey stood face-to-face with him and uttered two simple words: "Thank you."

11

GREY

When the fog rolled in as they rode further north, Grey had to shove away the echoing taunts of the fair folk from his dream. Not even the false sense of safety from the field helped soothe him with its winding paths. He tensed when a tall structure emerged from the mist—too tall to be a tree with how thin it was, standing parallel to its identical, slanted twin before it gave way to other beams. A bridge.

"The map didn't show a river, did it?" Grey asked, his skin jumping at every sputter of the bike.

"No, but it looks like there was one here at some point." Noel pointed them toward it, guiding the wheels over the bumps of metal rails and wooden slats covered in wildflowers and moss. "Old train tracks too..."

"You think the fair folk got rid of it?" His arms tightened around Noel as they drew closer to the bridge, trying to lift himself up some and glimpse the shallow ravine up ahead.

"Maybe. I bet they dammed it up from the mountains or one of the lakes. Anything to try to spite us, I'd guess..."

Each *thunk* of the tires against the slats sent a shiver through Grey, almost expecting that voice to whisper more honey-coated threats in his ear. The bike rolled over the rail again, and sped up alongside it, putting distance between them and the dried riverbed. Every distant tree through the fog put him on high alert, like it stood as a totem or a banner of enemy territory.

He shrank down, tensing when he thought something tugged on his hood. Noel hit the breaks. "What? What's wrong?"

"N-nothing," Grey said in a near-squeak. "I think the fog is playing tricks on me."

Noel twisted around, and Grey shivered, holding on tighter, as if that'd somehow protect him from getting torn off the bike and dragged away. The putter of the motorcycle drowned out the ambient noises around them while Noel surveyed their little pocket in the mist. And with an exhale, he tugged his knife a little further up in his boot before starting forward again.

The mist eventually gave way to a converted rail hub, surrounded by wrought-iron lattices. Box cars sat on parallel tracks through the fence, people jogging up and down the steps into and out of each one—dull greens and reds decorated with signs.

"Marks."

A stern-looking woman stood on the other side of the gate, a prominent scowl on her face with a polearm at her side. Noel began to push up his sleeve, and Grey tried not to tremble as he mimicked the motion. Her eyes narrowed on Grey.

"Hemomancers require gloves and tagging."

"Tagging?" Noel asked, digging around in his pockets for what Grey assumed were his gloves.

"If you want to enter, bring the hemomancer to the gate. Gloves on. Back to me."

He stopped, glancing back at Grey with concern creasing his features. "Are you okay with this?"

No, but it's not like I've ever had much of a choice. Grey nodded, his teeth chattering as he held out a hand for the gloves. He tugged them on and stumbled off the bike before making his way toward the bars separating them from their destination. Rubbing his arms, he turned his back to her, his bag thumping against the barrier.

"Hands on the bars. If you take your hands off the bars, you'll forfeit admission."

Grey fumbled to grab onto the iron, jolting as the woman grabbed his wrists and guided them. The flicker of metal passed in front of him, and then cold rested against his neck with a sickening, heavy *click*.

"Padlock and collar will be removed upon exiting. Do *not* tamper with the collar while you're here, and if you take off your gloves in public, you will be escorted out. Understood?"

"Understood," he whispered.

She tapped his gloved hands. "You're free to step away."

The itch to reach up and feel around the collar lost to Grey's urge to climb back on the bike for safety, hating how Noel watched him with pity in those green eyes. He fumbled to grasp Noel's jacket again as the gate screeched open, and they continued rolling parallel to the tracks.

"I'm sorry," he said over his shoulder. "It's temporary."

"I know," Grey mumbled. He swallowed as stray sets of eyes followed them with deep, disapproving frowns.

Noel shot them dirty looks and revved the bike past them, straight into the center of the rail yard city. Grey's heart sank the further they went as he read each sign that denied hemomancers from entry. He guessed that he shouldn't have expected anything different here. Gravel crunched under the tires as they stopped in front of the monolithic monstrosity in the heart of it all, and Noel kicked down the stand.

Grey stared up at the concrete building with its iron bars and his hands sweating in Noel's gloves. Straight out of one prison-like basement and into another. He hurried after Noel, sticking close on his way through the heavy, metal double doors. The lobby was a ghost town with dust motes twirling in the shreds of sunlight filtering through the windows high above. Grey supposed that was to be expected when a place filled with books was practically one bad day away from turning into a kindling reserve when people's priorities were firmly set on survival. Not that Grey and Noel's blight was all that different, though their needs for survival pushed them down a vastly different path.

The man at the front desk peered over his glasses, his mouth pressing into a thin line as they approached. "Can I help you, sir?" his question was pointed at Noel, a cordial demeanor slipping through the second he ignored Grey.

Noel put his hands on the steel table of a reception desk. "We're hoping to gain access to your library. A friend of ours is sick, and we think that one of the fair folk might've cursed her."

The receptionist tapped a stack of papers against the metal surface before laying them flat. "Spiral staircase behind the wall will take you down a level. There's an entire corner dedicated to fair folk." His eyes flicked back to Grey as his voice dropped to a warning grumble. "Please keep your hemomancer in check."

Noel's tight smile came with a sharp, "Of course." He grabbed Grey's hand and pulled him along. They passed grated shelves and strode over catwalks to the spiral staircase. Grey's stomach dropped when he glimpsed there were at least two more floors below them, all separated by interlocking metal links welded into frames.

Small tables were tucked into corners on the far edges, away from the catwalks and on solid ground. The soles of their shoes bounced against the floorboards in the midst of the fair folk archives with its stacked, floor-to-ceiling collection of books and journals crammed into every free space.

Noel grimaced, spinning around with increasing worry. "This... is going to take a while."

The Great Wild Hunt began at the turn of the 22nd century when Queen Mab awoke during a blood moon and shattered the veil between our realm and the Otherworld. Its destruction spread over most of the globe, save a few small pockets, deemed 'queendoms,' kept sectioned off to ensure none of Her Majesty's new subjects could revolt as she infused the land with renewed magic. Her terror lasted over a decade before she returned to her homeland with a promise that she'd hunt again.

Grey pulled the glove away from his face with a yawn, the leather peeling off his skin. He brushed the hair from his eye and hunched over the book's yellowing pages.

During her rule in our realm, magic soaked into the land, which eventually gave way to various types of mancers. Magic became a new, primary defense against the fair folk, and iron was further conserved to ward off more vicious, aggressive creatures that would wander out of the woods.

He flipped the page after glossing over the rest, catching on the praise of macharomancers and their gift of channeling through iron. A bitter taste welled up in Grey's mouth as he read more about their celebrated gifts before turning a few more pages until his sight snagged on *hydromancers*.

Originally one of the most powerful of the mancers, hydromancers were snuffed out during the first return of Queen Mab. Her Majesty warped the magic flowing through them to confine their power to that of blood: twisting them into beasts during the second Great Wild Hunt. The survivors were outcasted for many years.

Grey stared down at the page, frozen as the words sank in. Hydromancers: the one type of magic that could confine the fair folk to the forests or keep them restricted to their realm. His hand absently moved to the collar resting against his neck. How many people knew about this? Is *this* why everyone here looked at him like he was an abomination? Was he just some unhinged creature, bending to the whim of the fair folk? He flipped a few more pages, shoving down the uneasy feeling in the pit of his stomach.

After a century, Queen Mab retired to her realm with the decree of bringing six mancers, one from each sect, to be sacrificed to a Wild Hunt held within her realm. This would be the only way to pacify her, and defying this rule would result in tearing the veil once again. To ensure she received appropriate warriors for her Wild Hunt, we must always be prepared for her selected prey to be summoned to her battleground.

He sat back in the metal chair. His gloved fingers fumbled

through the rest of the pages, skimming word after word about the rules of the Hunt, depictions of the fair folk rumored to be involved, and the unfortunate 'winner' Queen Mab would send back to signal that her bloodlust was satiated.

Grey snapped the book shut and tucked it back onto the shelf, his gaze wandering over to Noel picking through the rows of books on the opposite end of the nook. He hadn't sat down for the past ten minutes during his rummaging and skimming through volumes. Grey bit his lip and thumbed over a few more spines until he came across one titled, *The Laws of Trade*. He leaned back against the table as the book fell open in his hands and the metal shuffling of other library-goers faded away.

Fair folk require trade, whether that be through trade to perform magic or through the simple balance of nature and humanity, there must always be an equilibrium.

He scowled down at the words, thinking of Atticus's rephrasing of the term to something more appropriate: sacrifice. Pages fluttered together as he tipped the book to skip ahead and stop when images of offerings to fair folk appeared. Expensive bottles of wine, sugary treats, unique trinkets. Grey tried to imagine offering one of those things in place of himself.

Something greater...

The book's cloth cover rubbed against the table as he set it down to retrieve another—one regarding fair folk's use of humans.

Humans lured or stolen away by the fair folk and taken to the Otherworld are primarily used as servants. Occasionally, children may be stolen away and replaced with changelings.

*It's assumed that these children are possibly used to entertain
the fair folk or temporarily raised as their own until reaching a
proper age to assist in servitude. However, some humans have
been abducted to participate in entertainment akin to the
Wild Hunt or for the purpose of one of the fair folk deciding to
take a mortal lover.*

Grey shivered, his grip tightening against the pages.

Don't cause a fuss, my little finch.

He prayed the latter wasn't the case, but the discomfort
pooling in his gut didn't want to risk assuming something less
than what it could be. Especially if his freedom was dependent on
an offering. For a second, he imagined trying to give this fair folk
an actual *finch*, but he shook the idea from his mind. They could
simply get their own finch, right?

Yeah, you.

"Any luck?"

Grey tensed as Noel stopped next to him, dropping his own
book on the desk.

"I don't suppose a really expensive bottle of wine would cut
us loose..." he said, folding the tome shut.

"Well..." Noel said, folding his arms over his chest and leaning
against the perpendicular edge. "There are things like sacrificial
rubies and faerie baubles, right?"

He brought his gloved thumb to his lips, tracing the bottom
of it in thought. "Or maybe more amethyst would ward this one
off? Maybe I could bargain with them to give them more of my
memories or something?"

Noel grimaced and shook his head. "That sounds pretty
unsettling. If anything, they'll probably argue that memories

won't do them any good, not unless they're using you for some sort of sick high."

His hands dropped, and he shifted to clasp them in front of him. "Part of the problem is that I'm not sure *why* they want me. I read all the reasons, but the worst possibility is that they want me for a"—he shifted uncomfortably—"a lover. Which is absolutely ridiculous," he quickly added, drawing his arms around himself in a hug.

That line of thought always left Grey uneasy, mainly because he'd never really felt that way about anyone he'd come across before. While he craved that deeper, emotional connection, he'd never really felt that urge to take up any of the propositions from some of the people back home to enjoy themselves. To try to find that sort of relationship from a fair folk lord or master sounded impossible and wholly carnal in nature—something that made Grey's skin crawl.

Grey cleared his throat. "They probably just want me to do their bidding. I can't imagine them wanting anything more than that."

"What makes you so sure?"

He reflexively reached for his eye, turning his head away with his fingers curling into a fist. "The fair folk only enjoy pretty things."

The table nudged some as Noel pushed away and moved in front of him. "I think you're being a little hard on yourself."

"I'm being realistic."

"By devaluing yourself?" Sorrow rippled his features.

"Noel, I'm a hemomancer." Grey tugged on the collar. "And other hemomancers only look at me with pity when they see or hear I've been tortured. Some people told me I deserved it or I had it coming. And maybe I did—maybe I *do* with reading things like hydromancers existing and then being changed into hemo-mancers, so we can't defy the fair folk. I'm just an abomination—just another monster..." He forced out a curling breath and tousled his hair, cupping his hands over his forehead. "If anything, this is all just another way to drag me into the Hunt. You had your dream to hand me over, and when you said no, the fair folk decided they'll come after me."

The quiet that settled in left Grey with a horrible ache, like his heart longed for another answer. Fingers wrapped around his wrist and pulled his arm away from shielding his face. Noel took a step forward. "You didn't deserve it. You don't deserve *this.*" He motioned to the collar resting around Grey's neck. "You haven't done anything to warrant my distrust, let alone any reason to make me think you'd use your hemomancy against me. And you've had plenty of chances to kill me and run to try to increase your odds of surviving—"

Grey quietly snorted. "If anything, my odds would plummet."

"Regardless," Noel breathed, "we'll find an appropriate trade. Something valuable this thing won't say no to."

"Maybe a finch *would* work," Grey muttered, fidgeting with his collar as he stared at one of the bottom shelves.

"A... finch?"

"They called me their little finch."

Noel's hand squeezed his wrist even tighter, taking him by surprise. He jerked his head up to see anger darken his features.

"Noel..." Grey began cautiously, trying to twist out of his hold.

His grip loosened. "Sorry, I... I don't think a finch will work, and I'm not exactly sure a fair folk looking for another servant is going to give them a pet name."

Grey pulled away and reached back for his books. "Like I said, Noel, I'm only useful as a servant." He moved past him to replace them on the shelves, sliding them back into their little nooks. "I think the better question is what sort of trade would get us out of this."

Noel rubbed the back of his neck and rocked against the table again. "I think it's going to be tricky to offer something up in place of us being in the Hunt."

"Especially since I guess we're technically offering something to Queen Mab," Grey said with a grimace. "She wants the Hunt to happen, so the only thing I can imagine her accepting is another person in our places."

"Maybe, *or*"—Noel snapped his fingers, his eyes lighting up— "maybe she'll accept something that shows our devotion to her as a ruler?"

He made a motion for him to continue. "With?"

Noel's excitement faded. "Um…"

Grey stepped past him, collecting Noel's book. "Maybe let's start with a meal and asking around? Then we can figure it out from there."

❧ 12 ❧

NOEL

L *ittle finch.*

Without a doubt, those were the two most upsetting words Grey could've uttered. Noel couldn't shake them from his mind as they started out of the archives and headed to dinner. He kept reminding himself that he didn't have a valid enough reason to be upset, considering he and Grey weren't... anything, really. Friends, maybe, but nothing more than that. Just a boy wearing his gloves and warming his back whenever they traveled—intimacy in the form of an awkward hug. And Noel felt sickened by the idea that this fair folk creature might be preparing to take him for their own pleasure.

Noel shifted to conceal Grey's presence in their corner booth, warding away the scowls while Grey tugged up his hoodie to hide the collar a little more.

"I would've ripped it off by now," Noel mumbled, running his thumbs up and down his water glass while they waited for their food.

Grey remained quiet for a moment as he gathered his hood around it. "I prefer wearing it over the alternative."

"You mean getting kicked out?"

His dark eye snapped up to meet his green. "Having someone decide to torture and kill me because they deem me as a threat."

Noel's heart squeezed in time with his fingertips pressing against the glass. He glanced over his shoulder just as the waitress started their way with a tray, a smirk tugging at her lips as the bar patrons made quiet jabs for her to watch herself. She shook her head with a quip that she could take care of herself, further adding to Noel's irritation.

She slid the tray onto the table, depositing each bowl of stew without so much as a look in Grey's direction before she left. No pleasantries. No additional kind words to let them know she'd assist if they needed anything else. A simple cold shoulder since they'd already paid.

Grey tucked into the food anyway, slowing to blow on it and take sips of water between bites like a starved animal. Noel continued stirring his while he tried to ignore everything wrong with Grey's reserved behavior in the face of death threats. Outside of his panic at the obelisk—

Noel paused. That *hadn't* been the only time he'd shown panic. He'd been inconsolable under the oddities shop before Doctor Cavan had trekked down the steps with his goons. "Grey."

He stopped mid-chew, staring at Noel in question.

"Back in the basement—"

Grey shook his head, swiping his sleeve across his mouth. "I didn't mean to get you hurt—"

Noel shook his head. "That's not what I'm trying to ask. I was actually wondering why you reacted so violently until the doctor showed up."

Grey hesitated and lowered his spoon handle to the rim of the bowl. "When... when I was twelve, macharomancers killed my parents and locked me in a cellar for a month. They said it was because someone from their town was murdered and we were the only ones that lived close enough, so we were guilty by proximity. They never allowed hemomancers in, so..."

He shrugged, nudging some of the meat chunks around the stew. "At first, the woman that kept me there made her children practice macharomancy on me. I couldn't really heal without touching something to trade with, so they usually caught and dumped mice down there for me. But, winter hit, and she decided I'd be easier to deal with if I couldn't see anymore because I kept trying to break the basement windows to escape. I ran out of mice."

Noel's stomach turned over, losing his appetite from the mere thought that the fear he'd seen in Grey's eye back in Doctor Cavan's house of horrors had been the same look a younger Grey had given his captors years ago. "But you didn't do anything... Why would she—"

Grey bit his lip. "I think it's a lot like how I'm treated in this town, or like how hemomancers are depicted in the archive. Perception is all that matters. I'm a thing: a threat, child or not. I don't help in a way that could protect from the fair folk."

"But you can heal."

A puff of unamused laughter. "You're the first person that's trusted me enough to allow me to, let alone countless other hemomancers that'd undoubtedly try to help our fellow mancers. They just see our destruction when we defend ourselves and when we trade, so that's what we are: forces of destruction."

Noel swallowed. "So, how did you escape?"

"My aunt—my guardian that I call my aunt—found me. She was scouting the city for a while because apparently other hemomancers had gone missing, and her husband had recently been accused of killing one of their livestock. She confronted my jailor since she was one of the town leaders, and I cried for help. Or—I guess I screamed at the top of my lungs until I passed out. When I came to, I was wrapped in a blanket and a coat in the back of a car with my uncle saying everything would be all right and that we were going home."

Noel scooted closer. "I'm *so* sorry—"

"You didn't do it," Grey whispered. "Don't be sorry. I just learned it was easier to behave whenever my warden appeared to hurt me because it wasn't drawn out and to throw a fit whenever they left, so I might have a chance to escape."

"You shouldn't have even needed to learn that anyway," Noel hissed, scolding himself when Grey flinched. "The fact that someone did that to you is downright disgusting. And you being pulled into the Wild Hunt seems unusually cruel, especially hearing what you've gone through."

Grey winced, dropping his voice to below a whisper. "I don't think Queen Mab cares who she chooses as long as they put on a good show for her. Maybe she knows I'll run until my legs give out or heal myself over and over again until my body gives up."

"Or that you could possibly offer her something so great she'll dismiss you?"

Grey opened his mouth, then shook his head. "We can only hope."

Noel's heart sank as Grey went back to his dinner, picking through it much slower now, but keeping a steady pace, like he wasn't sure when his next meal was. He supposed neither of them knew when their next meal would be, so he began to dig into his too.

The squeal of the tavern door came with a raucous laughter and a squad of leather jackets bearing iron spikes and shoulder guards. The leader—his halomancer brand on full display—called out to the bar as his companions piled into the corner booth on the opposite end of the dining hall. "Round of drinks for my crew."

"Good haul?" the barkeep asked, a grin splitting her face as she motioned for the waitress to help her.

"Probably the best one yet," he said with a chuckle. "We'll have to take some of it to the appraiser in the morning, but we got more gold, so I can't complain."

Noel exchanged glances with Grey, his heart hammering in his chest with each detail of their looted treasure. This group might just be their ticket out.

❦

"Wait!" Noel jogged after the looters while Grey threw up his hood and hung back. Every step he took away from him felt like a step of abandonment and betrayal, but the crew turned around. "I work for a guy in Woodhurst, and he's interested in artifacts anyone might've found from faerie ruins."

Their leader perked up, grinning with a motion for him to follow. "Then step right up and take a look. We have quite a few artifacts you can peruse through back at our storehouse." He jabbed a thumb behind him.

Noel hesitated, glancing back at Grey, who rocked on his heels under an awning with his head down. He cleared his throat. "I also have an associate my boss sent with me. Would it be okay if…"

He trailed off, earning a shrug so he could omit the details. So, he waved him over, and Grey ducked his head to hide the collar.

"Let's go then," the guy said, rounding up the group. He clapped Noel on the back, spouting off some impossible journey through the wilderness, filled with wolves, bears, and vengeful fair folk—all warded off with their magic and iron.

But all Noel could think about was the possible treasure they collected. Guilt pulsed through him as they climbed the steps to their little boxcar, which happened to be a few boxcars deep with side doors slid open when he stepped inside. Their austromancer put on a kettle while the halomancer leader and a macharomancer brought them all the way to the back, where they threw back a curtain to a set of locked trunks.

Each one snapped open, and the leader set out each unique piece on the rickety side table. Grey gingerly lifted up a wooden box, engraved with an intricate tree emblem, and removed the lid with a frown. "It's empty."

The leader shrugged. "Sorry. There was gold inside, so we sold it off. The box is an older piece no one's wanted to take yet."

He replaced the lid and set it down as both he and Noel reached for one of the others. Grey went for a delicate-looking tea-cup-sized bowl with hand-painted flowers decorating it while Noel retrieved a thin, leathery case. He bent it slightly and slid its contents free, finding a small, green-tinted blade tucked inside.

"Pretty nice, huh?" the macharomancer said, elbowing him. "It's not iron, but it's quite a beauty."

Something suitable for the fair folk to use in the Wild Hunt...

"How much?" Noel said, unable to catch himself.

"Well, well—" A chuckle slipped from the halomancer as he strode over to stand between Noel and Grey at the table. He plucked the blade from his grip, turning it over a couple times. "I think the appraiser said this was worth a thousand, right?"

Noel's stomach dropped. "A thousand?"

"Yep. Sound fair?"

Based on the wide-eyed look Grey shot him, they likely didn't have more than a hundred pieces between them. "It's... a little out of our price range," Noel said.

Grey held up the bowl for him. "What about this?"

"Six hundred."

He put it down, his gloved hands hovering over another piece before recoiling. Noel took a step back and turned to the halomancer with an apologetic smile. "We might need to discuss it a bit with our employer first. He can be a little frugal, so we'll talk it over and get back to you if that's all right?"

"Of course," he said, beaming. "Just keep in mind these won't be around forever."

"Oh, trust me, we're well aware," Noel said, his smile pained as he grabbed Grey's arm and guided him out.

The kettle's whistle pierced his ears as he jogged down the steps, and Grey's shoulder bumped against his on the gravel pathway.

"Well, shit."

❧ 13 ❧

GREY

When Noel shut the door to their inn room, Grey rubbed his arms and scanned over the room's recycled, falling apart and threadbare furniture. The bed's sheets and blankets were snagged, the night table was propped up by a door wedge, the pillows were flat, and the windows were taped up.

And they were back to one bed. A single-person bed.

Noel's soles scraped the rug next to him. "Here I thought we'd at least get a full-sized bed with how expensive the room was…"

"Why don't you take the bed?" Grey said. "I at least got a mattress last night at Cavan's, so I don't need—"

"No, you shouldn't—"

"And you've been driving—"

"But you've been healing—" Noel shifted, cutting himself off and half tucking his hands in his pockets. He pulled them back out before he bit his lip and started for it. Grey relaxed, relieved he'd convinced him until Noel spun around, bent down, and threw him over his shoulder. A yelp escaped him, and he flailed as

Noel dropped him onto the mattress. "You get the bed," Noel said sternly. "I'll make myself comfortable on the floor."

Grey's hand shot up to the collar, regret settling in his gut about telling Noel the darkest part of his past. But Noel strode over to the closet. If he'd seen him react, he hadn't noticed it, and began to pull down the extra linens stored on the shelf.

"If this is out of pity, then—"

Noel's head whipped around, the spare comforter and pillow nearly falling from his grasp. "What? No—Just—" He scrambled to drop it all next to the bed. "You've sacrificed a lot so far to go along with all of this, so try to rest. I've barely traded anything, except for when we escaped the wardens, so I think you deserve an unobstructed, good night's rest. That's it." The way the last words strung together sounded stiff and fake, but Grey gave him the satisfaction of a slow nod while he reached to tug off his boots.

Watching Noel drop to his knees and spread out his makeshift bed, Grey dumped his shoes over the end of the mattress and curled up for sleep. Every adjustment against the thin pillow made him squirm with the collar digging into his neck. The strange blend of nickel and patches of smoothed crystal lining it pressed rectangles into his skin. After a few attempts to have the collar hang off the pillow, Grey finally found a tolerable position before Noel turned off the light.

Black consumed the room, save the trickle of light from under the door and the diffused town lights glowing in the window at Grey's back. So, he closed his eyes and focused on Noel's breathing—a gentle lullaby guiding him into sleep.

Where are you, my little finch?

Grey stumbled backward, hitting a wall with a wince. He peered into the dark, unable to find any signs of movement while he tried to pry his hands apart. Every twist of his wrists resulted in sharp pain that reverberated in his chest, just in the form of panic. He tried to stand, his legs shaking uncontrollably as he swallowed down his biting words for the fair folk prowling around beyond his vision to leave him alone. If he kept quiet, maybe they'd give up and head somewhere else.

Don't be scared. I won't hurt you. Just follow my voice.

Grey's knees buckled at how close it sounded. His pulse thumped in his ears, pushing every other soft movement of his hunter to the background. He bit into his hoodie sleeve and his mouth filled with the tang of sweat and salt from dried tears. The panic-inducing squelch of Grey's boots creeping along the perimeter of the room made his head spin until a single, horrible thought pierced his mind: the room wasn't dark; he just couldn't see.

Grey's teeth sank into his arm as he collapsed into the corner and tried to stifle a sob. All that pent-up hate from his series of jailers had finally taken the piece of him he cherished the most—the one sense he relied on to create and pour his soul onto paper with hands people feared touching. Now he'd forever be a creature of pure destruction. Another living thing that might as well be fair folk.

He flinched as the floor creaked in front of him, hair standing up on his arms as a feather-light touch grazed his cheek. "There you are, my finch," they cooed, their voice crisp in clear in comparison to the ghostly echo he'd been trying to run from.

Warm tears spilled down his face. They clicked their tongue before gently wiping them away. The sharp edge of what felt like a fingernail made Grey jolt. His core tightened as his mind raced, trying to piece together what he'd actually felt from their inhuman hand: a claw.

"Shh, don't cry."

The mere mention of it caused Grey to hiccup out a quiet, distressed sob as he tried to bury his face in his arms. Plastic dug into his skin, choking the backs of his hands. "Please let me go."

A shiver worked through him as the claws ran through his hair. Grey bit down on his tongue, trying to hold back his revolution.

"Humans are such selfish, hateful things," they said, venom bubbling to the top before spilling into curiosity, "and yet you'd rather continue dwelling among them than accept me?"

Grey paused, his own breath suffocating him in his little curled cocoon.

"Look at what they've done to you, Grey." They forced their clawed-tipped hand under his chin, prying it up to stare into the void. "What would stop them from taking more?"

A stray tear met the dip where claw dented cheek, reminding Grey that this fair folk could easily squeeze and break his jaw if it wanted to. His throat bobbed as he remembered the sound of the macharomancer woman's heavy boots coming down the stairs and the pattering of her children's slippers. Bile threatened to coat the back of his tongue as he recalled retching at the base of a tree after fighting off his attackers trying to collect him for the Hunt.

To people: he was a potential threat. To the fair folk: he was pure entertainment.

He could fight back in the world he knew, even if he wasn't strong enough to survive in the end. In the Otherworld, he'd be a mouse in a maze, waiting for the trap to snap whenever he thought he'd found reprieve.

"At least—" Grey breathed, every word quivering in the face of certain retaliation. "At least I have a fighting chance among my own kind, rather than at the mercy of faerie whims."

The silence that followed left him to imagine what sort of reaction they might be making until that curious tone returned. "And what makes you say that?"

"Y-you want me for the Wild Hunt, don't you?" Grey forced out, hating how small and pained he sounded, like a tolling bell on his life.

A dark chuckle sent him jerking back, trying to escape the disturbed bemusement. The vice-like grip on his jaw clamped a little tighter, forcing him to his feet, where his whole body trembled.

"You want to run from the Wild Hunt? Then I'll be happy to give chase until you surrender, little finch." A taunting purr that made Grey's heart plummet.

"Why?" Hurt seeped out like blood from a wound.

The scent of cypress pressed in on him as cool breath tickled his skin. "Because if anyone gets to hunt you, it should be the one you belong to."

❧

Grey jolted awake, his hands clasping around the collar digging into his throat with a sharp gasp. His head spun, and tears sprang to his eyes at the sight of streetlights peeking through the windows. He could see, but he was still being choked by something trying to keep him pacified.

A shadowy figure pooled at the edge of the bed, and Grey scrambled backward, panting as dim yellow poured over green eyes. "Grey, what's wrong?"

He shook his head, his vision blurring. "I-I don't want this—"

"Don't want what?" Noel carefully climbed onto the mattress.

Grey sucked in a breath as it dipped, his mind trying to correct his fear that the boy in front of him was the fair folk stalking his nightmares. "They're hunting me. They won't stop until I give up because I belong to them, and I don't know what to do." He was reduced down to a scared child again. No Atticus and Ingrid to save him from the cruelty waiting on the horizon.

Noel grabbed Grey's sweatshirt and pulled him forward, despite Grey trying to push away. Arms encircled him, and Noel laid down, his thumb tracing small circles along Grey's spine. "I got you," he whispered as Grey's cheek settled against Noel's chest. "They can't take you when I have iron to fight them off. They won't be hunting either of us soon. Just breathe."

He sucked in a shaky breath, driving away the thoughts of the collar as he focused on Noel's soothing touch. "I'm s-sorry."

"Don't be. I'm scared too. But we're not alone. We're going to take care of each other."

He half-nodded against Noel's shirt, soaking up his warmth and calm, even breathing. And after a few more minutes of tranquil quiet, sleep took him again.

14

NOEL

Noel stared up at the stained ceiling with an arm tucked behind his head and the other absently running along Grey's back. The gentle rise and fall of Grey's chest finally told him he was sleeping, but a sour tang in Noel's mouth kept him wide awake, imagining the fair folk might break into Grey's head again.

He didn't belong to that *thing*, let alone have the right to torment and threaten him like this. Noel almost wished this fair folk would show themself so he could hunt *them* instead. Ripping into them with an iron knife sounded like music to his ears after the way Grey flew into a panic. Here he was, putting on a brave face and giving up more and more to keep trudging along, only for sick bastards like Doctor Cavan to make things worse.

His hand drew away from Grey's back as he glanced down to his sleeping form curled up against him, and he tried to tuck some of Grey's short, black, wavy locks behind his ear. They popped free almost immediately, making their slow slide toward his face again. Noel chided himself for indulging in that moment as his mind invented a world in which his Calling was to travel like his father had.

Maybe he would run into a few hemomancers and realize none of them were all that bad, and then maybe they would invite him back to their town, where Grey would be living. They could meet when Grey was out shopping or—

The prompt stumped him, and Noel racked his brain to piece together what else Grey might be doing back home. There weren't any medics in a hemomancer town, for obvious reasons. He conjured up the contents spilled from Grey's bag in Doctor Cavan's office, recalling a banded journal and a small, charcoal-stained tin.

It clicked like a puzzle piece when he stared back up at the ceiling again, a smile tugging at the corner of his mouth. Grey would be capturing the scenery somewhere nearby, and Noel would find him by accident. That's how it'd start.

Fate would bring them together, just in a kinder way than it had when they'd been driven to the obelisk. They'd sort through their fears naturally, rather than out of necessity, and then it would all unravel from there, spanning out into years of give and take, like his parents always reminded him relationships needed.

His smirk faded as the watercolor daydreams evaporated back to the rusty stains of reality, and his hand dropped back down to Grey's back. He could fantasize all he wanted, but it wouldn't do either of them good in the end. Instead, he had to focus on the here and now—the path out of the dark woods they'd wandered into.

What they needed was money to get that special fae knife and bowl. Either that or for them to be able to collect something similar for themselves. Noel chewed on his lip as he let that thought settle in his mind, rooting with each thump of Grey's heartbeats against his palm.

Iron.

If they had iron, they could go into the ruins themselves—a much cheaper alternative that might yield them a greater profit, either way. Then they could walk free once they made their trade to escape the Wild Hunt.

Problem solved.

That could work, couldn't it? Or was that far too simple? Maybe they were just overthinking the whole thing to begin with, and the answer was right there in front of them: give the fair folk and Queen Mab back what's theirs.

❧

Sneaking out of bed turned into a challenge with Grey clinging to him for over an hour until he shifted. But even when he moved, Noel warred with himself over getting up, slipping on his shoes, and wandering out of the inn.

He tucked his hands into his pockets and shivered against the wind sweeping through the streets between the lines of boxcars. Off-key songs spilled out of taverns, driving pinpricks of irritation into his soul. They were running for their lives while the rest of the world continued on like nothing was wrong.

Gravel crunched with Noel's every step on his way past metal-sided storefronts. He jogged up the steps to a shop illuminated with a bluish, daylight hue. The door pushed open, and a woman looked up from the counter with bags under her eyes and a steaming mug in reach. "How can I help you?" she asked, the macharomancer mark on her arm peeking out from her sleeve as she moved to wipe down the iron dagger on the table.

Noel scanned the small boxes organized along the back wall, the labels barely legible with messy ink strokes. "Do you mind if I take a look at the pieces you have to melt down?"

She nodded and pulled down a bin, setting it in front him. "Have at it."

He picked through the iron pieces, turning each one over in his hands until he came across an old-fashioned skeleton key. Noel held it up, getting the shopkeeper's attention again. "How much?"

15

GREY

The smell of warm cinnamon roused Grey from sleep, along with the *clink* of a tray against the night table. He popped up and swiped at his eyes while Noel scooped a bowl up and offered it to him.

"Sleep better after the nightmare?" he asked as Grey relished the heat against his bare palms.

"Yes," Grey whispered. "Thank you, by the way. I'm sorry I woke you."

"Don't be sorry." The bed complained as Noel perched next to him with his own bowl of oatmeal. "I'd feel worse if I'd left you to deal with it alone."

Grey began stirring in the cinnamon as he replayed Noel crawling into bed last night to comfort him. Every deliberate movement and careful touch made him shift to try to shake off the intrusive thoughts of safety mixed with that weird sensation in his core.

Don't overthink it. Why would he like you like that?

The mere notion of Grey entertaining a relationship *now*, of all times, made his stomach churn. And with a macharomancer—a fellow member of the Wild Hunt. Grey shoveled a spoonful of oatmeal into his mouth, savoring the spice while they ate in silence. The final scrapes from the bottoms of the bowls pierced through it, and Noel sighed as he set his back on the tray, the spoon rattling against the edge.

"I got you something."

Grey tensed, his heart beating wildly as Noel pulled something from his pocket—an old key strung through a braided leather cord. Confusion pressed in until Noel drew closer, and Grey gripped his bowl, unsure what he was doing before Noel lifted the makeshift pendant over his head. It skimmed the collar, falling over his hoodie, where he reached to feel the worn iron against his palm.

"Hopefully that'll help with the nightmares." He pried the empty dish from Grey's hands and set it on the tray with his own. "But I was also thinking it'd help protect you if we have to go in the woods."

Grey's hand fell away, his ridiculous ideas tossed to the back of his mind again and locked up for his own safety. He grimaced, trying to keep his exhausted tone firm. "Trin said not to step foot in—"

"I know, but we're running out of options, Grey." Noel's pleading look needled at him. "If we head into the ruins, we have a chance to get something just as good, if not *better* than what we saw yesterday, or maybe gold to pay for one of those items. We have to try, or we're as good as dead, right?"

You want to run from the Wild Hunt? Then I'll be happy to give chase until you surrender, little finch.

Grey hugged himself, fighting back that knot in his throat.

He wished Noel wasn't right, but they couldn't afford not to take risks. Not with whatever waited for them in the Otherworld.

Noel's hand clung to Grey's shoulder, tilting him to look him in the eye. "I know you're afraid, but I won't let anything happen to you, okay? If it turns too dangerous, we'll run. Fair?"

His gaze drifted to the bedding still strewn about the floor, thoughts of his night locked up in Doctor Cavan's spare room sending phantom chills running up and down his arms. He wrapped his fingers around the key hanging around his neck again, its quiet pulse of power anchoring him.

"Okay," he breathed. "Fair."

Grey craned his neck to take in the looming presence of the forest as Noel rolled to a stop on the outskirts. The motor purred in the face of danger while Grey tried to conjure up a disturbing image of what might be hunting him inside. His mind rattled off everything he knew that had claws until the list was disrupted by Noel's, "You ready?"

"Y-yeah," Grey answered, his arms tightening around Noel's body, like he was bracing for impact.

A gentle pat from one of Noel's hands against his own gave him the smallest dose of reassurance before the bike lurched into the unknown. The slow roll through the narrow trail made every shadow look like a creature in the corners of Grey's vision. The stink of moss permeated the air, further feeding his anxiety with the suffocation of the fair folk's influence.

When it all gave way to a stream, Grey relaxed some. That is, until Noel turned off the bike.

"What are you doing? Are we not going to look for a bridge somewhere?"

Noel shook his head as he climbed off and started for the stream, his shoes squishing against the mud at the water's edge. "See the stone up ahead? I think we're right on it…" He pointed past the trees shading the other side, and Grey hopped off.

Tangled roots and soft green consumed the ancient walls of what remained of the buildings and monuments in front of them. Pillars stood with crumbled chunks around them, like a tree shedding leaves.

A shiver worked through him as Noel took the first step onto one of the rocks. Water lapped at his soles on his way to the next. Grey followed behind, like this was a child's game of exploration he vaguely plucked from his memory, always chasing after someone he couldn't remember.

Once they were on the other side, Grey turned back to the bike with a frown.

"Come on." Noel tugged on his sleeve, ripping him from his urge to escape from this place and the unease settling in his stomach.

The brush of grass transitioned into the tap of well-worn stone beneath them, set among ransacked destruction and decay. Threadbare banners were snagged on doorframes and ripped along the sides, almost as if someone had removed the trim. Grey bet it was probably gold, considering the gaping hole in the center of the flag where the emblem once sat.

Alchemic symbols matching the ones tattooed on their arms were scratched into the wall plaques they passed once they ducked inside the first, partially-roofed building, along with half-torn notes begging for curses to be undone.

Take away these nightmares, one demanded.

My mother is sick because of this curse. Please spare her, cried another.

I did what you asked. Take it away, read the third. *You have my son, now free me from this wretched blood bond.*

"Nothing comes without sacrifice," Grey mumbled under his breath, like a mantra as he rubbed his arms and wandered after Noel through the debris of the collapsed roof.

The former garden sat before them with upheaved paving stones and a toppled, eroded fountain. Noel slowed as they passed it and clicked his tongue. "Figures there's nothing in it."

"We probably won't find anything unless we go pretty far inside," Grey said, staring down the dilapidated, covered path up ahead where stone met mountain. The spaced columns holding the entrance together leading into the inner sanctum might as well have been beckoning them into a massive cathedral. He grabbed at the key around his neck. "I don't think this is a good idea."

Noel ran a hand through his hair with a grimace at the yawning maw of the fair folk shrine. "I know it's not a good idea, but we're sort of out of options." He motioned for Grey to walk with him, and they started into the shadow of the overhang, straight into the depths of the teeming dark.

They stopped on the threshold of the entrance for their eyes to adjust to the dim, cavernous dome of a main hall. Chandeliers hung among the beams, candles frozen mid-drip without their flames to whittle them down. Two were missing, tiles cracked below where they once hung, but their remains were nowhere to be found.

Picked clean.

That was the only real way to describe this place with how the recessed candle holders and sconces had been ripped from their nooks and off the walls. All that remained were less dusty outlines of rugs and seating had once rested before it'd been ransacked.

And Grey couldn't help but feel a twinge of remorse for all the destruction others had left behind. That pang of sadness pressed in on him, and as Noel started forward, pulling his flashlight from his belt, Grey grabbed his arm. "This feels wrong."

He cocked his head and flicked on the light. "Grey, it's a fair folk shrine. They want to kill us for sport. I don't think they'll give a shit if you feel guilty about it. You'd rather live, wouldn't you?"

Grey shifted, letting go of Noel as he traced the trail of the flashlight beam. The far-off memory of his mother pulling him into her lap while they watched distant, dancing lights unfurled in his mind. One that came with the reminder to respect the fair folk as she brushed his hair from his eyes.

Those were words that'd stuck with him through the years, grounding him with his actions and observations. It's why he steered clear of those who would harm him and cause more damage to a world that he'd be fortunate enough to be born into —to try to immortalize through sketches and musings without consuming more than the fair folk would balk at.

"Yes," Grey said, his shoulders sagging as Noel led the way again.

Chunks of broken tile slid underfoot in their travel down the far corridor, Grey's key digging into his palm with every shuffle forward. The beam swept over open door after open door, catching on the glint of beady little eyes before they scurried away with a chorus of squeaks.

They turned down another hall, and Noel slid to a stop in front of a closed door. A quick test of the handle: locked.

"You don't suppose someone relocked this at some point, do you?" he whispered.

Grey shook his head while Noel ran the light over the door's intricate pattern, though it was missing hexagonal tiles.

"No keyhole..." he muttered, taking a step back as Grey stepped forward.

He traced some of the green-tinted metal set into the door, his fingers stopping at the missing piece. "What if it needs these parts to be filled in? Maybe those are the keys?"

Noel hummed and shone the light at some of the nearby doors. He nudged one of them open to a couple of trunks sitting on the floor, and Grey braved a look into another room a little further down the hall. The door creaked open to a beat-up desk and shelves folded in.

Grey stepped inside, and the world brightened every-so-slightly. The desk and shelves stretched out of sight; the room spread out like butter on toast with its creamy hue turning everything shiny and new again. His legs locked up, stunned by the sudden magic before he spun around. The door was gone.

"Hello, Grey."

He yelped and whipped back to try to catch a glimpse of the voice's owner. An echoey chuckle enveloped him when he found the space empty instead. Grey's shaky step backward was met with hands gripping his upper arms and quickly turning him toward a mirror, where he recoiled at the blurred, ever-changing features of that fair folk.

"Look at you," they purred, lightly swiping Grey's hair from his face.

His eyes went wide when their hand—claws—fell away, and Grey reached to push it back again. The color was there, that familiar gray-brown in place of the near-white he'd grown used to.

"Always selling yourself short." Their cool breath curled against Grey's ear. "You're such a gentle creature, respectful of things that are so much bigger than you. You just want to create, don't you?"

Grey paused, his fingers letting hair slip through as he noticed his hoodie and jeans had been traded for flowy, dark, ethereal garments that reminded him of vague depictions of fair folk in some of the books he'd flipped through.

"An artist needs a patron, of which I'd be happy to oblige. I'd love nothing more than to give you all the paint and canvas you could ever ask for in exchange for the beauty that is the end result. Much like you, my finch."

He tensed and tore free of their grasp, spinning around again to nothing. His heart hammered in his chest at the sight of an easel and palette set up by a balcony overlooking a pink-tinted horizon with rolling hills and waterfalls.

"Come now, Grey," they cooed, sending goosebumps down his arms. "I'd prefer not to wield your name against you, but the longer you resist, the more impatient I become. I'll give you whatever you wish for. I'll even free you from the Wild Hunt."

Grey sucked in a breath and shook his head. They hummed in dissatisfaction, a low note of disapproval that made him sick to his stomach, like the sharp tone of a bad omen.

"Suit yourself, little finch. When you call for me, I will send whomever I must to claim you if it comes to that. Don't think I'll stop hunting you."

He froze as their voice drifted to an echoey remnant at his back, and he turned one last time to a horrible, tall shadow taking over the doorway. It started toward him.

"W-wait—" he choked out, panic fluttering in his chest as he grabbed for a key that didn't exist in whatever plane he'd been tossed into. His ankle twisted on something he couldn't see, and he toppled backward.

If this was a dream, the pain radiating from his leg, his side, his spinning head—it all felt *very* real. His heart kicked up speed as the creature's darkened form stooped into a crouch. Grey kicked at it and scrambled away, gasping as his back smacked against a wall. A wall that shouldn't be there.

"Would you like my name, little finch?"

Grey's jaw quivered before his magic kicked in, ripping whatever he could from the nearest source to heal, even though he'd been told that the last thing he should pull life from was fair folk. The creature swayed, his ankle throbbed as it reset itself, and Grey shoved off the wall, pushing himself to his feet. "I-I don't w-want your name," he called out, flinching at how it echoed.

His head swiveled around to try to find a door that didn't exist before it landed on the balcony. He tensed as the creature rose again, and Grey sprinted forward, past it to the only exit.

An arm hooked around his waist, and a cry tore from his throat. "Stop!"

"Grey!"

He stiffened, letting the voice cut through the rest of confusing scenery as it began to undulate and warp.

"Grey," it panted, "calm down. You need to calm down."

He knew that voice, despite being unable to place it, and his body relaxed as he squeezed his eyes shut, letting it consume him.

"What's going on? Did you see something? Are you okay?"

Grey shook his head, gritting his teeth as he twisted around. Sure enough, he felt denim graze against his palms before he shoved his face against soft cotton. "Make it stop."

Something clasped his upper arms, and he flinched. But these weren't talons this time—these were warm, gentle hands. "Can you walk?"

He nodded into the shirt, not able to pull his face away or open his eyes just yet out of fear of what he might see. But he was carefully pulled away from it all, guided along uneven floors until he was commanded to open his eyes.

When he did, he was in the hallway of the ruins again, that door he and Noel were trying to unlock sat a little further down the passage where they'd come from. Grey spun to face Noel, and his heart plummeted. Blood dripped from his nose, but those green eyes were stuck on Grey, filled with nothing but concern.

"I-I didn't mean—I'm so sorry—" Grey reached up to try to fix it, but Noel went for his sleeves, jerking his arms down.

"It's okay. What happened?"

He stared into the room, finding only a desk visible in the doorway once more. "They..." Noel's grip tightened. "They took me somewhere else. I thought you were fair folk." Grey shrank down. "I'm *so* sorry—"

"Where did they take you?"

He opened his mouth, barely any sound coming out. "I-I don't... The Otherworld? I was trying to escape through the balcony."

"Grey, that was a wall," Noel said, his tone firm. "I think they wanted to confuse you so you'd hurt yourself enough that you'd be stranded here, or" —he bit his lip— "maybe drain me."

Blood drained from his face, his arms trembling as Noel finally let go. "Noel, I didn't mean to—"

Noel shook his head, a small spark of concern still prominent in his features that Grey couldn't help but write off as worry that Grey was becoming more of a problem than he was worth. He swiped the blood away from his lip. "It's okay. Just stick close to me from now on, okay?"

Dread pooled in his core as Noel peeked into the room again, quickly rifling through desk drawers before ripping a basket from the shelves and dumping it out in the hall.

Look at you.

Yeah, look at me, Grey thought bitterly, his hands curling into fists with pressure building at the backs of his eyes. *A nuisance and a monster.*

16

NOEL

Noel picked through the baubles piled on the floor while he fought back a wave of nausea. The longer Grey hovered there, standing over his hunched form, the worse Noel felt about it all. He shouldn't have let him wander off by himself in the first place—what a stupid idea to take his eyes off of him when some crazed fair folk was enjoying themself.

Grey dropped down to his knees in front of him and began sorting through the pieces Noel hadn't gotten a chance to touch yet. "I'm sorry," he breathed, barely audible over the scraping and rolling of trinkets against stone.

"It wasn't your fault, so stop apologizing." The words sounded harsher than he intended, immediately wincing as Grey crumpled in on himself. Noel pushed away several pieces of junk and was rewarded with a hexagonal tile. "Found one." He shot up and jogged over to the door, slotting it to finish off the missing portions while Grey quietly rose to his feet behind him.

He pushed down on the handle, and the door creaked open to

the darkened room beyond. All of Noel's hope faded away in an instant, his heart dropping at the sight of an emptied pedestal that only bore a single, inky-black feather. "All that for... *this?*" He started inside, staring down at their reward.

"We shouldn't touch it," Grey said, his voice wavering as he rubbed his arms. "I have a really bad feeling about messing with something like that."

Noel sighed and ran a hand through his hair. "Fine, I guess. Let's try elsewhere." Grey backed up, his head on a swivel as Noel dragged himself into the corridor again. "This is so fucked." He kicked a couple of loose trinkets against the wall, and Grey grabbed his arm.

"You shouldn't do that either," he hissed.

"It's faerie shit, Grey. Relax."

Grey's hand fell away, taking Noel's heart with it as he hunched back in on himself and rubbed his arms. "Maybe we should just go? I feel like we're being watched," he whispered.

Noel stepped over one of the baubles, starting into the dark corridor up ahead. "Come on. I know you're creeped out, but we can't leave empty-handed. Just... stick close."

Quick, quiet shuffling sounded behind him, and Noel glanced over his shoulder to find Grey on his heels. He swept the flashlight over the stone and creeping plants prying through doorways. It finally opened to another domed room, flourishing with flora beneath the shattered greenhouse windows. Dim rays of sun cutting through the clouds made Noel flick off his flashlight and stare up at the arched stone beams, gawking at the craftsmanship of this nature shrine.

Grey stopped next to him, pushing his mess of hair back from his good eye and tracing the tall windows towering around them. The illuminated shards of stained glass that remained left pulses of reds, pinks, blues, purples, greens, and yellows floating around the conservatory like butterflies. "It's beautiful," he breathed, squeezing Noel's heart with the sheer whimsy escaping him.

Noel cleared his throat and motioned for him to follow in his skirt along the edge of the foliage. "Let's try a little further in. I don't think they'll want anything in here."

The scrape and crunch of glass underfoot made his hairs stand on end as Grey caught up. Noel's urge to reach back and grab his wrist pressed in with every creep of darkness closing back in on them. There was a wrongness to this place among the stillness and oppressive reminders of their absent rulers. Two playthings to gods wandering through sacred halls, left disturbed by greed, rather than cries of desperation.

He trained the beam on toppled chairs and upended, emptied chests lining their pathway with a disturbing sense of dread. But he kept going anyway, reminding himself that fear was the least of his problems. Chills pulsed through his veins as they reached an intersection, and he panned his light over the blackened recesses of the infinite labyrinth they'd walked into.

Noel side-stepped the corner and peered inside one of the doorways with its cover torn off the hinges. Claw marks left trails carved into the stonework of the frame, but he crept closer as light shone over the corner of a trunk mostly covered with a ratty cloth, shredded to bits along the edges.

"Noel..." Grey whispered, his voice quivering as Noel gently took him by the arm and led him in after him.

"It's okay," he said with more bravery than he felt. He pressed the flashlight into his hand. "Hold this for me."

The beam bounced around the room until Grey stopped violently trembling. It pointed down to the box, and Noel knelt down in front of it. He tugged the cloth free, and beetles scattered all over the walls and floor.

Grey gasped, scampering back, but Noel bit down on the inside of his cheek and flipped the trunk lid open. Rows of teeth poked out of gray, goopy flesh, and a large tongue—as wide as both his arms together—shot out. Noel fell backward, kicking away from it.

"Grey, run!" he called, twisting his dagger from its sheath and swiping at the grotesque, spindly hand grasping at his leg. It screeched, and he scrambled to his feet, sprinting toward Grey in his panicked backpedal into the hall. The shock of Grey's hand slipping into his gave him that boost of extra adrenaline he needed with a mimic nipping at their heels.

"Are you okay?" Grey called over the pounding of their soles hitting the rough stone and echoing through the corridor. "Did it get y—"

A yelp, and his hand ripped from Noel's grasp, pitching him forward with the counter momentum. The flashlight busted against the floor, the light spasming as Grey flailed in the grip of some towering, twisted tree-like humanoid.

Spriggan.

Grey wrestled his iron key free from the folds of his clothes and the creature screamed in pain, letting go of him. He hurtled toward Noel and fell face-first into his chest with a gasp as the flashlight rolled backward underfoot. Noel yanked him back to his feet and ran.

His pulse whispered *go* with each thump and Grey's wild panting at his side. Everything faded to black at the edges as they sprinted back through the conservatory, dodging Spriggans peeling themselves from the walls and emerging from the faux forest. Through the hall, where they fumbled over trinkets and baubles.

Don't take my finch from me, came a venomous threat digging into his skull.

Noel gritted his teeth. *Fuck you.* He squeezed Grey's hand tighter as they flew through the main hall and with large spider-like creatures casting undulating shadows along the domed ceiling in their menacing descent.

Faster.

Over the downed trees and weaving through the broken hovels, they made one final push to the stream. The sound of its calming trickle was music to his ears: safety. Like a barrier between them and the fair folk. And all they had to do was hop across.

"Almost there," Noel panted, slowing only once they reached the edge. He let go of Grey's hand and ushered him forward on shaky legs while Noel looked back at the horrific creatures closing in behind them.

A scream. A splash. Noel turned back to see Grey's hands clapped over his ears as a cry pried from him. "*Stop!* Leave me alone!"

Noel quickly laced his arm around him and pulled one of Grey's hands away from his ears to wrap around the back of his neck. He hoisted him up, half-dragging him to the other side. "You're okay. We're okay. We need to get to the bike, and we'll be safe."

Grey's sob cracked his heart in half.

"I won't let that faerie bastard touch you," Noel hissed, glancing back at the creatures now halted a mere meter away from the bank. They swayed and paced from side-to-side like Noel might come back and submit to them. His fingers dug into Grey's ribs as they shambled over to their ride, and then he sent them flying through the woods.

❧ 17 ❧

NOEL

"I am *so* sorry," Noel finally said as they passed the tree marked with a royal blue ribbon tied around the most prominent branch—a sign that they were almost back to Ivywood. He wasn't sure if the silence had finally gotten to him or if it'd been the realization that he'd have to say *something* before they wandered back into the city to bargain for the only goods that might be able to free them. But he knew that guilt had carved into him the longer Grey leaned against his back.

"It's okay," he breathed.

"No, it's not okay. I should've realized that damn fair folk would find a way to mess with you, and that it was too much of a risk."

"You act like we're not destined to die anyway, Noel," he mumbled. "I should've been more careful."

A scoff slipped from Noel, immediately regretting the dismissive way it sounded as Grey started to pull back. "This isn't your fault. We just keep getting screwed in all of this." He shook his head. "We'll get back to Ivywood and bargain for some of the items those looters had. There's got to be an alternative form of payment—"

"I'm not sure they'll be willing to part with any of it for anything that's not money, and if they do, I don't... I don't..." His voice dropped to a trembling whisper as he tightened his grip on Noel's jacket.

He had to resist the urge to cup one of his hands over Grey's in reassurance. "I'll get it worked out. Relax. I'll take care of this for us."

"Maybe we should just try somewhere else? Somewhere further away? I feel like the news has to have made it to the Grand Capital by now, which means that it'll start to spread. If we waste too much time here trying to convince..."

Grey's voice faded away as Ivywood came into view, and Noel took in the sight of the gate in the midday sun. Old, rusted, and holding back a small crowd of people—one of them turning to reveal a familiar face that made Noel's stomach drop. "Oh no."

"What?"

"*Hey!*"

Noel hit the gas, whizzing around the crowd as that hulking macharomancer Daz and his creepy Doctor boss sprinted to climb into their van. Screeches from bystanders leaping out of the way almost drown out the adrenaline-inducing boom of the Doctor's shouted order for them to stop.

Like hell he would.

"Hold on tight," Noel called back to Grey as he rocketed down the path.

Grey pulled back slightly, like he was twisting around to keep his eye on their pursuers. "Shit," he hissed. "They're catching up."

"Brace for some turns," Noel growled, leaning forward with Grey pasted against him again. His vision tunneled as the horrid clunking of the van's engine closed in behind them during this reckless pursuit.

"Don't run, you little shit!" Doctor Cavan called, his hair whipping around his head in Noel's cracked mirror. "Give me Grey, and I won't have you ripped to pieces."

Grey's arms tightened around Noel's torso, giving him just the boost he needed to play a little more reckless.

Fuck you.

He made a sharp turn and tore off the trail, his tires ripping through the grass and bumping over stones in the wake of squelching tires pressing into the earth behind them.

"Give him back, you fuck—Goddamnit." A quick glance in the mirror again showed the doctor's retreat into the passenger's seat, and his head bobbed down to vanish behind the dash.

Hot breath curled against the back of Noel's neck. "If they knock us off the bike—"

"They won't," Noel snapped.

"But you have your knife, right?"

"In my boo—"

His heart hammered in his chest as Grey reached down and ripped the dagger free. "If they get too close, I'm going for the driver."

"You're going to fucking stab the driver while we're on a bike? Have you fucking lost your mind?"

"I'm not going to stab *him*—"

Noel gritted his teeth. "Oh, hell no—Grey, put the knife back."

"I'm trusting you, so I'm asking you to trust me."

"I trust you, but you're saying you're going to stab yourself to try to siphon some asshole, and I'd rather you *not* do that—"

"Then lose them, and I won't have to," Grey breathed, his

tone carrying a resigned, serious edge as he shifted against him. "But I'm not letting them drag me away to that *thing* without a fight."

"And what if you accidentally drain *me* instead?" Noel demanded, the memory of Grey's stunned expression in the depths of the basement and his lightheaded realization that he'd tapped into the doctor's lifeblood, rather than his. He couldn't tell if it'd been intentional or not, but then he was dragged away. And Noel was locked up with the heart-wrenching visual of Grey's panic before it ebbed into a numb fear. How much control he actually had there, Noel didn't know.

"I won't."

"Give me a chance to lose them first," Noel breathed, jerking the bike around a tree and aiming for the narrow gaps. The van fishtailed behind them, swerving through the larger openings before a shot rang out and birds sprung from the trees up ahead.

"Holy shit—" Grey winced. "He's got a gun."

"Fuck."

"Stop the damn bike!" Doctor Cavan shouted, a murderous glint in his eyes reflected in the mirror.

Another shot, and they ducked. Noel gritted his teeth. "Is he fucking crazy? He's going to kill us both."

"Just keep driv—" A yelp cut through as a bullet whizzed past and smacked into a tree up ahead.

That's when he saw the final obstacle: a wall of brush and brambles with the smallest gaps cut through. "Oh, fuck me," Noel hissed. "Brace yourself."

"What?" Grey's voice rose in panic as Noel leaned forward, holding himself steady in the wake of a gasp like a breath before hitting water and another gunshot rippling through the air.

Thorns ripped through denim and pierced flesh, too quick to sting on impact on their way through.

The van rumbled behind them and crashed into the brambles with a horrid series of snaps and pops before wild yells and curses fell into the distance. Noel's wounds receded as the tall grass along the path browned and drooped for a few feet. Grey's face fell against Noel's back, and a sigh of relief tore from his lungs as they sped off further into the woods, out of the line of fire and into the shadows of the fair folk's domain.

18

GREY

*D*on't *step foot into a single forest, and don't reply to anything you can't see.*

Grey sank further into his seat and kept his head on a swivel as Noel navigated the woods. The anticipation for that fair folk to tickle the back of his neck with phantom breath and haunting words made his stomach clench. Fog crept in all around them, caressing his skin and sending shivers down his spine as the bike slowed to a near-crawl.

"Don't stop," Grey whispered, fighting against the irrational fear that he might disturb the forest or worse—accidentally summon the fair folk hunting him with how eerily it matched the first dream he'd encountered them in.

"I'm not, I'm just... trying to figure out where we are," Noel said quietly, craning his neck.

Every bump of the uneven ground turned into an additional jitter Grey couldn't shake until they rolled into a clearing. Despite the mist clinging to the edges of the field, Noel kicked down the stand and hopped off.

"I want to make sure we're on the right track, okay? Let's just stop and catch our breath for a second while I check the map."

He unfolded it while crouching in the grass, and Grey glanced around, rubbing his sweaty palms on his pants before stumbling off and stretching his legs. Pain throbbed through his limbs from how tightly he'd been holding on, and his fingers trembled as he started to dig through his belongings. His worn notebook's soft, leather cover anchored him the second it caressed his hand, taking him back home.

The urge to sit down and let himself be consumed by the foggy blanket of the forest overwhelmed him until Noel crouched down. "I think we're here?" he said, doubt creeping in as he pulled out his compass. "Which means that if we keep going in the direction we have been, it should dump us out in this little town, here." He jabbed a finger to a marked point east of Ivywood. *Far* east of Ivywood.

"Are you sure we'll even make it there before dark?" Grey asked, his brows knitting together as Noel held out the compass in front of them.

"If we're quick, yeah." The needle wobbled and pointed dead ahead of them, dipping Noel's concentrated look into a frown. "That can't be right." He jiggled it, and it spun to land somewhere between its previous mark and the way they had been heading. "What the hell?"

"Maybe we veered off the path some?"

"If it was a *little* off, I'd buy it, but there's no way we've been traveling northward this whole time."

"Then why—"

The needle moved again, spinning around once and landing in the complete opposite direction. "Motherfucker," Noel hissed. "Get back on the bike. I bet that damn doctor is messing with crystals or something to get us lost long enough for him to catch up."

Grey rose with Noel, glancing around the edges of the misty clearing. "I think he'd have to be pretty close to do anything like that. I can't imagine he would've caught up by now. Don't lithomancers have to be practically next to someone to do anything to them?"

"I don't know," Noel hissed, seizing Grey's arm and pulling him back to the bike. "Looks like we're going to fumble our way through the woods with my sense of direction to hopefully guide us out."

Grey hesitantly climbed back on, watching Noel as he crinkled the map in his hands and flipped it over a couple more times. He mounted the bike again and revved the engine once he tucked the map into his bag. A whisper under his breath, and they started back into the trees.

Everything sounded muffled and disturbingly quiet as he strained to listen to whatever wild animals lurked in the depths of the leafy green foliage they rolled past. No chirps of birds or skittering of chipmunks. Grey searched for eyes hovering in the dark recesses of the far-out trees, and he sank down against Noel while praying nothing peered back at him. The odds of it being something mundane dwindled with each passing second. His ears pricked at each revolution of the tires against the underbrush, and his heart hammered a little harder as the fog ebbed to show the sun hidden behind the clouds.

The gentle chatter of insects interrupted the mechanical noise left in their wake, finally lulling Grey into a somewhat relaxed state. He closed his eyes and absorbed each little chirp like a familiar chorus he'd soaked in before bed every night.

Kay. Kay. Kay.

Hey. Hey. Hey.

Grey. Grey. Grey.

He tensed, his eyes flying open and searching for the source of the noise. It was bugs. Just bugs.

A giggle cut through that explanation.

Poor little Grey. So tired. So distressed.

The hair on the back of his neck stood on end. Whatever this was, it didn't sound anything like the first fair folk that had been hunting him. Instead, this one was cheerful and bright instead of husky and dangerous.

Why don't you just come sit for a while? Come rest.

Revulsion worked through him, and his arms tightened around Noel just long enough for him to glance in his mirrors. "Something wrong?"

"You don't hear that?" Grey breathed, licking his lips as he swung his head around to find the creature taunting him.

"Hear... what?"

His stomach sank like a stone. "I-I..."

Noel cursed under his breath and sped up, but the giggling continued.

Reign.

The word stretched into the void with how many cheerful voices whispered it in unison, making his head spin from the sheer force of magic pressing in. Sweat started to bead along his brow, and it felt like his sinuses might pop.

Call for Reign.

"What?" Grey whimpered just as Trin's words crashed into him: *Don't reply to anything you can't see.* He swallowed back the rest of the questions lingering on his tongue: what did 'Reign' mean? A person? Fair folk? Was that the name of the fair folk hunting him?

A darker, velvety chuckle bubbled up over the others, the voice dipping into a coo like a hand caressing his cheek. *You're delaying the inevitable, little finch. Call for me, and I'll relieve you from this burden.*

Grey gritted his teeth. "Drive faster."

And just like that, Noel leaned forward, launching them further into the woods.

19

NOEL

Have we seen that tree before? Noel scowled as he flew past a trunk carved with two long claw marks ripped down to the roots. He shook his head. He was imagining things again, clearly. They'd been going in a straight line for the past hour, so there was no way it was the same tree.

Was it?

"Noel?" Grey's voice was barely above a squeak.

"Nothing. It's nothing."

He kept his gaze pinned dead ahead, straight into the foggy trail that would eventually dump them out into a field or a road somewhere—something that *wasn't* trees and brush for a change. Another tree with two long claw marks.

"What the hell?" he mumbled.

Faster. He shot forward, and sure enough, the damn tree sat dead ahead, mocking him. The bike coasted to a stop, and he sat up, feeling Grey's arms loosen around his torso. "What's going on?"

Noel pointed at the marks along the trunk, frustration building. "We've passed this damn thing at least three times now."

Grey shifted behind him, his browns knitting together in the mirror. "Are you sure?"

"One hundred percent." He reached into his bag and tore out the map while they idled. The shadows at the edge of his vision undulated, making his stomach twist as he panicked to find where they were on the page. "Fuck." He flipped it over like the answers might be marked on the next panel, but it was impossible to tell.

Grey's arms moved in the mirror, and Noel tensed as something slipped over his head. The iron key he'd found for Grey.

"Calm down," Grey said quietly. "Maybe this will clear your head."

"What? No—" He grabbed at it, trying to pull it back over while Grey tugged it back to stop him. "*You* need it. What if—"

"I'm with you, and I can take your knife if we think we might be in danger, but it won't do us any good to keep roaming aimlessly around the woods with fair folk creeping around. Take it."

Noel forced out a shuddering breath as the key clinked against his jacket zipper. Inhale. Exhale. He rolled his shoulders and stretched his neck, looking up at the overlapping branches. Small silver and wood medallions swayed against the ribbons strung from one tree to another with braided twine, feathers, and blown glass baubles alternating between each one.

"Talismans," he whispered, pointing upward. "But why would someone put these all the way out here?"

Grey softly hummed behind him. "Maybe someone was being followed and put this up? Or maybe there's a secret path someone's trying to hide?"

Noel revved the bike with a grumble. "Well, they're screwing everyone else over with this." He ducked his head and pushed forward again, glad when the scenery changed, and the fog rolled away along the edges.

The blue-black sky greeted them once they hit the tall grass and rolling hills, bringing equal parts relief and dread. He sped up, and the scenery fell away in heartbeats—each thump a brave new world under the ever-brightening stars. Beautiful and terrifying, much like the fair folk.

Twinkling lights in the distance turned into the grand finish line, despite its alarming placement near the woods. The little hovels tucked into the chain linked fences and corrugated metal walls looked like they might collapse at any second. But a haven was a haven, and Noel wasn't about to turn down someplace for them to seek shelter, rather than risk spending the night outside with Doctor Cavan and whatever creature he devoted himself to hunting them.

He cut the engine just short of the gate when one of the guards pointed a shotgun at him. "Who the hell are you two?" he demanded, his gruff voice slightly muffled through his face mask.

"Relax," Noel said, holding up his hands, catching Grey mimicking the motion out of the corner of his eye. "We're travelers. We got a little lost in the woods, or else we would've been here sooner."

The other one glowered at them as he readjusted his bandana to rest on the bridge of his nose. "Marks," he called, waving a pistol. "No mark, no entry."

Noel rolled up his sleeve, displaying the black inked mark in the glow of lamplight until he was waved away for them to get a look at Grey's. The one lowered his gun and went for the latch. An ear-splitting screech sounded as he pushed it open and jerked his gun toward the threshold.

"Inside. Park the bike there," said the other, pointing to the nearby cinderblock garage missing doors.

He rolled it inside and turned it off, him and Grey dismounting while the gate screamed again before it locked.

Bandana pointed a pistol at them. "Hold out your arm, hemomancer."

The guy lowered his weapon as Grey started toward him, but Noel stepped forward, his body going into fight mode. Bandana snapped to aim the gun at him. "Stay there. Hemomancer first. You next."

Noel gritted his teeth as the guy holstered his gun while Face Mask hovered nearby, at the ready. An iron coin emerged from his pocket, and Bandana pressed it to Grey's hand. Then he was ordered to stand by Face Mask before Noel was told to step forward. He held out his hand, and the coin grazed his palm for a second before the guy seized his arm. The other grabbed Grey, and they were led toward the main road.

"Where are we going?" Noel asked, resisting the urge to shove them away.

"Quarantine. People around here have been getting sick, so outsiders stay in a cell for twenty-four hours."

"Sick?" Grey piped up, his voice barely above a whisper. "Sick with wh—"

"Quiet," came Face Mask's gruff reply, shaking Grey slightly.

Noel's hackles rose. His hands curled into fists as they passed a few run-down buildings until they were dragged through a door hanging off its hinges. Grey was pulled back behind a wall, and then Noel was forced to turn the corner to where a row of cells sat —some with barred windows at the very top of their back walls. His stomach clenched as Grey was pushed into one of the cages with the door locked behind him.

Noel pitched forward after a sudden shove sent him into the next cell. He stumbled inside and spun around just as his door latched shut with a resounding *click*. "So you're going to keep us here for a full day? What about if we want to leave?"

Bandana shook his head. "We'll come back with rations if you don't have any, but you two are staying here until tomorrow. If you want to leave, you can leave after we release you. I'll be back in a couple hours to check on you if you need anything." Heavy boots clunked against the cement floor on their way out, leaving Noel grabbing onto the cool bars as he watched them leave. A slam of the front door later, and his hands fell back to his sides.

"Shit..." Noel paced, his palm cupping his mouth as he walked the length of his cell. "What are the odds that Doctor Cavan ends up here too? What if they throw him in the cells with us?"

"Well, then I guess we'd hopefully get a head start if they also decide to keep him in here for twenty-four hours, right?" Grey said with a slight shrug as he sagged against the back wall. "It's better than being stuck outside for the night, I guess."

Noel watched him slide down to the floor by the bars, and he started over to him, pulling Grey's key free from his neck. "Here." He dropped down next to him, holding it out to Grey.

He took it, turning it over in his hands. "You don't think this can unlock the cell, do you?" he asked, a teasing glint to his eyes that made Noel's heart pump a little faster.

Here they were, stuck with a row of bars between them and complete uncertainty about whether or not they might be handed over to the Grand Capital in the morning. He prayed it wasn't the case since they seemed to be more anxious about some sort of plague going around, but for all they knew, it could easily be a plot.

He swallowed and forced out a chuckle. "I think that would be a little too convenient to have a skeleton key on you."

Grey popped up and jogged over to the door, weaving his arm through the bars and trying to jam it into the lock for about thirty seconds before giving up. He pulled the cord over his neck and slunk back over to the corner.

"It was worth a try," Noel commended, warmth tickling his side as Grey dropped down next to him again. His dark hair skimmed Noel's shoulder as his head leaned against the bars. So close yet so far—a tease of all his hopes and foolish wants in the face of encroaching death.

But this was a *hemomancer*. Was he settling simply because this was the person he happened to rush in and save for his own selfish reasoning? Wouldn't it be better for him to cut ties to give them both a better chance at finding a way out? How stupid was he to chase this thought that it'd somehow work out for them in the end?

His eyes flicked down to Grey's mop of hair, resisting the urge to twist one of the stray waves around his finger. The one thing stopping him from bringing it up was the fear he'd seen etched into Grey's features every time that fair folk reared its ugly head. He lightly thumped his head against the bars and blew out a sigh, pushing it all from his mind as he closed his eyes and basked in the silence.

Rest. That's what they needed right now after the chaos of today. Then they could face whatever waited for them in the morning. He hoped.

⚜ 20 ⚜

GREY

"I'm sorry for getting us lost," Noel mumbled against the bars, disrupting the silence pooling between them over the last half-hour. Drowsiness seeped into his voice and tumbled into Grey's heart a little too hard, pushing him away from their shared cell wall.

"It's not your fault."

"It certainly feels like it," he said with a sigh. "And now we're stuck without anything to trade, along with being at the mercy of these people…"

Grey pulled his legs up to his chest. "We just got to hope that word hasn't spread from the Grand Capital yet."

A joyless laugh escaped him. "We're definitely short on time there. If it hasn't reached this place, it'll be here soon."

Misty cold licked his skin, seeping in from the barred windows and sending shivers through his body. "Then we'll have to be quick once they let us out—"

"*If* they let us out," Noel interjected.

"I don't think they'll know before tomorrow," Grey said with a shake of his head. "Considering how quick they threw us in cells, I can't imagine they'd take a random messenger in to spout off the news that there are new sacrifices for the Hunt."

Noel hummed and leaned back, his throat bobbing while his green eyes searched the ceiling. Grey dropped his cheek against his knee as he watched him. For the first time, he tried to imagine him among a flock of macharomancers. Strong-willed, skilled, and pretty, even when he was speckled in dirt. The fact that Grey was even taking his looks into consideration made his stomach flip.

He remembered Uncle Atticus's little story from several nights ago and its romanticizing of some macharomancer knight coming to the rescue, despite Grey only knowing pain and fear whenever he encountered them. The one thing that made Noel different was that they were both on the chopping block—both doomed to die at the hands of a common enemy. But if they were face-to-face without that threat, would Noel even bother saving him? Would he consider sparing him a glance? Or would he viciously rip him apart like the others?

To imagine Noel as his ally now left an uneasy sensation worming through his gut. Everything he'd ever believed slowly turned on its head in the face of the fair folk—all the times he'd wandered out into the woods as a child went from tasting of sweet adventure to bitter dread.

He'd gone so far to respect the world around him, even though his magic destroyed it in his careless actions. Like the time he scraped his knee stumbling over a log and drained the life from the most gorgeous patch of wildflowers he'd ever seen. The colors bled out while his skin knitted back together. His heart sank heavy in his chest as his mother called out his name, and she clicked her tongue when she found him mourning his kill.

"Grey, sweetheart, what happened?" she asked, crouching

down in front of him, her appearance fuzzy in his childhood memories. "Are you hurt?"

But he continued to stare down at the drooping petals while she brushed his hair from his eyes. "It was an accident," he whispered. "I didn't mean to…"

Her fingers danced over the blossoms and each one slowly popped back up, its color returning before Grey jerked his head up to take in those soft, kind features on the blurred edge of his thoughts. "No harm done," she said, the words smooth and sugary like honey.

Whatever died in their place, Grey never found, but a part of him always feared it'd been plucked straight from her own flesh. Not that she'd ever admit it. Not that she ever could now. Not that he'd be able to continue her legacy either.

All while he'd be immortalized as yet another nameless sacrifice, rather than for anything he could create.

Create.

You just want to create, don't you?

Grey perked up and crawled over to his bag, trying to ignore Noel's sudden shift on the other side of the bars. "Something wrong?"

He rummaged through his things until he scooped out his journal and charcoal. "The fair folk like pretty things, right? And they love natural creation, so what if I drew them something that captured that essence?"

Noel scooted forward along the bars, sitting across from him as he flipped through the messy pages to find a blank one.

"You really think they'd take that in exchange for your freedom?"

"Maybe," he breathed, pausing with his charcoal hovering above the parchment. His shoulders fell as he looked up and worried his lip in thought. "They said they'd be my patron, but what would they want me to draw?"

Noel squinted and set his jaw. "Who? That thing stalking you?"

Grey bit down on his tongue. "Yeah."

His hands wrapped around the bars and his brows furrowed. "I'm not sure that you should listen to anything they say—"

"We don't exactly have much else to go off of," Grey said, a sigh slipping through his teeth as he let his hands take over. "I'm just afraid that a crude drawing might not be enough. If I had paint, that might appease them a little more, but it's hard to know for sure."

Small, upward strokes turned into the outlines of stems, leaves, petals—a reimagining of the small patch of flowers he'd killed and his mother breathed life back into. He could picture the colors each one should be, but he didn't have the heart to shade them in.

Grey sat up straight again and scowled down at his sketch before his shoulders fell.

"What?" Noel asked, that confused concern accompanied by his hand falling from the bars and landing on Grey's side of the cells.

"I don't think it's going to work without color..."

"Let me see." Noel held his other hand out, and Grey's grip on the journal tightened.

This—his journaled art—was such a fragile, intimate thing he'd always kept close to his chest after Uncle Atticus gave him his first sketchpad to ease the time he'd been tended to in the confines of his small room. It wasn't much bigger than the cot they set up for him, but Aunt Ingrid insisted he stay there so they could keep a close eye on him until he adjusted to his new home. His new life. His new reality with a new family.

This was his personal form of therapy that was never pried from him without permission. His fingertips ran the slope of the pages to the cover, like sand in an hourglass. Before he knew it, the leather was pressed into Noel's grasp.

The upturn of his lips and glimmer in his bright green eyes as they danced across the page made him squirm. Seeking approval from Noel should be the last thing he wanted, but he craved that small reminder he wasn't completely useless—that he had his own talents and strengths.

"I think you might be onto something," Noel said, offering it back to him. He ripped open his own bag for the map and spread it out on the floor. "I think I know a place that makes paints—by the delta." He jabbed his finger to a spot marked near one of the offshoots of the river. "Here."

Grey crawled over, his cheek grazing the bars while his eye focused on that pinpoint. He swallowed. "Isn't that lithomancer territory?"

"Yes, but we'll be in and out before that bastard catches wind of us. For all we know, Cavan could've flew out his damn van window and got impaled on a tree back there." Noel waved past the building's walls. "We get you some art supplies, we corral ourselves in an inn for a couple days, and then we see what we can come up with."

A small, scared squeak of a laugh pulled from Grey's lungs. "And what if I can't get it just right? What if they don't take it? Where do we even bring something like that to trade?"

Noel's excitement dimmed as his grin twisted into a grimace. "Um... Well..." He smoothed out the map a little more, like the creases in the paper were obscuring all the answers he needed. "I think it's the best idea we have to go off of, and what you made in a short period of time is incredible by itself, but I do recall seeing spots on the walls of the ruins where portraits and stuff had to be before they were stolen and scrapped. So maybe we return something like that to a shrine? Or ruins?" He shrugged.

Grey rubbed his hands together, smearing the remnants of charcoal staining his fingertips. "Then maybe a landscape isn't the best choice? Maybe one of the fair folk instead?"

"And have you actually ever *seen* one in person?"

He opened his mouth, paused, and bit down on his tongue. "No. Fine, I'll do a landscape."

Noel began folding up the map. "Then it looks like we'll be on our way the second they let us out of here."

NOEL

Noel nearly ripped the map in two as a shriek tore through the silence in the early hours of the morning. The glow of dawn hadn't even crested the horizon before he and Grey scrambled up from the floor of their cells to glimpse the commotion from the bars of their windows. A man shambled through the streets with a dark stain spreading under a palm pressed to his shirt.

"Help!" he wheezed. "There's something wrong with my wife—"

A guard jumped off the porch of one of the shops and another started out of the dark recesses on the other side, pulling their mask down over their face. The second the first guard was within reach, the injured man snapped up to attention and lunged. Grey jolted and ducked down while Noel's grip tightened on the bars, his hackles rising as more guards poured out of their hiding places along the walls.

Orders barked out as they converged on the feral individual, and Noel felt a tug on his sleeve. He turned to Grey, finding him pointing at a spot just beyond the wall. "Fair folk," he whispered, barely a rasp.

His blood ran boiling hot as his head whipped back around to the lanky silhouette with piercing, glowing pink irises. The creature paced back and forth with its entourage of unhinged faerie monstrosities panting for flesh.

"Fuck," Noel mumbled, just in time for the alarms to start blaring. "Is that them?"

Grey winced and crouched, his breaths coming out harder and faster. "I- I don't know—"

He bit down on his tongue and bolted back to his bag. The contents spilled along the floor from coins to trinkets to rations until his fingertips skimmed the rough surface of a nailfile. It pressed into his palm with yips and howls growing ever closer. "Shit, shit, shit—" Noel shoved himself up and jammed the file into the lock.

Grey gasped the moment the lock clicked free, and Noel shoved the door open to work on Grey's. It took everything in him to ignore his shaking as Grey started scooping everything back into Noel's bag and tensing at every guttural noise from outside.

"They're not going to take us, Grey," he hissed. "Just stay calm."

"What about the gate? What if—"

The lock popped, and Noel gritted his teeth at the squeal of the hinges. "We're sitting ducks in here." He grabbed his bag and helped haul Grey to his feet. "I think it's better we take our chances before they figure out we're part of the hunt."

But instead of letting go, Noel squeezed Grey's hand even tighter as they hurried past the cells with the growing shouts, zips of electricity, and cries of malformed faerie things making his heart pump faster with each passing second. He glanced back every few steps, the corners of his vision darkened by adrenaline. Grey's breaths started to slip into hyperventilation as they reached the door outside with a raucous fight breaking out just on the other side.

"We can't—"

Noel spun around and dug his thumbs into Grey's shoulders, nearly nose-to-nose and trembling in the low lamplight of the concrete jail. "Fair folk show no mercy. I know you're scared but stick close and keep quiet. I'll get us out of here. Trust me."

Grey's now-free hand wrapped around one of Noel's wrists. The fear reflected in his colored eye might as well have been a thousand knives running him through before he took his hand again—an anchor he refused to deny himself. All his previous fear of Grey pulling the life force from him immediately vanished when he ripped the door open, and they stumbled out into the dirt.

Noel's eyes went wide at the circle of guards past the building and further toward the center of town with weapons drawn and orders for the townspeople to stand down. His knees locked up for the briefest moment until he caught a slicing arc of pink in the distance. A quick jerk of Grey's arm, and they bolted toward the garage. Distant cackling chilled him to his core. He took a sharp turn around the garage's overhang and skidded to a stop, throwing up his hands, Grey's still firmly tucked into one.

The muzzle of Bandana's gun pointed straight at Noel's face. He swallowed. "Please just let us leave, and I promise we won't cause any more trouble."

A dark, warped chuckle slipped from Bandana, and he shook his head. "You're not going anywhere."

Every hair stood on end. This wasn't the voice of the man

they'd encountered earlier. This was something else—something animalistic and dual-layered in a twisted way he couldn't quite describe.

Grey bumped against Noel's side. "There's something wrong with his eyes," he breathed. God, he was right. They were oozing black at the corners, eating away at the white.

In a flash, Noel and Grey jumped back, tearing their hands apart while the guy slumped forward with a resounding *crack*. Another shadow took his place: thin, shorter, with tanned features and a mess of dark brown hair in short, messy waves cascading over her face. Wide, gold eyes contrasted the steel sheen of the bat in her hands. "*You*," she whispered, tendrils of loose hair getting caught on her chapped lips.

His gaze flicked to the tattered black denim jeans, studded belt, and dark gray plaid flannel shirt tied around her waist. He recognized that checkered flag in its blurred sprint into the woods by the obelisk all those nights ago.

She bared her teeth and pointed the bat toward the garage. "Get the fuck out of here. Both of you. Why the fuck are you two even here together?"

A howl jolted the three of them from their confrontation, and the girl whipped her head around to find the source of the noise before jogging toward one of the motorcycles.

Noel started for his own, fumbling for his keys while the girl pulled at wires. Her scowl shone through tangled hair when Grey climbed on behind him.

"Get your own fucking ride, dumbass. If they catch any of us together—"

"We know the risk," Noel snapped.

"Yeah, and the longer you two stick together, the more likely the wardens will kill two birds with one stone. Fucking. Split." Her engine revved with another cry from inside the city.

"It's our decision," he ground out, his argument solidified with Grey's arms wrapped around him as he began the backward shuffle from the garage. "We're going to break it."

She guffawed. "Break this curse? You two seriously think you can outwit the fair folk? Goddamn you're fucking stupid." She backed up and rolled past them. "Suit yourselves. It's your funeral." Then she was gone, through the gate in a heartbeat with the cackling howls of beasts chasing after her.

Noel punched it forward and drank in the first glimmer of morning grazing the edge of the horizon and shot southward in search of freedom.

The snapping of jaws ratcheted up Grey's heartrate ten-fold as they hurtled past trees and brush. He dared a glance back to the horrid pink glowing dots jerkily bouncing above their mount, their body anchored low with a greenish blade in their hand. The jagged, feral grin pasted on their face grew deadlier the closer they drew.

Grey sucked in a sharp breath and turned back around, searching up ahead through the forest with a single word lingering on the tip of his tongue: *Reign*. Would he even be able to call them off if they were the fair folk pursuing him and Noel? Or would it toss them further into a frenzy? A coppery tang started to spread in his mouth, followed by a pressure threatening to pop his skull.

Come now, little finch.

The cackle that loosed behind them forced him further against Noel's body. He gritted his teeth and fought against the clashing sounds of Reign pushing into his thoughts and the more feminine shriek tearing from the fair folk giving chase.

Decidedly *not* Reign, then.

"Leave me alone," Grey hissed, his voice drowned out by the roar of the engine.

A lilting, husky chuckle echoed in response. *Surrender yourself to my fellow hunter, and I'll ensure she brings you to me unharmed.*

His heart fluttered in his throat as he weighed their escape. "Will you let the macharomancer go?" he asked, barely above a breath.

The Wild Hunt requires prey, dear finch.

"Then no."

We shall continue our chase then, hm?

Grey's head spun until his vision doubled, and his stomach threatened to heave.

The forest is our domain, remember? Surrendering will end this torment.

He buried his face in Noel's jacket and squeezed his eyes shut. His breath came out in short, shallow gasps until the splash of water kicked up around them. The sudden mist lightened that weight pressing into his mind, triggering Reign's echoey snarl before whatever claws they'd sank into him pulled free. Grey's head whipped back, and he watched the pink-eyed fair folk scrambled to a stop at the edge of the creek between them. She screamed in rage, but Noel didn't so much as flinch as he threw them further into the depths of the light-touched forest.

Grey's body was stiff from how tightly he'd held on during the remainder of the ride. The clearings that'd once been a quiet reprieve no longer felt safe. When the bike engine cut, Grey shakily hauled himself off and collapsed into the tall grass and white wildflowers. Dewy blades caressed his face as he laid down on his side and drew in deep, even breaths to slow his panic.

"Grey? Grey, are you all—"

"Spent," Grey rasped.

He jolted from the gentle pressure against his back, and his head snapped up to Noel's worried features. The moment his hand pulled away, all that surprised relief evaporated. Grey propped himself up on his elbows while Noel shifted to sit cross-legged in the grass.

"I might actually be able to eat in a few minutes now that the adrenaline's finally fading," Noel said with a nervous laugh. His hands trembled as he rubbed his palms against his knees.

Grey's head dropped back into the grass with a sigh. The early morning sun started to pierce his ratty sweatshirt and tattered jeans. He curled into a ball and flinched away from the shadow pooling over his face.

"You're not okay," Noel said.

"I'm fine. I just need a moment."

Fingers dug into his shoulder, and Grey's eyes flew open again. "You're not okay," he repeated.

His heart ached from that simple gesture, imagining Uncle Atticus looking after him at this very second, rather than a macharomancer—a macharomancer that had done everything to keep him alive in all this. A macharomancer that wouldn't have cut it so close or have been ruthlessly chased down if it hadn't been for Grey's existence. A macharomancer that would have a better chance without whatever strange curse hovered around Grey like a storm cloud. Grey's throat constricted before he shoved himself up and swatted Noel's arm away. "That girl back there was right," he said. "We should probably spit up."

Noel's jaw dropped. "What? Grey, what are you—"

He pushed himself up on wobbly legs. "I'm a liability, and I'm putting you in far more danger than if you travel alone."

Noel scrambled to his feet, shaking his head. "That's not tr—"

"It *is*," Grey snapped. "If it weren't for whatever Doctor Cavan saw back before we were tied up in that basement, you might already have everything you need to free yourself from the Hunt."

Noel's face crinkled into a scowl. "And what about you?"

Grey threw up his hands. "I don't know! I..." He rubbed at his eyes. "There's something wrong with me. They tested me because they thought I was fair folk—part fae beast—a changeling —or *whatever*, but I'm not. I'm something cursed and just lingering around me is affecting you."

"What? Grey, that's ridiculous." Noel reached for his arm.

He tore away from his grip and stumbled back. "Look at me! I'm nothing *but* bad luck. People *hate* hemomancers—They hated me so much they stole my eye. We're just a step away from being fair folk in the minds of everyone else, so yeah, she's right —" Grey's next step away was met with a lunge and Noel squeezing his biceps, forcing them to stand face-to-face. His heart caught in his throat as he stared into those bright green irises.

"I don't hate you." Those four words were spoken with such conviction that Grey stood rooted to the spot. "And you're not bad luck. I really do think we wouldn't have made it this far if we hadn't been looking out for each other. So, please don't leave just yet."

Pain blossomed in his chest between the pleading and the phantom echo of the fair folk continuing to haunt him. "What about *them?*" he forced out.

Noel's grip tightened, his face darkening in a way Grey

couldn't determine whether it was anger aimed at him or Reign. "They want to split us up and hunt us. That'll always be their end goal. That's not your fault. So please stick with me?"

Grey's head dipped to stare at the grass, catching sight of the iron key dangling between them. The thought of it being just as useless as he was flitted in and out with a single breath before he closed his eyes and forced himself to nod. Noel's palms skimmed Grey's sleeves while Grey reached for the key, praying for it to anchor him.

It might not keep Reign out of his head, but maybe it could buy him or Noel some extra time with what little they had left.

23

NOEL

The rush of water nearby was the biggest, most refreshing signal to take a break and enjoy a light breakfast after another few hours of riding post-chase. His stomach growled as he kicked down the bike stand, and they rifled through their bags for a rationed meal. But God, the cookies still tasted just as good, despite going stale.

He still craved the sugar after the last bite was gone and cursed himself for staring at Grey's lips when he licked away the final crumbs. Noel wiped his hands against his pants and shoved himself to his feet to keep himself from acting on that urge. So he scooped up his bag and found his small container of soap.

"I'm going to go wash off in the waterfall," Noel said, clacking the tin in his hands and fidgeting uncontrollably.

Grey absently began to nod before reaching for his own bag. "Yeah, I should probably clean up too."

Heat coiled in Noel's chest, spreading outward way too rapidly for comfort. "I'll be quick then," he blurted, trying to ignore Grey's confused look. He jogged off toward the small cluster of trees around the river and started tearing off his shirt. Muttered curse after muttered curse slipped out, faster the second he heard footsteps trailing behind him.

He tore off his pants before he could stop himself from getting decision paralysis and dumped his clothes behind a bush, only taking a chunk of soap with him into the cold depths. Noel ducked under the falls, scrubbing at his face and keeping his eyes closed as he rinsed away all the dirt and grime from the past few days.

Just don't think about Grey.

He shook out his hair and swiped water from his eyes just in time to catch Grey dunking his head into the river. The arch of his slender frame resurfacing gave him pause, like he was watching fair folk indulging in the woods. Noel snapped to attention again and hurried out to collect his clothes.

At least he felt refreshed by the time he strolled back to their small camp, but when he collapsed into the grass, thoughts of fair folk replaced all his fantasies of Grey. He plucked at the soft, green blades pinned under his legs and thought of the dagger that fair folk wielding, along with its sibling in the possession of those looters.

He sighed and fell back with a grimace, throwing an arm over his face until he heard the light crunch of boots against the ground. Noel focused on Grey's face outlined by the midday sun in a halo of light, driving another knife through his heart.

"Are you okay?" Grey asked, crouching down as Noel pushed himself up.

"Yeah. I'm fine. Just... thinking about what to trade since I think you're a little more prepared than I am."

"What do you tend to do with your free time? Do you write? Forge?"

Noel huffed out a laugh and ran a hand through his damp hair. "I typically *hunt* in my free time. Or hike. Or..." He shrugged. "Pretty much nothing that I can physically give to the fair folk without pissing them off because I killed something sacred to them."

"O-oh..."

Noel shifted and glanced away with his hand massaging the back of his neck. The more he thought, the more he cringed at just how little he had to offer to the fair folk, let alone to Grey—which, in itself, was a ridiculous notion. How long were they going to be alive for him to actually be able to act on those feelings? How would he prove to him that he'd be worthy of being a safe person for him to embrace? How long could he keep his mouth shut before he acted on that suppressed urge to touch him?

He had to hold back a laugh at the idea that Grey could very well not want anything to do with him, and he could only imagine what the horrified reaction would be if he presented a hemomancer to his parents when they'd constantly warned him over the years. But this one had sacrificed flowers to knit Noel's wounds back together instead of prowling outside the town gates for hours like a crazed animal with darting eyes.

Noel stood and brushed himself off. "We should probably get going before we waste too much daylight." He spared Grey a glance, and his heart ached with longing at the concern written all over his features.

Soft, damp waves curled around his brows, dipping toward that bad eye without completely obscuring it like it usually did. Not a single mark outside of that, in contrast to his own collection of discolored scars. He really did look like something from the Otherworld when his skin was only smattered with freckles instead of dirt.

Noel's fingers twitched, attempting to revolt from his stern self-instruction not to cup Grey's face. So instead, he grabbed up his bag to busy them and motioned for Grey to hurry up.

☙❧

The sun was halfway gone at the edge of the world by the time they reached the hulking obstruction of a city along the trail. Towering buildings connected with cables and cars pulleying up and down each pathway left him slack-jawed, but he was even more stunned by the line in front of the gate for entry. Trucks and cars idled nearby with people perched on hoods or gates. Smoke puffed from two men's lips before they flicked their cigarette butts on the ground, and a low hum of displeasure emanated from Grey—something akin to a whine or a wince.

"You need to stop caring so much about what the fair folk think," Noel whispered, rolling to park alongside the others.

"They're part of the reason why the Hunt exists in the first place," Grey muttered.

Not really something Noel could argue, considering it was blatantly disrespecting nature. Grey squirmed when Noel cut the engine, and their bodies finally pulled apart after another long set of traveling hours in which Noel fantasized about being some sort of mercenary and medic team wandering through the land as if they wouldn't potentially be hunted again tonight.

A woman, flanked by two men, tucked a clipboard under her arm and motioned for the first vehicle in line to head inside. Sputtering dark smoke poured out of the exhaust, and Noel's leg started to bounce. Another car let through, and he began tapping his keychain dangling from the ignition. His eyes darted to the sunset. "They need to hurry it up," he hissed.

"Will they turn us away if night falls before we get in?" Grey asked.

Noel hesitated. They wouldn't, would they? He automatically shook his head, mainly to keep Grey pacified, but that little inkling of doubt spread through just as the woman pointed to the horizon and dismissed one of the vehicles.

Grey nudged him. "What is she doing?" Panic rose in his voice. "Why are they leaving?"

Noel suppressed that instinctual reply of 'I don't know' in favor of sitting up straight and craning his neck as the woman moved to the people waiting in front of them. Another car sent packing. Grey clutched a chunk of Noel's denim jacket, tugging on it as they were approached and the shadows of dusk set in.

"Traveling?" the woman prompted without preamble. "Unless you're here for work, in which case, there aren't any jobs available."

"Traveling," Noel said, settling back into his seat with relief.

She hummed and flipped through a couple papers with her mumbled next request for their names and marks. The glimpse of Grey's shaking forearm in the corner of Noel's vision turned into a domino effect of the woman scowling and her two assistants exchanging looks.

"We don't normally allow hemomancers inside. Too much of a liability."

Grey's arm dipped with Noel's heart plummeting in his chest. "He won't cause tr—"

"That's what they all say," snapped one of the guards as he uncrossed his arms to reach for the holster at his hip.

Anger bubbled up within Noel, his hands curling into fists.

But before he could open his mouth to argue otherwise, Grey had already grabbed a chunk of his sleeve. "Let's just go," he whispered. Defeated. Afraid. Every emotion that slid smoothly and cleanly through his ribs before feeling that sharp sting.

His hesitation to argue gave way to a shift in the woman's features—her scrutiny ebbed into remorse—*concern*.

"Is he your partner?"

Noel blinked with surprise as he heard Grey sputter. His hand shot back to latch onto Grey's knee, immediately feeling guilty for how quickly he went tense. "Yes," he blurted. "Sorry, we're just really exhausted. Not a lot of places take hemomancers without some sort of caveat, so we've been trying to survive on the outskirts of the woods where we can. We won't be around for more than a night to catch our breath, I promise."

One of the guards pursed his lips, but the woman's brows knit together in sympathy before she scribbled something onto her clipboard. She released two sheets of thick paper and held it out for him. "Don't lose these. If someone asks for your papers, you'll be required to show that you've been allowed admittance. Don't go over the allotted timeslot either, understood?"

Noel nodded. "Thank you *so* much. We promise not to cause any problems." He slid the documentation from her grasp, and she stepped aside, ushering them into their temporary haven before the last gasp of daylight was snuffed out.

24

GREY

The fifth-floor motel room they snagged was a barebones thing—every piece of furniture constructed of black pipes and planks with thin mattresses and minimal décor. It boasted cleanliness from the distinct lack of dust and the scent of lemons, but when they shut off the lights and drew the curtains, the clangs and whirrs of machinery pried apart Grey's mind with the undulating shadows of hanging cars zipping up and down nearby buildings.

Cold and mechanical.

The quiet, rhythmic breathing from Noel in the other bed wasn't soothing enough for him to drift off, not when this felt more like a prison than the one they'd escaped from the night before. His head turned to see Noel's arm tucked under his pillow and his face half-buried, all while Grey replayed the last few days over and over again in his mind.

He'd done nothing but slow Noel down from one place to the next, sinking him like a stone with Grey's hemomancy jerking them to a halt every other step in this journey. And that didn't even include Doctor Cavan's furious chase or Reign's crazed hunt. He tried to push down that overwhelming idea that he should've left yesterday instead of allowing Noel to draw him back into that unspoken promise of protection that Grey couldn't repay.

Guilt nagged at him until he finally slipped out of bed and tugged on his shoes, his stomach gnawing before he reached the motel room door. So, he tucked one of Uncle Atticus's small chunks of rations in his pocket and set out onto the metal catwalk outside.

The crisp night air stole the breath from his lungs with its chill. As the city ebbed and flowed in the dead of night, Grey climbed. Every step to the next landing brought a gentle breeze to ruffle his hair and nip at his face. Each rung of the ladder to the roof of the monstrous metal contraption brought an ache to his arms, but it was worth it when he stood among the tallest structures of the city and drank in the world beyond.

Tall trees, hulking mountains, and ominous cliffsides through the jagged Old Trail made him feel so small in the grand scheme of things—a speck in a stolen world that showed no mercy to the creatures fighting within it. He dropped to sit on the edge and tapped the heels of his boots against the steel siding, cheesecloth-covered chunk of dried fruit and granola in hand under the soft light of the moon and stars.

The bite of cranberry tasted of home: a harsh place carved out for caring people who sugar-coated their little nooks to combat the unforgiving reality beyond their walls. Tart but savory—palatable. His vision blurred as he thought of his loft overlooking the place he loved—a place he'd likely never see again without putting everyone he cared about in danger. His heart squeezed at the memory of Atticus and Ingrid's arguments that the wrath of the machromancers he'd been rescued from might destroy them all.

And here he was, running from something that would absolutely demolish so much more.

His chewing slowed, all the sweeter notes going sour as he began to fold up the cloth again. How much more destruction and strife could he bring before people would spit at him for not surrendering because he was too selfish and fearful? Didn't that categorize him as a monster? As monstrous as the fair folk that pursued him?

He swallowed and closed his eyes, trying to focus on the amplified white noise of the city around him, but every sound rang hollow with its lifeless tune of the artificial comforts humanity had constructed. So Grey focused on the more melodic sounds of rustling leaves, imagining himself when he was much smaller and trying to catch frogs in a pond with the quiet chuckles of his mother warming him with every attempt.

A sudden *squawk* pitched him forward, and he quickly rocked back with his heart hammering in his chest as he twisted to take in the gleaming, purple-glinting feathers of a raven beside him. The creature's head tilted before opening its beak to complain again.

"Are you hungry?" Grey whispered, subconsciously unfolding the cloth to break off a piece. He crumbled it between his fingers and dumped it in front of the bird like he was letting sand slip through his fist.

The raven hopped forward and nibbled at his offering with ruffled feathers, bringing a smirk to Grey's lips. It scooted a little closer after picking through the choice pieces and cried again. "Sorry, little guy, but I probably need to save some for myself."

The self-loathing that washed through him as he bit off the last word pulled him to his feet.

So selfish. Such a burden.

Grey unfolded the bundle once more and sprinkled another chunk for the bird before he could convince himself otherwise. He shimmied back down the latter as the raven gobbled it up, and he rubbed his arms while he quietly jogged down the steps. By the time he reached his door, he jolted at the shadow fluttering by the railing.

Caw.

Grey sighed and shook his head. "Go home. It's late."

The bird cocked its head but hushed when Grey stepped inside and waved for it to leave. It didn't, deciding to pace side-to-side along the rail. He shut the door and waited for his eyes to adjust to the shift in darkness, letting out a breath when he saw Noel's still evenly rising and falling chest beneath the blankets.

Call for me, and I'll relieve you from this burden.

Grey gritted his teeth and shook Reign's words from his mind as he stooped to tear off his boots, tuck the ration back into his bag, and climb into bed. The bird's shadow through the curtain became the sole source of his attention until the world faded away to sleep.

"Grey, wake up."

Grey eyes opened to Noel shaking his shoulders and panic written into every line of his face. He shoved himself up as Noel backed away and scooped a bag off the floor.

"What's going on?"

"There's guys in the street wearing Grand Capital emblems going door to door."

Panic seized Grey's chest, and he threw back the covers to collect his own bag. "What time is it?" He winced as he nearly tripped over his boots.

Noel pushed back part of the curtains. "Dawn. It's still dark enough we can use it for cover, but they clearly don't give a shit about traveling at night, which means they must be desperate to find us."

His arms shook while he pulled on his boots and hoisted himself back to his feet with the help of the bare-bones dresser. Noel popped open the door and motioned for Grey to follow. They stuck close to the wall and hurried down the steps, trying to muffle the *clangs* of their footsteps. Every story made Grey tremble harder until they reached the street below.

The muffled pounding of their soles against the packed dirt sounded in time with his heartbeat in their sprint behind the motel. Grey recoiled at the sudden, flitting shadow out of the corner of his vision and bit back a gasp. Sure enough, that large, curious raven perched on the railing of the fire escape from the second floor, and let out a sharp, echoing *caw*.

"Go," Grey hissed, trying to wave it away when Noel skidded to a stop and spun around.

"Fucking bird," Noel growled. He grabbed Grey's wrist and dragged him out of view of the alley. Grey stumbled after him, finding his pace with a shadow gliding along the corrugated metal wall.

His pulse pounded in his ears in time with their panicked breaths. Every darting turn became a new gauntlet with a quieter cry from the raven giving chase. Noel cursed and ducked through a doorway, pulling Grey inside to the cluster of vehicles, including his bike standing at the opposite end.

The world elongated in Grey's view, like a never-ending tunnel toward their escape—or the second leg of their escape. Another shot of adrenaline kept his knees from giving out with another sharp *squawk* ringing out from the entry. Noel pulled him onto the bike behind him and revved the engine before he slumped against his back and hugged him as tight as he reasonably could.

He held his breath as they shot through the garage and into the early morning, zipping toward the manned gate, where one of the guards held up her hand. "Papers, please."

Noel cursed under his breath and swung his bag around, rifling through it. Grey twisted around to catch sight of a cluster of people filing out of a building, donning those Grand Capital patches on crisp blazers and well-tailored clothes.

"Here." The shuffle of paper snapped Grey back to attention.

The guard flipped through them, her mouth moving to whisper out each name. "Marks?"

Grey quickly shoved up his sleeve in the midst of Noel saying, "I'm Noel. He's Grey."

She nodded, folded the papers and turned back to the gate. Noel readjusted his bag, and the gate folded inward. The bike revved as Grey glanced back again to see the cluster of Grand Capital officials dusting off their sleeves and sticking up their noses at their guides while clustered along the road—unbothered and oblivious until one's head swiveled to the source of the tell-tale screech. That slow-growing frown fell in time with their arms falling to their sides, then they started straight for them, opening their mouth to shout an order.

But the motorcycle lurched forward, and they were gone in a heartbeat.

25

NOEL

That eerie raven shadow swam through the grass before they hit a dirt path and it flattened out, beginning its slow circles when they slipped into the most relaxed town by-far. The gates were completely peeled back, and carts were rolled out along the main road. Noel parked the bike off to the side before the raven fluttered down to the striped awning and cawed.

"Damn flying rodent," Noel hissed. He scooped a pebble off the road and wound up his arm to throw it.

"No! Don't!" Grey lurched toward him and grabbed his wrist.

"That thing is going to give away our position if we don't do something about it."

Caw.

Noel gritted his teeth. "Come down here, you little bastard."

"Noel, it's just a bird. It's just following because I couldn't sleep last night, and I fed it a little. Don't hurt it."

"You *fed* it? Grey—"

Grey's brows knit together. "*Yes.* It probably just wants more food."

"*Your* food. Don't feed that thing your rations when you need them."

He drew back and rubbed at his arms. "I... I'm really starting to think that we should reconsider splitting up, especially if the Grand Capital—"

Noel threw the pebble down. "We're not discussing this right now," he breathed. "Come on. Let's go find some paint and get the hell out of here before they catch up." He turned on his heel and stalked off toward the multi-colored sign over bolts of dyed cloth.

The skittering of Grey on his heels made his stomach twist with guilt, but he shoved his way through the door to dust motes stirring up in the pale sunlight among small, mismatched jars of colors, fabric swatches, yarn, canvas, and brushes. When the door jingled shut and the room stilled, Noel glanced back to Grey's wide, dark eye tracing the shelves before he crept toward it, like it was some wild animal he might scare off. He plucked up one of the jars and turned it over in his hands.

"Can I help you two?"

Noel's head whipped around to the beaming shop keep with soft, dark eyes and a kind smile marred at the edge by a long scar down her cheek. Grey stiffened along the shelves, gripping his potential prize a little tighter. Noel strode up to the counter. "Yes, actually. We're looking for some pigments and canvas."

She grinned and tucked her limp bob behind her ear. "I'll get that all cut up for you. Do you need it stretched, or—"

"No," Grey piped up. "We can do that ourselves. Could we get a couple squares of it? Like"—he held up his hands—"this wide?" He slapped on a tight, painful-looking grin, and Noel turned back to the shop keep with a hesitant nod.

"Right away," she said, beaming as she reached for one of the rolls lined up along the back shelf.

Noel watched her unroll it across the countertop and slip her scissors into the metal groove. The rhythmic cutting might as well be the ticking of the grandfather clock in his parent's living room counting down the minutes until dark, but now it might as well be the seconds until they were found. Sweat beaded on his palms, making his hands sticky against the wood counter while he waited on Grey to decide on his pigments and brushes.

The shop keep nudged the rolls toward him and rattled off a price that almost flew over his head when Grey stepped up next to him and rummaged through his bag. Coins on the counter. Supplies tucked into his arms. A jingle of the bell before feeling the heat of the sun on his face again.

"Do you have any ideas on where there's a field of flowers we'd be able to spend some time in?" Grey asked. "I know a lot of places like that are usually by faerie circles, but there are a few that aren't…"

Noel bit his lip and shook his head. "Isn't there something else you could paint? Does it have to be flowers? Can't it be something else?"

"The fair folk glorify nature, remember? And finding something with a ton of colors will probably be the best to capture that because it's a taste of what they fought to preserve."

Noel's shoulders sagged as they came to a halt next to his bike, the raven preening itself on its striped temporary roost to taunt him. "There's bound to be one near the delta though, which is probably the safest place to do anything since we can just cross the river if something finds us."

He jumped at another shrill *caw* from the bird and gritted his teeth. Instead of shrinking back like Grey had at just about everything else that posed a threat, his shoulders fell as he turned his face to stare up at the creature with a worried look. The way those beady little eyes peered back down sent an uneasy feeling through Noel, so he grabbed Grey's arm.

"We should get a move on."

Grey shook his head and pulled free. "Noel, I don't want to drag you down with everything. If you don't want to joi—"

His heart seized, and then he ripped some of the supplies from his arms. "Don't talk like that. Get on the bike." Noel jerked his chin toward the seat with a scowl.

The pain reflected in Grey's eyes ripped him apart at the seams, but he climbed on anyway while Noel tucked away as much as he could into his bag: an insurance policy for him not to take off at a moment's notice. When Grey's arms encircled him, Noel forced out a long breath and revved the engine.

Gravel rumbled under rubber and the town fell away into the eerie serenity of the distant, looming woods and raven shadows. The sciomancer's warning for them to split up slowly surfaced to the forefront of his thoughts, despite how he desperately tried to will it back—to cover it up with his newfound argument that they'd be stronger working together as a unit than peeling off in two different directions.

His grip tightened on the handles, squeezing the worn silicone coverings while imagining some feral, lanky fair folk creature prowling after Grey at the edge of the woods. Those bright pink eyes glowing in the dark, forever seared into his memory as a living nightmare of what awaited them on the other side of the veil in the Otherworld. Something the Calling had lured them toward until this very moment when they'd broken free.

Grey's face rested against Noel's shoulder blade, and he nearly melted, his legs going slack for a mere breath and hiccupping their acceleration. His jaw set, and he relished the rush of wind through his hair—that taste of freedom he'd always taken for granted not all that long ago, back when he quietly feared the thought of encountering a hemomancer.

Now he knew better. Now he understood that the fair folk had pitted them all against each other for a laugh. All just to watch them squirm and squabble—to spill each other's blood without so much as lifting a finger.

To keep them separated.

To keep them scared.

To keep them pacified.

Noel swallowed, reimagining his fantasies of meeting Grey in another timeline that he'd never get now. *But you can offer a sacrifice to keep him.* Guilt gnawed at him, nudging forward that horrible reminder that Grey might wish to be left alone or—*worse*—that Grey might still be intimidated or fearful of him when all was said and done. Sure, trust among being hunted was one thing, but when they were free, what would he do then?

The offering of a cookie after their initial escape. The feel of Grey's magic knitting him back together in exchange for the grass all around them. The night Grey jolted awake with nightmares of being hunted, wearing a suppressing collar.

Sacrifice after sacrifice, all made for the sake of their survival—*Noel's* survival—and yet, Grey's hesitation said that it wasn't enough. But it was. It was more than enough, and Noel felt like everything he'd done for them paled in comparison. And here he was, selfishly hoping to keep Grey to himself when all was said and done.

Noel shook the idea away. This would be his sacrifice: protecting Grey until they were free from this wretched game.

26

GREY

Dark closed in before they reached the delta. Grey's legs ached as they peeled themselves off the bike from the long ride, and Noel led the way to a hole-in-the-wall tavern with its doorway covered by a sheet. Jewels clinked together along the other side when Noel pushed it back and they stumbled in. Smoky trails of incense permeated the air, and cushions scattered the floor around squatty mismatched square and round tables. Tea kettles and liquor decanters lined the back wall alongside flickering candles dripping down to the dregs.

Noel took a hesitant step inside, peering around the draped sheer fabric dividers on his way to the ornate bar. Not a soul in sight. It ramped up Grey's anxiety more than he cared to admit, but he ran his palms up and down his sleeves to try to calm himself. "Maybe they're closed?" he whispered.

Almost in answer, a wood-beaded curtain drew back, and Grey jumped, nearly toppling into Noel as his shoe caught on a cushion. A slim, tall woman with pouty lips and narrowed eyes scrutinized them on her way behind the counter—each step a sashay that made him scoot behind Noel like he might use him as a shield.

Such a coward. So selfish.

"What can I help you two with? We're closed for the night, so if you're looking for a drink—"

"We're actually looking for a room, and maybe a warm meal if you can spare us the kitchen to put something together? We don't want to inconvenience anyone if—"

She held up a hand with eyes closed, her shimmering sterling charm bracelet jingling in apparent dismissal. Grey's heart sank.

"Leave the kitchen to me, assuming you two have enough to pay."

The stress in Grey's shoulders ebbed away while he rummaged through his bag, scraping out a few metal coins from the pouch. God, the bag was teetering on dangerously light. He dropped them on the counter anyway, and the woman slid them into her palm, one-by-one. That horrible thought that he'd wasted so much of their money on frivolous art supplies made his stomach clench as he watched the proprietress pluck a key off a hook in her little lockbox. Its slam shut snapped him back to reality and pushed every nerve on edge.

"Follow me."

Steps creaked on their way up the slim staircase, his shoulders grazing the walls. Two flights up, she drew back a curtain to a just-as-narrow hallway with a door off to the side and one at the dead end—the latter their clear destination since she ignored the former. A *click* of the lock, and she pushed it open to flip on the light. The flickering bulb hung at the foot of a single, wood-framed bed, neatly made with the scent of lavender permeating the air.

"I'll bring up your meals in a bit. There's a washroom for you two to clean up in the meantime."

"Thank you," came Noel's stronger reply, overshadowing Grey's mumble.

And just like that, the door shut, leaving them alone again.

Noel's heaving sigh and backwards flop onto the mattress made Grey instinctively rub at his arms, shame needling at him with every passing second.

"Noel, we don't have much money left."

He groaned and covered his mouth to stifle a yawn. "How much?"

Grey shifted, letting his bag droop down to his elbow to dig out the pouch. He set it down on the bed and glanced out the window to the strung lights zipping from building to building. The gentle sway back and forth moved in time with the slow spin of the water wheel. Grey fidgeted with his hands as he listened to the *clink* of their treasure in Noel's grasp.

"We can find something to sell if it comes down to it."

Grey's head fell into his hands, and he sucked in a deep breath. "Like?"

"We'll figure it out."

He spun around, his fingertips grazing his pants again. "If that fair folk wasn't chasing me, you would've been able to find something to trade by now. You shouldn't be so focused on helping *me* when I've been nothing but a burden since—"

Noel's mouth fell open in time with the coin pouch thumping against the bed. "*Burden?* Grey, we've only made it this far because we've been looking out for each other—"

"And I've been siphoning your resources—"

"*Our* resources."

"No, *yours*," Grey snapped, his voice rising as his vision

glossed over. "Yours because nearly every step I've taken further from home, I've been met with nothing but rejection and distrust. The only reason we're here together is because *you* saved *me*." He pointed at Noel's chest the second he rose. "I'm a *thing* —a monster wearing someone's skin according to them, all because of this corrupted magic running through my veins. If I were you, I'd cut your losses and trade me, just like when they offered you shortly after we met."

Noel paled when Grey held out his wrists, expectantly waiting for him to bind them together. Hot tears threatened to spill with each passing second. Grey's gut knotted with anger—anger at himself for drawing everything out this long. Anger for telling himself things would get better somehow, despite always getting worse. Anger because he couldn't remember his parents' faces anymore, and their loving words, gifts, and sentiments were all too far out of reach for him now. He had nothing.

Nothing to gain.

Nothing to fight for.

Nothing to love or be loved by in return.

"Sell the supplies," he rasped, swallowing back the hollow feeling seizing his throat. "I'll give you the name the fair folk told me, and—"

He tensed as Noel grabbed his upper arms and forced them to stand eye-to-eye. "No." That single, sharp word radiated through him like venom, paralyzing him with his hands clumsily folded between their chests. "I already told you—"

"I don't want to die, but the world doesn't want me to *live*, Noel." A trail of warmth slid free, running along his jaw before another joined. And another. And another. "The more I fight back, the worse it gets, and I'm not strong enough to keep going. So *please*—"

"Please *what?*" he growled. "Please save myself? Fuck that, Grey. You're probably the gentlest person I've ever met, and you really expect me to drag you over to the fair folk and sacrifice you like a sheep to a den of wolves?"

"Ye—"

"*No.*"

Grey choked back another sob and squeezed his eyes shut. His shaking legs buckled against the wall, and his back threatened to slide against the window with only Noel to keep him pinned in place.

Noel's drawn-out exhale tickled his skin as he greedily gulped down breaths between fits. "Look, Grey," he whispered, his vice-like grip slowly losing its pressure. "I... God, I wish you and I met in another life. You have no idea how much I've stupidly thought about it since we've started working together, but I know that I wouldn't want to trade meeting you with anything else in the world."

Grey forced his eyes open and blinked back the blur to find the remorse written all over Noel's face.

"I don't have many friends," Noel continued, "but I consider you to be one, even if you're unsure about me. I hate seeing you like this, so if you can't press forward for yourself, do it for me, please?"

A friend.

The very last thing Grey expected to gain after cutting himself off from so many people—so many *hemomancers* for so long. Even those relationships had been difficult with the ups and downs of people coming and going day in and day out while he kept to his perch in that dreary apartment and darkened his hands with charcoal. It'd been impossible to consider trusting anyone to that extent after witnessing the cruelty he had, including seeing hemomancers turn on each other for the sake of image amongst their other mancer neighbors.

Grey fell forward as pressure built at the backs of his eyes again and buried his face in Noel's shirt, savoring the embrace that followed—a touch he'd missed after so long. One that was just as comforting as his uncle's before he'd left.

❧

The hot meal had forced Grey into bed the second the last bite had been scraped off his plate, and he succumbed to the dark for a flickering instant before jolting awake to voices drifting up from the window. Every muscle went taught—his entire body on high alert while he slowly pushed himself up and locked onto the swaying bulbs piercing the sheer curtains.

He glanced over his shoulder to find Noel's back nearly grazing his, but he didn't stir in sudden agitation like Grey feared he might. Instead, his chest evenly rose and fell, even as Grey shimmied from the covers and attempted to peer down to the source of the voices below. The proprietress's frame stood mostly obscured by the street-side awning, along with that of another woman, baring a patched sleeve he couldn't make out.

Grand Capital?

Grey stole another glance at Noel's undisturbed form and tiptoed over to his shoes. The last thing he wanted to do was wake him for a foolish false alarm after travel fatigue and this place likely being their final comfortable room to sleep in a long while. He cracked the door shut behind him and crept down the narrow hallway, winced at the creak of his weight on every step, and pushed open the door to the alley, where the crisp night air greeted him, laced with the fresh scent of river water.

The slow crawl to the main road left him straining to hear the exchange, words cutting in and out until his back was pressed against the brick at the intersection.

A chuckle slipped free from the proprietress. "You know moving to the Grand Capital is easier said than done, right? I have an entire business here. I can't just—"

"But I can help you with it, and it'll be even better than before. Please just trust me on this, Nisa. I don't want to be a Grand Capital messenger forever, but it's also my home."

Grey's head lulled back against the building, relief washing over him. It was just a discussion between friends or lovers—not an interrogation to find the Hunt's prey.

Right before a shadow stirred just beyond his bad eye's blind spot, and a gloved hand clamped over his mouth. "There you are, you little brat." *Daz.*

Grey tried to rip away, throw his elbow into the macharomancer's gut, bite through the leather before a meaty arm constricted around his waist and hoisted him off the ground. Panic rippled through him with every flail and struggle to peel either arm off of him—a struggle that grew more frenzied the second they passed the inn door and Doctor Cavan appeared at the opposite end of the alley.

"You've been quite the quarry, haven't you?" Cavan seethed with Daz mere steps away.

Grey gasped as he was dropped to the smooth pavers and tried to break into a sprint, but Daz grabbed the back of his shirt and hurled him against the building wall. Air rushed from his lungs with a quiet cry while Daz shoved an elbow into his back and seized his arms. Cavan's sudden, viper-like grip on Grey's jaw lightly scratched his cheek against the brick. A deliberate move not to break the skin and get his attention.

"You will *not* run from me again, understood?" Cavan growled.

His gloved fingertips dug harder into skin and bone until Grey winced out a, "Y-yes." Pain radiated from his wrists with the sickening zip of the plastic ties, and Cavan let go. His nose pointed up with a haughty irritation in his turn to open up the back of the dirt-spattered van.

"Let's get a fucking move on."

❧ 27 ❧

NOEL

Caw.

Noel grimaced and pushed himself up in bed, his stomach immediately dropping the second he twisted to glance out the window. Grey wasn't in bed. His head snapped to the bathroom door. Open. Their room door. Cracked.

Caw.

He cursed and threw back the covers, his mind racing as he pulled on his boots. His hands shook as he scooped up his knife. The world warped around him as he started into the hall, hating how heavy his breathing sounded to his own ears until his sights caught on the fluttering from the window by the stairs.

Caw.

The damned raven paced back and forth on the railing of the next building over, its beak pointed downward to the beat-up van idling on the side of the street. Noel lurched forward, eyes wide and breath fogging the window. Cavan and Daz. Hauling Grey into the back.

"Oh, *fuck.*"

Noel shoved away and sprinted back down the hall to the room. Both bags were slung over his shoulders. Every pulse turned into another fraction of a second in his run down the hall, the stairs, through the tavern-lobby and onto the street.

Caw.

The rev of an engine might as well have been a gunshot through his heart. He gritted his teeth and pushed through the weight threatening to drop him like a stone, but by the time he reached the corner, the van was already rattling away.

Caw.

Wing shaped shadows spread along the pavers, gliding after it. Noel followed after and dipped into the garage. The *clink* of his keys against the ignition returned a much sweeter purr.

"I'm coming for you, Grey. Just hold on."

The methodical grind of metal sliding against stone again and again became Grey's sole anchor during the bumpy ride. Cavan pursed his lips as he sharpened the blade, a single leg outstretched while the other bent like a makeshift gate between Grey and the doors of the van. Grey's face pressed into the eroded metal coating of the floor and simply watched him.

Cavan's nose scrunched up with every passing second until he finally snapped. "*What?*" Those furious eyes pinned on Grey.

Grey tore his gaze away again and bit his tongue. A slow countdown began as that lingering question floated to the front of his mind: "What do you get from trading me?" he finally whispered.

The scrape of the blade against the stone stopped. "I'm loyal to the fair folk, as should the rest of humanity."

"You say that like you're not motivated by greed."

He emitted a sharp bark of a laugh. "You don't understand what it's like to wield true power. Once you taste that, there's no going back. The fair folk offer so much more than our feeble minds can comprehend. It's no wonder your kind succumbs to it so easily—how quickly you all go mad with power."

Grey's wrists strained against the ties. "That's what I'm worth to you?"

"That's all anyone is ever worth: power. Power to climb the social hierarchy. Power leftover from the fair folk's return. Power bestowed by our rulers and gods." Cavan hummed and turned the blade over, examining the sheen. "You should be grateful I'm offering you to them. Considering their interest, I take it you'll serve them well for as long as they'll have you."

Bile crept up his throat, but he choked it back. "What if I don't wan—"

"Shut up," he snapped, his cheery façade a far-off thing from when they first met. "Your wants don't matter. The fair folk's wants trump all, and the sooner you learn that the better. Especially if you want to survive the Otherworld in their good graces."

The van rocked to a stop, and Grey's heart leapt into his throat. "So you're a zealot," he hissed, finally feeling brave enough to fight back now that his fate was sealed.

Cavan *tsked* and pushed himself up. "I know my place. Know yours, hemomancer." He seized Grey's arm and hauled him to his feet.

Just the right opportunity for Grey to spit in his face. Cavan jerked back with a twisted grimace as he wiped it away. But he didn't hit him—not like he'd expected after everything he'd ensured at the hands of other monsters like him wearing human skin.

The mere thought of Noel waking up without him anywhere in sight kept him going. Down a single, horrible friend who couldn't even keep a promise to press forward for him. If he wouldn't fight for himself, he'd fight for Noel, even though guilt nagged at him from Cavan's sentiment. The fair folk were meant to be respected and feared, but *worshiped?* That was a step beyond Grey's comfort.

He stumbled out of the van in a blur. Sparkling lights hovered in the air like fireflies—blue winking in and out in a mesmerizing display that rooted him to the spot until Daz grabbed him by the back of his shirt and dragged him further into the trees. A swift kick to the back of his leg, and Grey's knees hit the grass, his breath catching as his shirt collar caught around his throat. When it loosened, Grey shifted his weight to scramble to his feet, but Daz had already seized his ankles.

Mushrooms and flowers decorated the small patch of grass he'd been dropped into, instantly turning a whimsical faerie dream into a panic-inducing nightmare. This was it. This is where he'd leave and never come back. This was the beginning of the end —where death awaited him in the form of a long, painful demise. And he was sure it'd pale in comparison to that macharomancer who'd stolen his eye.

"Let me fucking go!" he yelled, squirming to graze his skin or draw blood to make it stop.

"Shut the fuck up, you dumb brat," Daz growled as the final zip sounded, trapping him like in that little faerie door he'd tried to free himself from in a dream all those nights ago.

Boots pushed down the grass in front of him before Cavan stooped into a crouch and grabbed a fist-full of Grey's hair. "If you leave this circle before you're claimed, I will drive my damn knife through your foot and into the ground, got it?"

Grey gritted his teeth, trying to fight back the pain from how hard he was pulling at his scalp. "I hope whatever they give you for me kills you so slowly you don't notice until it's too late."

Cavan's eyes narrowed, but he let go, giving him a small pat on the shoulder with a nearly-imperceivable smirk in the glowing dark. "Spoken like one of the fair folk."

His stomach clenched as Cavan stood, the order for Daz to follow barely registering with Grey's racing heart. He sat there, frozen to the spot while those words turned over and over in his mind. Grey shook his head, squeezed his eyes shut, and forced himself to think of Noel's last comforting reminders before he'd gone to sleep and woken to this nightmare.

You're probably the gentlest person I've ever met, and you really expect me to drag you over to the fair folk and sacrifice you like a sheep to a den of wolves?

Grey desperately wished it'd been Noel trading him instead of Cavan now. At least it would've been a welcomed goodbye after finding someone Grey trusted as much his adoptive family. He should've stayed in the damn room. He should've woken Noel up. He should've started packing the second he assumed danger had found them—

Snap.

Grey jolted at the sharp break of a twig nearby, his eyes flying back open to peer into the dark woods up ahead. Those blue bobbing lights were joined by glinting gold irises this time— several pairs hovering between the distant trees. The feather-light graze of gloves brushed across his forehead, momentarily pushing his hair away. Grey's heart stopped.

"It's time to go now, little finch."

The world spun with the swift hook of an arm under his knees and behind his back by a force on his blind side. His body tensed in the cradling grasp of his captor while the trees began to move past—*they* strode forward. Grey's shallow breaths tingled in his chest and turned stifled against the heavy, silky fabrics of a suit-cut jacket, a garment far fancier than he'd seen the people from the Grand Capital wear.

Morbid curiosity clawed at him as he let his good eye trail a little further up to the thin ribbon bow drooping over the elegant, black-and-gold-patterned vest climbing up to their partially-lifted jacket collar. He swore he stopped breathing when he finally took in their face though: near bone-white skin and hair, the latter looking as if dipped-dyed in ink just past his ears. Ears that tapered into a fine point and were adorned with jewelry that ran alongside slender, cerulean antlers. Where the whites of a normal person's eyes would be, theirs were solid black around blue and a small circle of green around that pinprick of all-seeing coal.

This was the most beautiful and horrifying creature Grey had ever seen. Reign's focus remained dead-ahead with every stride forward, completely oblivious to Grey's awe and surge of sudden panic. But now, every fiber of his being screamed for him to *run*.

He bucked, and Reign *tsked*, their claws cushioned by gloves as they held on tighter through the squirming. Grey's heart worked even harder as he panted, forcing out, "Put me dow—"

"Now, now, finch," Reign chided, finally deigning to spare him a glance that sent a shiver through him with how much *want* lingered there. Power and control lurked behind every vice-like grip and coo of a word, turning Grey into a panicked bird in a cage—just like the finch they called him.

Grey's arms screamed in agony between Reign's hold and the zip-ties keeping his hands at his back. His wrists burned and threatened to push out of place while he blinked back watering eyes. Reign growled and jostled him for what he assumed was to get him to quit struggling. But an ear-piercing scream made Grey seize up shortly after, ripped straight from Reign's throat as Grey fell free and tumbled into the grass.

He gasped and squirmed as a warm hand clasped his wrist. "Hold still."

Noel.

Tears threatened to spill with how much relief spread through him at the sound of that familiar voice, accompanied by the snap of zip-ties and pressure fading from his wrists and ankles.

"You filthy little *creature*," Reign seethed, voice dripping with malice as Grey was yanked to his feet. He only got a glance of Reign doubled over in his now-soiled fancy, black garments, head lifted to bare their teeth at Noel.

Then Grey was running hand-in-hand with his friend, who still gripped a bloody blade at his side. "There's a bridge up ahead," Noel said through heaving breaths, his head whipping around with the rapid shuffle of grass growing closer. "*Fuck—*"

Something hard slammed into Grey's back, shoving him face-first into the ground. The air tore from his lungs before he could manage to scream. Dark fur appeared on the edge of his vision, followed by a quick clamp of teeth on the back of his neck—enough pressure to be a threat, though it didn't move farther than that as more creatures shot past. Straight toward Noel.

Grey struggled to move, finally croaking out a pathetic cry when a snarl emitted from the offending creature's muzzle like an order: *stay put.* Likely one of Reign's barguests, ready to maim on command.

A yelp followed. Then another.

He tried to move his head to take it all in, but Reign's gravely, warped growl cut through Noel's fight with the rabid fae-wolves: "I can't wait to hunt you like a rabbit in my domain and skin you alive to teach you not to touch what's *mine.*"

Grey grabbed at clumps of grass and gritted his teeth as he

attempted to squirm free again. Teeth dug deeper into his flesh, on the verge of puncturing skin.

"*Run!*" Grey screamed, fighting every instinct to yell Noel's name and give his captor another weapon to wield. Fear tore through him with the sound of every shambling step Reign took.

"No, *stay*," Reign hissed, their voice growing closer and more deranged. "It'll be my pleasure to spill your blood here and *now*."

A rush of footfalls through the grass, and Grey squeezed his eyes shut. His pulse pounded hot in every dimple of teeth until the creature's jaw suddenly released. When his eyes flew back open, he glimpsed the spray of gold sprinkling the grass before the barguest fell limp with a final whimper. Noel's face—spattered with fae blood—drew close to his, every feature pained as he helped him back to his feet with greater urgency than before.

No more words, save the echoing rage of a shambling Reign trying to catch up. The rush of water almost started a torrent of relieved tears down Grey's cheeks—a feat to hold back the second planks from the hanging bridge sounded underfoot. He gasped and stumbled forward from a single, offending swipe at the back of his shirt.

"Grey," Reign growled, "*stop*."

The bridge swayed back and forth, forcing Grey to catch himself with a hand wrapping around the rope at his side. But when Noel tried to pull him forward, his legs screamed in agony, like they'd been run through with a million needles.

Noel spun around, eyes wide before narrowing on whatever lurked behind Grey—undoubtedly Reign—and quickly grabbed his shoulders. "Come on, we need to keep moving before this fucker does something to the bridge."

"I-I can't," Grey whispered, forcing back the wobble to his voice.

"What do you mean you can't? Grey—"

"I can't move my legs." Tears finally fell then, like the overwhelming sense of doom closing in. There was no escaping this—no escape from the fair folk nipping at their heels every step of the way. Any time they struggled, they simply ended up closer within these creatures' reach.

The chilling, even tone of Reign's next words might as well have been a nail in that coffin: "I don't want to hurt you anymore, Grey. Turn back, and I'll let that dirty-blooded mongrel go, *for now.*"

Noel's mouth twisted into a snarl. "Don't listen to them," he hissed. "Bastard's afraid of a little running water turning them into a useless little sprite." He leaned forward, hoisted Grey up over his shoulder with a surprised yelp, and flipped Reign his middle finger before launching into a sprint across the bridge.

Grey clung to the back seams of his denim jacket and held his breath as the pain in his legs subsided, even despite Reign's glower laced with pure rage. But they didn't pursue—they simply stood there without trying to cut the bridge loose or pacing to find another way across. And after Noel took a sharp turn into the woods, Reign was out of sight, though *far* from out of mind.

29

NOEL

Noel refused to put Grey down until they reached the brush where he'd stashed his motorcycle. Every complaint his body made up until that point, he ignored in favor of the adrenaline keeping him upright. Adrenaline that was also siphoning more and more magic by the second, practically eating him alive from how much energy he'd spent slicing through all those fae-beasts—let alone the iron blade he'd plunged straight into that fair folk's back. Seeing the well of blood pour out and stain that bastard's fine clothes hadn't been enough to satiate him, but Grey had been the priority.

And now they were both a trembling mess trying to situate themselves on the bike and pulling bags over their shoulders. His heart raced when Grey's arms wove around him and tugged on the opening of his jean jacket. Right where he belonged.

"Oh no you fucking *don't*—"

Noel's head whipped around toward the sound of that dreadfully familiar voice. The *click* of a gun's hammer being pulled back only served to tighten Grey's arms around him in the face of

Cavan standing mere meters away with red-hot hatred consuming his features.

"Grey, get off the damn bike, and I'll only shoot to harm your wretched little friend instead of killing him."

The sudden, rough pull of his jacket, and a quiet wince from Grey stopped Noel's heart. He glanced down to the zipper track to find streaks of blood and red-stained palms. "Grey—" he choked out in a panic, right as he caught Cavan swaying on his feet, and the gun dropping from his hand.

"*Go!*" Grey snapped.

Arms folded around him again, no longer attached to his jacket as he shot the bike through the woods, weaving past trees and thorns with another engine roaring somewhere behind them. Every extra push of gas sent his mind tumbling through all the horrible possibilities—possibilities in which Grey would be ripped from him and he'd be left for dead. The irony that Grey had just saved his life while in the midst of Noel saving his wasn't lost on him, but he desperately wished he had the ability to make all these problems go away on his own.

He gritted his teeth and pressed forward until the worst possible noise carried over the sound of the van: *caw.*

Caw. Caw. Caw.

A chorus of screeches broke out in the trees, nearly drowning out Grey's panicked, "Oh, no. No, no, no—"

Forms swooped down in a cascade of nightmarish shadows. Black birds shot in front of them, around them—talons dug into Noel's scalp and beaks nipped at his fingers. He batted them away and tried to wave to where Grey pressed further into his back.

The van swerved in his cracked mirrors, nearly consumed by the cauldron of ravens. Noel peeled off to the left and zipped through the narrow path. Only then did the birds fly away, drifting higher in the sky. Noel panted and tensed at the echo of two screams before the sharp smash of metal colliding with earth. Noel slowed, feeling Grey's head lift away from his back as he peered into the dark beyond the row of trees at their side.

He wove the bike through and slammed on the breaks. Rocks from the edge of the cliff slipped free as he gently rolled the motorcycle backward, and his stomach clenched at the sight of the van at the bottom of the ravine.

"Oh, fuck," he whispered.

Grey's shuddering sob of relief almost cracked his heart in half as he turned the bike back onto the narrow path. The grinding of dirt against the wheels became the sweetest melody as Noel spirited them away from Cavan, Daz, and the terrifying creatures lurking on the edge of the Otherworld.

30

GREY

Grey's arms shook by the time they stopped in the early-morning shadow of crumbling brick duplexes and stripped cables dangling from glass-less window frames.

No gates.

No corrugated walls.

No chain-link fences.

The slow roll through an alleyway stacked with debris along the edges left every nerve on edge until Noel pulled up to a half-closed garage. It's metal shutter glinting pink in the first gasp of light. He got off, and Grey stumbled after him, the two ducking inside while Noel wheeled the bike in.

Grey's eyes adjusted to the dim, dusty box. Peg boards were half-torn off the walls and trash sat crumpled in the corners. "Do you think it's safe to rest here?" he asked, ringing his hands and scraping off the dried blood from his palms.

"Not sure, but we need to rest." Noel paced along the garage door and tried to pull it closer to the cracked pavement. The thing groaned like something straight from the Otherworld until it finally dropped down a little further. "Close enough," he grumbled, dusting off his hands on his pants.

Grey laid his bag on the floor and collapsed to rifle through it. He pulled out a bunched up spare shirt to turn into a makeshift pillow as Noel sat down next to him. Worn, familiar fabric rubbed against his cheek, his body finally relaxing while Noel sifted through his own bag.

"I'm fucking starving," he mumbled.

Grey nudged his bag closer to him. "I still have some rations."

Noel scowled. "Those are *yours*."

"But you need them," he said with a tired sigh. "Take it as a thank you for saving me, especially after all the trouble I've caused."

"You're not—"

"I know. I'm not because I'm your friend. I just... feel like I am."

Noel's bag buckle clanged against the concrete and scraped as he shimmied closer and laid down next to Grey. "You're not." His leafy green eyes pierced through him, prying into his soul. It made Grey squirm until Noel turned his face up to the bag again.

"Thank you," Grey whispered through the rustling of Noel hunting down his trade-snack.

He hated how he couldn't look away when he started breaking apart his granola bar. Or when he propped himself up to eat and take in their makeshift shelter like it was some fascinating new world. A world that Grey felt completely disconnected from when all he could think about was Noel refusing to let Reign take him. That was something he doubted any of the people he'd ever known would've risked for him.

Grey bit the inside of his cheek, debating if he should sleep or say something. Another thank you didn't feel like enough, but he wasn't sure what else felt more appropriate. A hug? A kiss? *God, Grey, do you really think he wants a kiss from* you? He wrapped his hoodie string around his finger so tight it started to turn white. Too many confusing feelings and not nearly enough time to sort through them all.

He shoved himself up and pulled his journal from his bag. When he flipped to the back page with its miscellaneous scribbles, he jotted down a single word and held it out for Noel with a nudge of his elbow.

"Um, that's their name."

Noel's eyes narrowed on *Reign* written there, and his mouth twisted like he'd tasted something sour. "Too bad saying it just causes more trouble, unlike if any of those things get our names," he grumbled. "I'd make them unable to use their legs and cut them up. I still can't fucking believe how close we came to the Hunt and" —he absently motioned to the air— "everything else." He popped another chunk of granola in his mouth and chewed.

Grey closed his journal and sat it to the side. His shoes slid against the floor like the dry wood planks of his loft as he pulled his knees to his chest. "I want to thank you for saving me from them. You put yourself in a lot of danger when you could've gone on without me, especially after I sort of admitted defeat."

His chewing slowed as those green eyes drifted back to Grey. "Friend," he said, pointing to Grey's chest. "Remember?"

A nod, though Grey wasn't sure it could be considered a nod with how little he'd moved his head out of uncertainty about how to react. But when Noel's hand pulled back, Grey finally let go of his knees and wrapped his arms around him. "Thank you," he mumbled into his shirt, regret washing over him the second he noticed how rigid Noel had gotten. He quickly pulled back.

"Sorry if I made you uncomfortable, but I'm... I'm really glad you didn't give up on me. Thank you for being my friend."

Noel's body swayed forward with hesitation before he pulled Grey into a hug—one that Grey fell into like he was being welcomed home. He tensed as Noel rocked back and they dropped against the floor. Huddled together. Safe.

Grey relaxed into it all, reminded of the night Noel comforted him in the midst of his panic episode. Before he knew it, he quickly slipped straight into sleep.

31

GREY

Grey jolted awake to a *clang* reverberating through the garage. Noel ripped himself away in an instant, his dagger scraping against the concrete as he shoved himself to his feet. Grey recoiled at the bright light flooding into the square cavernous space around the silhouette of a scrawny figure in baggy clothes.

"Oh, fuck *me*," came a sharp feminine whine as the shadow's head tipped back with a sigh. "And here I hoped I could camp out here for a bit because it's supposed to be fucking *abandoned.* Didn't I also tell you two to split up? What the hell is this?"

Noel's arm fell back to his side with a groan. "Look, we've had a rough night—"

"With each other?"

Grey felt heat creep up the back of his neck as his ears met his shoulders. He wrapped his arms around himself and stared at the floor while the girl from that plague-ridden town ducked inside.

"*No,* not with each other," Noel snapped. "We ended up

having to travel last night, so just ignore us and continue your looting or whatever." He waved the dagger at her.

She rolled her eyes and scowled in her survey of the garage. "Apparently there's not a whole hell of a lot here anyway, and since you two are fucking up my chances of getting caught, enjoy your remaining cuddle time."

The woman swung her bag around to her back with a wince, and Grey's gaze caught on the red-stained cloth wrapped around her hand, barely peeking out of her sleeve. He pushed himself up to stand, stumbling as he took a step forward. "Are you hurt?"

She shot him a dirty look and pulled her hand past the cuff to hide it. "I'm fine. I'm taking care of myself. Just like you two should be doing. I'd rather be a little scraped up than dead or dragged away to be hunted."

"I can—" Grey bit his tongue for a split second. "I can fix you up before you leave if you want." He wrung his hands.

She sniffed, looking him up and down. "What kind of hemo-mancer ends up missing an eye?"

Noel stepped in front of him. "One who's been pushed to his limits and still manages to walk away mostly in-tact. There's a fucking reason why I'm still in one piece right now."

The woman snorted. "And you're keeping him around for bandages and bonus cuddles?"

Grey sputtered and pushed past him. "It-it's not like that."

"Uh huh..."

"Do you want our help or not?" Noel snapped.

She rocked back and forth on her heels before heaving out a sigh and rolling up her sleeve. "Nothing funny, or I'll give you a raging headache, got it?" She shuffled toward him and held out her arm.

Grey took it and slowly unraveled the white strip of cloth

from around her wrist and palm. The red-brown stain peeled back to a nasty gash and adjoining scrape. "Come on," he said, leading her outside to a patch of wild grass and weeds poking up through the gap between the garage and the building.

He knelt down next to it and beckoned for her to join him. Her mouth tipped into a skeptical frown, but her knees met the pavers. Noel's shadow painted the ground beside them as he took her hand again and began knitting her skin back together.

Relief flooded her face. "You... thank you," she breathed, flexing her hand. "What's your name?"

"Grey."

"Grey," she said, a hint of a laugh slipping into her voice while Noel towered behind him. "I'm Cyanide. Call me Cy. I... don't suppose you'd be willing to patch up my back too?" She gave a sheepish wince.

✦

"You two don't seriously think there's a way out of this..." Cy started, her brows knitting together. She tossed down another collection of twigs and crumpled paper in Noel's stone circle outside the garage.

"The fair folk deal in bargains," Noel said, "so if we give them something of value—"

Cy scoffed. "Funny. You act like there's anything they'd be willing to take over enjoying a Wild Hunt. They're blood thirsty."

Noel grimaced and dropped to his knees with a match. "You say that, but don't they also value stuff more than they value us? We're just human filth to them. We're disposable in comparison to anything we could give them."

"That's quite a bold statement," she muttered, folding her

arms over her chest as the first of the paper began to burn. "Not to mention that we're marked for death because of the Calling, right? It doesn't make much sense to fight that. We can only really delay the inevitable."

Grey hugged his knees to his chest, noting how Noel was biting his tongue in favor of skewering one of the fish he'd come back with. That slow dip of the sun on the horizon might as well have been sand draining from an hourglass with Cy's combative words against anything Noel tried to argue.

"Well," Grey began, clearing his throat, "if there *was* a chance, would you at least try it?"

She worried her lip and crouched down next to him, nearly sitting on her bag just behind her. The sputtering sparks reflected in her thoughtful, dark eyes while Noel turned the fish over in the fire. "I don't know," she finally admitted. "I guess it depends on the price."

"What do you mean?" Noel asked with a frown.

"They hate us. They hate what we've done to a world that isn't theirs, but they claim it anyway. So I guess my only assumption is that they'd want us to trade our humanity in the end—to give up who we are in favor of bending the knee to them. Complete surrender."

Grey shifted. "Well, the fair folk didn't break through the veil all those years ago until we destroyed enough to anger them, right? So, we were thinking to give them something back that once belonged to them or by creating something in offering, rather than destroying."

Her lips pursed, quiet settling in around them, save the gentle crackle of the fire.

"You do have a point..." she muttered, her eyes sliding over to meet Grey's. "So what are you planning to trade?"

NOEL

Cy's relentless chattering with Grey overshadowed Noel's relief of gaining another ally. Every second he focused on cooking or eating, he scooted closer to Grey, millimeter by millimeter until the soft calls of owls signaled for him to put out the fire.

Crawling back into the garage hadn't fixed that small seed of jealousy from planting itself like he hoped—not when Cy had stolen Noel's place next to Grey. He considered dragging his bag around to the other side of him and selfishly pressing his back to Grey's, but when he considered the small opening between the garage shutter and the concrete, he laid down to face it. Putting another body between Grey and any potential intruder seemed like a wiser decision than leaving it up to Cy, who'd been so adamant on separating them in the first place—who'd planted that horrible idea in Grey's head while he was being hunted by *Reign*.

Sleep took its sweet old time to greet him while Cy's irritating whispers and strange new sounds kept him on edge. When his eyes finally closed, the image of Cavan's van smashed at the bottom of the ravine was etched into the back of his mind, sending him spiraling through a series of wild dreams until he jolted awake at the first light of dawn.

Cy and Grey didn't stir as he got up and stretched, unable to tear his gaze away from the rise and fall of Grey's chest—hating how his sights quickly snapped to Cy's curled up form facing him. He ducked under the garage door and sighed. Of course Grey would hit it off with her. Earn her trust. Survive with *her*.

He ran a hand through his hair on his way down the main road until he came across a closed, green-painted door and stopped. It might as well have been the door to his parents' townhouse, crammed between a bakery and a seamstress's hovel of a workshop. His mother said the green would keep away the fair folk since it blended it with nature, despite how his father rolled his eyes. Green eyes, the same hue as his own. The same eyes that people said made him lucky because that meant he could trick the fair folk into believing he was blessed by them—a lie, but a kind, hopeful one.

He stepped up to the threshold and tried the handle, his heart hammering in his chest when he found it locked. A few minutes and some finagling of his dagger later, the door popped open with a buckling *crack* to the remnants of a dwelling not all that unlike his own. The major difference was that this one kicked up dust motes wherever he stepped and the plates sitting on shelves above the sink didn't have the little hand-painted flowers he used to trace at dinner.

Which is why the task of looting the pantry left a sour taste in his mouth. But it wasn't like someone would come back in the next few minutes to hold him up for it. Whoever had lived here before certainly didn't need it now, but Noel did. Well, assuming he'd find anything at all.

A sharp scrape of a shoe against the plank floors, and Noel smacked his head against the inside of a cabinet. He winced as he scrambled to his feet, only to find Cy standing just inside the house.

She scowled. "What are you doing out here by yourself?"

Noel grimaced and continued rubbing the spot as he shook his head, stooping back into a crouch. "Finding food. Supplies. Anything useful."

"Stuff to trade?"

He scoffed. "You really think the fair folk want—" Noel pulled a bottle of some mysterious pale liquid from the back of the cabinet and uncapped it. He reared back and coughed. "Vinegar?"

"Think we can convince them it's alcohol? I hear they go nuts for that stuff."

Noel choked back a chortle. "It's your life to gamble with, I guess."

Footfalls trailed a little closer toward him. "Considering the sorry state of this place, I feel like whoever lived here last did about the same... Throw yourself smack in the middle of the delta so no one can touch you and suffer the consequences the second they find a way to strike." She ran her fingertips along the countertop, rubbing them together when they came away coated in dust.

"Pretty sure this is why we have iron walls now," he muttered.

She snorted. "You don't think they'll eventually find a way past those too? They're crafty little fuckers. I think they're more than capable of destroying those barriers, given enough time."

"Something we're decidedly short on." He stood and dusted his palms off on his pants.

"What are you planning to trade, anyway?"

The question took him by surprise. He'd been almost certain she'd keep up the doom and gloom, but instead, she watched him with dark eyes, waiting for his answer. Noel bit the inside of his cheek. "I'm not sure yet. I'm sort of hoping to get ahold of something like a weapon to give back to them—"

"Poetic," she mused with a smirk. "And Grey?"

He had to refrain from pinching his lips into a thin line. "Did he not tell you with all your talking last night?" Surely that *had* to have been a topic of conversation. What the hell else would they be talking about unless she was feeling him out?

Cy shook her head. "Nope. He didn't tell me."

Noel bit back a sigh and opened his mouth to explain, halting at the quiet melody tickling his ears. "What the hell?"

Her brows knit together. "What? I said he didn't tell—"

"*Shh*—" he snapped. "Listen."

Her eyes slowly grew wide before she spun on her heel toward the door—a door, in which, Noel suddenly realized she had walked through *alone.*

"Where's Grey?"

❧ 33 ❧

GREY

Grey's warped reflection in the ripples of the pond fueled his curiosity as his small hand dropped another silver coin in, his dark eyes following its descent until the depths took it. The water lapped against the mossy edge, and the coin reappeared beside him once more. His mouth tugged down at the corner as he picked it up to try again, thinking that surely *this* would be the time he'd catch a glimpse of what lurked below.

"Grey, sweetheart."

He fumbled the coin, and the usual, graceful *plunk* turned into a splash that rolled into a bemused giggle from his mother as she crouched down beside him.

"What are you doing?" Her voice held that teasing lilt, just like it always did when she found him lost in wonderment.

A lap of the water, and Grey whipped around to find the coin right back where it started. "Hey!" he cried, his disappointment aimed at the ripples left behind.

His mother's bubbly laugh cut through his momentary frustration as she brushed back the messy locks pouring over his face. Each touch banished another layer of his sulking.

"I don't think this faerie wants to be seen, sweetheart."

"Why? I just want to be friends…" Grey rocked back and hugged his knees, resting his chin there. He searched the pond for movement, but all the ripples had stilled, leaving nothing but a smooth mirror of tranquility.

"I'm sure they want to be your friend too. Why else would they be playing little games?"

"I feel like they're teasing me like the other kids…" Grey pouted.

"Other kids?" she echoed.

"They called me weird for drawing a pixie." He sniffed and swallowed back the lump in his throat as he buried his face, trying to hold his tongue about the part when they ripped it from his hands. The sparks from the small iron fireplace tucked into the corner of the classroom had eaten through that scrap of paper too quickly for him to react.

It'd hurt. It'd hurt more than he cared to admit, but he'd refused to cry when he'd numbly dropped back into his seat after the teacher returned.

You shouldn't draw that kind of stuff anyway, said one girl, her nose wrinkled in distaste.

Who would even want a drawing of that? chimed a boy.

The gentle trace of his mother's nails along his scalp threatened to spill all the suppressed emotion. He was sure he'd break if she pulled him into a hug—that warm, loving embrace he constantly longed for but didn't have the heart to request.

"You're not weird, Grey," she cooed. "You're just very special —unique." She propped up his chin, forcing him to look at her.

"You're a wonderful, respectful young man. You're doing every-thing perfectly, so ignore what they say, all right?"

Her tune dipped into a melodic hum, lulling him into a soothing state of serenity. Like when she'd woven flowers into his hair or told him a faerie story when he'd lay down in the grass.

"*Grey—*"

He closed his eyes, letting himself be swept away by the tune.

"*Grey!*"

Grey's heart lurched as a hand clamped around his arm. His eyes flew open to the warped planks of a footbridge stretching ahead of him. That haunting melody pressed in on his skull, threatening to split his head in two.

Tears spilled as an arm hooked around his waist and dragged him back to the pavers, his glossy vision distorting those bright green eyes that stared back at him.

"Holy shit, are you okay?" Noel asked, gripping his shoulders a little too tightly.

Grey choked back his initial reply and fought back the tremors. That '*no*' on the tip of his tongue was snatched away by the sudden halt of the far-off tune, exchanged for silence. Crushing silence. No birds, mice, or frogs stirred when those glowing pink eyes pierced through the woods at the far end of the bridge.

Noel must've noticed between Grey's sights pinned on some-thing behind him and Cy grabbing a fistful of Grey's shirt. The dagger at Noel's side slid free as he stood in front of Grey like a shield.

"Well, well," came the feminine, sing-song voice of the fair folk. "I remember you, machromancer. Quite a resourceful thing... Or *lucky*." She paced from one tree framing the path to the other, her face splitting in a feral grin. "Why don't you come over and face me? A precursor to our dance on the sacred hunting grounds. Maybe I'll even be able to convince Reign not to cut off your hands for touching their claimed prey."

Grey bumped against Noel as he defensively slid a foot back, sandwiching him closer between him and Cy.

"You and that bastard can rot," Noel growled.

She threw her head back, releasing a spine-chilling cackle. "Oh, you'll be *fun* to break. No wonder Reign was so enraged. You came so quickly to the little hemomancer's aid too—what's your name again?" She hummed, her head tilting. Those violent pink irises bore into his and rooted him to the spot as he peeked from behind Noel. "*Grey?*" He flinched, and that wicked smile returned. "Reign gave me some treats to offer you if you come willingly, Grey."

How quickly her voice shifted to a playful purr made his skin crawl, but it was even worse to have her try to coax him out like a stray pet.

Cy shifted behind him. "Fuck off, you piece of shit faerie!"

The fair folk bared her teeth. "I wasn't talking to *you*, you little mutt. I was talking to *Grey*."

"Keep his name out of your mouth," Noel snapped.

A grin. "Come over here and make me."

Grey grabbed Noel's elbow and tugged him back, trying to ignore the fair folk's jeering as they started toward the closest building to break line of sight.

"I'll have you know you're surrounded," she called. "Let's not waste any more time."

"Fuck," Noel hissed, glancing over his shoulder. "They have to be bluffing, right? We would've been ambushed by now if—"

Cy shook her head. "She might not be. The only way to get here is over bridges. There are a couple pretty far back toward the dense woods the delta falls into, but she could've easily stationed something there if she discovered that Grey ended up here."

Grey rubbed his arms as he fell back against the brick façade and stared down at his shoes. "I don't think she'd be here if it weren't for me," he mumbled. "This is my fault."

Noel's sudden turn on his heel made Grey's head snap back up to watch him pace. "There's bound to be some fucking iron in this town, right? More of it than what I have on me, considering how it hasn't been picked clean?"

Cy shrugged. "Maybe. I've only searched a single building on my own since I got here. It's worth a shot, but I'm not completely sure if we can hold this crazy bitch at bay—not if she has some tricks up her sleeve. And seeing how she's specifically hunting *you*" —she jabbed a finger at Noel's chest— "I think it's fair to assume that she's more skilled than the average fair folk. A designated hunter for the Wild Hunt could mean we're fucked here."

He turned one last time, his footsteps slowing to a stop with his thumb pressed to his lips to go with his furrowed brow. "I think we're out of options if we want a shot at the master plan."

"We don't even know if that'll work," Cy sputtered. "As much as I'd like to think it might, we don't have any proof." Her hands flew to her hair, tangling chunks in her fingers. "This bitch wants Grey. She even brought stuff to lure him out. What if she's trying to pick us off with our names? Then we're *fucked*."

Noel's face screwed up. "We're not giving up Grey if that's what you're suggesting."

"It's not what I'm suggesting, it's what she clearly is here for. I know we can't see them, but I remember her having a fuck-ton of barguests back in that fucked up town. So, even if we do find more iron, do you know the odds of surviving a barguest attack?"

Grey swallowed. "Well, Noel fought off a small pack of them the other night."

Her arms fell against her thighs. "You've got to be fucking joking."

Noel glanced away and rocked on his heels. "Look, I know I'm not invincible, but Grey was in danger, and—"

"Can hemomancers actually *heal* those kinds of wounds? I thought they were too tainted."

"It doesn't matter—" Grey blurted, feeling like a tea kettle screeching that it was done. "Noel, I know you don't want me to give myself up, but—"

His eyes widened for a fraction of a second before he seized Grey's arm. "You're not going to do this."

"They're not going to stop! You know they're not going to stop until they get me, so trade me and save yourself!"

"*No!*"

"Fuck no," Cy echoed. "Let's say we hand you over. She could refuse a deal with us, and then we'll be double-fucked."

Grey pushed down the lump in his throat before Noel finally let go.

"We scavenge the buildings and return here in the next thirty minutes. We're bound to find something to get us the hell out of here."

34

NOEL

Every piece of random trash stuffed in the back of a closet or crammed under a floorboard turned into a second of hope until Noel unwrapped or dusted it off to reveal nothing of use. His pulse continued thrumming in his ears like a war song, telling him he was at the end of his rope. When he popped open a box, he recoiled at the tinkling music that poured out—an uncanny match to the fair folk's song used to lure Grey—and hurled it against the floor. He panted while he stared down at the shattered remnants and immediately regretted not considering whether or not the faerie bitch would've taken it.

Trade me and save yourself.

Noel's fingers curled into a fist. What would be the point? What would be the fucking point if he gave up the one person he'd grown attached to—the one person he'd been unable to picture himself without? He fell back against a closet doorframe and stared straight ahead at the peeling paint coating the walls. Noel wished Reign was after him instead. Taunting him. Stalking him. Needling at him each and every turn. Noel knew he could take that, which made his anger settle that much hotter in his gut.

His head fell into his hands. The pain of knowing if they couldn't escape from this trap that he'd never be able to confess to Grey with the promise of a tomorrow shattered him. Hell, he didn't even know if Grey would ever look at him the same way. A hug was a hug, despite how Noel wanted to accept it as more.

Seeing him next to Cy might've flared his jealousy, but it'd also reminded him of the harsh reality that Grey wasn't promised to him. Just like how Grey wasn't promised to Reign either. His head thumped against the frame, sadness welling up in his chest.

Why don't you come over and face me? A precursor to our dance on the sacred hunting grounds.

She wanted a fight: a taste of what to expect when they clashed again. Noel closed his eyes and drew in steadying breaths. He could do her one better. She couldn't take Grey, but Noel could hand himself over to buy them both more time. After all, *he* was the threat. *He* was the one that still had nothing to give. *He* couldn't create like Grey could.

As much as Grey lamented about being a monster, Noel couldn't help but succumb to that feeling that he might be fueling this false hope they'd all indulged in. Hope that could very well be their downfall. Hope that ate away at what little time they had left without some sort of sacrifice along the way.

His boots dragged against the floorboards, each step piercing his heart as he surrendered to the thought of facing his fate. Not like he could run forever anyway when it relentlessly came to collect everything he'd ever chosen.

Stairs creaked, threatening to break under his weight—poetic, considering how much rested on his shoulders with this single, horrific decision. But the thought that weighed even heavier was whether Grey would stand silent as Noel crossed that bridge or if he'd scream the words he'd secretly tucked away in his own thoughts.

There was a fine line between love and infatuation, and the further Noel went, the more uncertain he felt about which side of that border he stood on. Was it infatuation with someone who always came to his aid? Or was it love for a person he never expected meeting in his lifetime—love for someone that complimented every flawed piece of himself in the same way he believed he complimented the object of his affection?

The door screeched as the sunlight grazed his face. God, he wished it would warm his soul the same way Grey's hug had, but it remained surface-deep on the way back to the bridge—to the building beside it where Cy stopped with a small bag. She dumped it out on the ground, sending coins and trinkets rolling every which way.

"This is all I could find. Some of its iron, some of it might be."

Not a single item laying there was a decent enough item to trade though.

"What did you find?" she asked, her gaze drifting to his empty hands and his jacket, like he might've tucked some magical weapon within that would save their skins.

He had, but the weapon was *him*. It wasn't like she'd see that though, not with all the chaos surrounding a fight he'd rather extinguish for the sake of someone he barely knew and someone who held nothing but fear from how the world had chewed him up and spat him back out.

"I... didn't find anything," he said, even sounding distant and distracted to himself.

Cy's nose crinkled. "Are you okay? If you're having second thoughts about this plan—"

He opened his mouth to spill it all, but before he could manage the first word, the pounding of soles against the pavers cut him off. They turned to Grey running toward them, something clutched to his chest.

When he skidded to a stop, he was panting and holding it out for them to examine. "I found something we can try to trade for more time."

Sure enough, in his hoodie-covered palm, rested a crystalline shard. The undulating smoke trapped within shifted from pinks to blues to purples around the edges, uncertain of what to settle on. A piece of soul glass: a mirror that displayed one's inner-most desires like pinning a heart to their sleeve. Something wielded as a weapon by the fair folk to lure in victims and rip them apart piece by piece until the glass turned black. A cry for death.

Noel pulled a glove from his pocket and tugged it on, his pulse hammering in his throat as he took the faerie treasure.

Cy's breathless awe hitched as he started past her to the bridge. "Wait, what are you doing?"

"Making a trade."

Running followed on his heels, both Cy and Grey immediately flanking him. He flinched when Grey grabbed his sleeve. "Let me do—"

He ripped away. "Grey, you've done enough. *More* than enough. I know you believe you're the cause of all these problems, but the truth is that we *all* are. You shouldn't beat yourself up for that."

"But what if she doesn't take it?" he asked, that one clear, dark eye searching his in a way that could've melted Noel into a puddle.

That overwhelming urge to give into selfish wants here and now almost won out until the shard threatened to pierce the fabric of his glove. "I have another idea. Just leave it to me."

Noel started across before any of them could talk him out of it, including himself. The uneasy silence consumed everything around him as the pink-eyed fair folk pushed off one of the trees lining the path and grinned.

"Come to face me?"

He swallowed, stopping at the edge. Noel twisted the shard in his palm, keeping his other hand at the ready for his knife if all else failed in either of his two bargains. "I'm offering to trade you this to let us all go."

She quirked an eyebrow and reached for it.

He jerked it away. "To let us all go for *today* since I'm sure you'll be back in five minutes if I don't make that abundantly clear."

A twisted chuckle escaped her lips. "Clever thing you are..." Those pink irises danced with malice. "It's been a while since I've had a challenge. Every macharomancer before you has been all brawn and no brain."

Noel bit his tongue, seriously doubting that. If anything, she was trying to feed his confidence so he'd slip up faster. Perhaps she actually believed that, but what else could someone like himself do in their domain besides fight for their lives?

"Do we have a deal?" he asked, his grip on the glass tightening to stop himself from trembling.

"Deal, little fox."

He held it out, and she plucked it from his fingers. With a whistle, her barguests slunk from the bushes, and she turned to lead them away.

"I look forward to our hunt," she called over her shoulder. "Maybe you'll live longer than a day."

35

NOEL

"**H**oly shit, it *worked.*" Cy's breathy awe-struck words smacked Noel in the chest once he hit the pavers again. Her bubbly, disbelieving laugh tore through his stunned state until he looked to Grey.

Relief—Relief was written all over his face, woven into his sway, vibrating off every part of him that'd been wound so tight Noel had mistaken it for that freeze of not knowing what to do. "Are you okay?" Grey asked.

Noel nodded, trying to hold his head steady as he peeled off his glove. "Yeah. I'm fine." He forced a smirk and pushed down the fluttering in the pit of his stomach. "That bought us the rest of today, so we should move. The quicker we get out of here, the better."

"Let's get the fuck out of here then," Cy said, turning on her heel and heading for the garage.

Grey moved to follow, but with his slow steps and his neck twisted to look back at Noel, he could tell there was a lingering question there.

Noel frowned. "What?"

"Did the fair folk say something else? You don't seem okay..."

I was prepared to give myself up to save you because I'm too much of a coward to tell you how I feel.

He ran a hand through his hair and started alongside Grey. "It's nothing. I was just overthinking things. Letting my head get the best of me."

Grey nodded, his head dipping down while he picked at the ribbed knit of his hoodie sleeves. Was that the wrong thing to say? Should he have said more? Less? Maybe being honest would be the best choice—

Noel cleared his throat. "Thank you for finding that." A sorry excuse to speak, but one that he could at least put his heart into. Grey stood a little taller in the final stretch of their walk, feeding Noel a fraction of that pride by proxy.

The rev of Cy's motorcycle tore his attention back to the present task, along with a newfound hesitation as Grey continued past him to collect his bag. That pressing question of whether he'd rather ride with her instead choked him until Grey started for Noel's bike. So he scooped up his bag and jogged over to leave.

Winding trails up the mountain turned into an ascent of chasing sunlight. Cy's warning to stay away from the trees kept Noel on high alert with the shift of every shadow and rustle of every leaf. Grey, however, relaxed against him, almost like he was swept away by it all to a different world altogether.

When they crested the cliffside, Grey perked up as the three of them idled to take in the sight of the Queendom stretching north. Towns they'd visited were little specks among thick forests and rolling fields. Noel couldn't help but wonder if they'd be able to make out a little piece of his home if they made it to the top.

A small break to eat and refill their canteens at a stream, and they returned to the bikes to push uphill again.

"I'm getting a little worried about fuel," Noel said, tucking his bottle back into his bag. "Where are you taking us, exactly?"

"Macharomancer town," Cy said, throwing her leg over her bike. "It's maybe another twenty minutes, but I'm not sure if the Grand Capital has sent anyone up here yet."

Noel cringed, unable to refrain from stealing a look at Grey. "What if they have? How fucked are we?"

She shrugged. "I'd say fairly fucked, but there's only one was to find out. It's the closest place, not to mention that it's pretty out of the way, so it's possible we'll be fine."

Grey shrank down in his seat, his arms wrapping a little tighter around Noel once they were situated again. The engine purred to life again as he patted Grey's hands—a small reassurance that he'd protect him. Because he always would, so long as they stuck together.

When green gave way to the towering metal, cinderblock, and brick that pierced the sky like a beacon of safety, Cy slowed her bike to a crawl. Noel rolled up next to her just in time to catch her growing scowl.

"What?" he asked, glancing back at the corrugated metal walls. "Something wrong?"

"Do you hear anything?"

Noel paused and cocked his head, feeling Grey shift and pull away to look around. "No?"

"Yeah, that's what has me worried," she muttered, pushing ahead.

Grey's arms looped around him again, and they followed,

tracing a circle around the barrier until Cy's wheels skidded to a stop at one of the gates. One that was completely folded open without a single guard in sight—not a single *soul* in sight.

"What the fuck..." Cy murmured. She turned to roll inside, looking up and around like something might leap off a roof on her way through. Noel left some distance between them as he trailed behind.

Ash trays with half-smoked cigarettes sat on the railings of a bar's makeshift outdoor area. Flies swarmed knocked over trash bins. Doors swung on their hinges from the breeze.

Grey squeezed Noel's torso a little tighter. "I don't like this..."

Cy's engine cut after she pulled off to the fueling station, Noel parked alongside her and worried his lip. "Something's off here."

"No shit," she breathed, hopping off and starting up to the station door. It swung inward as Noel and Grey climbed off and glanced around before creeping after her, not getting very far when she backed up and gagged. "What the fuck is that smell?"

Noel reared back at the sickening sweet stench that assaulted him and pulled his tee-shirt up over his nose. "Watch the bikes, Grey," he ordered, pushing past Cy as she loosened the bandana around her wrist to tie around her face.

Dust motes cascaded downward in the rays of sunlight trickling through the windows. Washed out blue walls bore old-fashioned signs tacked or nailed to every centimeter of free space behind the counter. Sheets hung in the door frames, obscuring his view of the back of the shop.

"Hello?" he called, braving to pull down the collar of his shirt for a second.

The floorboards creaked as Cy shifted next to him. "Something tells me we're not going to get a response," she whispered.

She started around the counter, each step a scream in the deafening silence. Noel glanced over his shoulder to Grey rubbing his arms outside, his head on a swivel before he braved to follow her.

Cy drew back one of the curtains, straight to a locked storage cage and a staircase.

"Owner's apartment?" Noel guessed as she went for the lock, giving it a tug.

"Probably. I'd guess the key's upstairs unless they took off with it…"

Noel's brows knit together when he caught sight of the locked, wire-enclosed pantry of canned goods. "Why leave all th—" He bit his tongue, feeling goosebumps trail along his arms when Cy's gaze met his.

She jogged up the steps, throwing caution into the wind, and he ran after her. The smell slammed into him the moment he hit the second floor, eyes watering while Cy buried her face in her elbow.

On the floor laid a man on his side. Stiff. Bloodshot eyes. Blue lips. Dead.

Cy took a step back. "Fuck."

"What the hell happened to him?" Noel said through a cough. His eyes darted around the room, tracing untouched table-tops, neatly organized shelves, and well-worn furniture. Nothing seemingly out of place to indicate a struggle.

She shook her head. "Not sure. Poison, maybe?"

"From *what?*" Noel shuffled forward to peek through another doorway while Cy crouched down and began picking through the dead guy's pockets. A woman laid face-down in the next room. "There's another one, Cy."

"I'm betting something fucking happened with the water supply—like back where we met. I saw that crazy fair folk bitch drop something through the fence. Some sort of moss-looking thing." A jingle made Noel turn back around to find a set of keys in her hand. "When I tried to tell someone the night the fight broke out, they wanted to lock me up because they thought I was infected and seeing hallucinations like the others."

He pressed his shirt collar closer to his nose as she pushed herself off the floor. "These two didn't try to attack each other though. At least, not with the way everything looks here."

She shook her head. "Doesn't matter. Let's check for weapons we can take with us, refuel, and get the fuck out of here. No food. No water. Assume anything we could take for consumption could be tainted." He grimaced as she popped back up and started for the stairs. "Bet the other doorway behind the counter leads to the cellar or something," she muttered.

They clamored back down the stairs, and Noel's heart sank at the sight of canned goods locked in the cabinets. Here they were, low on food, fuel, and morale, only able to strengthen one at a time at the cost of another. She jammed a small key in the fuel cabinet's lock and pulled one of the doors free.

"Grab a canister. You and Grey can fuel up while I take a look in the other room." Cy hoisted a stained, yellow fuel jug from the shelf and groaned. "Fuck, this sucks."

Noel grabbed another, letting his shirt collar fall back into place and hurried to catch her. He grabbed at her canister's handle to pry it from her grasp "Let me take it. Go find the weapons cache, and I'll join you once we're done."

She nodded and disappeared behind the other curtain. He lugged the fuel around the counter before Grey spun around and hurried inside to help.

"Where's Cy?"

That little jealous monster threatened to come loose again.

"She's looking for weapons. Help me fuel the bikes." Guilt flooded him when Grey took one of the containers and stumbled under the weight. But he managed to get to Cy's motorcycle anyway, once again summoning that horrible feeling Noel couldn't shake.

"Where is everyone?" Grey whispered.

"Dead, probably."

Grey's canister sloshed, his face going pale. "What? I- How?"

"Two dead macharomancers upstairs," Noel said. "No sign of a struggle. Blue lips and bloodshot eyes. Cy thinks the food or water might've been poisoned." He tried not to take his eyes off the fuel gauge out of fear of wanting to comfort Grey somehow. *Stop it.*

"Oh." Grey's whisper barely hitched above a breath, like he was too stunned to add anything else.

Noel cleared his throat and capped the fuel canister while Grey fumbled to do the same. "I'll be right back with Cy," he said, taking the empty jugs back with him into the shop.

He didn't even wait for any sort of reply like he normally would have, simply driven into autopilot mode for survival—a horrible attempt to detach himself from it all, to ignore the stench of decay closing in, to ignore the fact that he was looting the homes of the dead. But he still replaced the canisters on the shelves instead of dumping them. Closed the grated doors but didn't lock them. And scrounged around for a notepad at the front desk as Grey dropped to sit on the front steps.

Caution: do not eat or drink. Take only what you need. Safe travels.

36

GREY

ead, probably.

D The loose brick under Grey's foot wobbled with every backward dip of his heel as he stared down at the jagged edge freeing it from the others. Was this his fault? Did that fair folk come here and poison them all because Grey had found a way for them to escape? Would this have happened if he'd just handed himself over?

Guilt gnawed at him. The loose brick tilted down.

You can't control what the fair folk do. Up.

Yes, but you didn't exactly give them much of a reason not to do it. Down.

What about Noel? Up.

It feels like he's having more regrets by having you around. Down.

You wouldn't have been around to help Cy though. Up.

An echoing *slam* somewhere by the open gates smacked the brick back into place, and Grey scrambled to his feet. His heart thrummed in his chest as he craned his neck to peer around the barrier and identify the source. A car? A van? A—

Something pressed against the back of his head. "Hands up."

Grey's mouth went dry as he shakily raised his hands to level with his head. "I- I don't have much—"

"We'll be the judge of that," came a second, gruffer voice before worn gloves pawed at the sides of his hoodie in a pat-down. More figures emerged at the gate—all covered head to toe in fabric and protective gear like goggles, knee guards, and heavy boots.

Sweat began to break out along the back of his neck while he silently prayed for the man holding the gun to his skull to point it away, especially at the sight of many more rifles and pistols headed toward him in holsters or slung to their sides.

"Please," Grey whispered, wincing when the muzzle pressed a little harder. He bit down on his tongue, waiting patiently for the gruffer man to finish his inspection.

When he finally came into view, Grey took in the slashes of scarred flesh through stubble and a hardened jaw. Possibly the only parts he could use to identify this guy, outside of his towering height. Amber goggle lenses reflected the buildings behind him, narrowing down to Grey's scared face.

The man reached for the string around Grey's neck, his mouth tipped down at the corner as he pulled the iron key free. "Is this it? Where's your weapon?"

"I- I don't really have a weapon. Just a pocket knife in my bag for survival."

He let out a low hum that rang closer to a growl as the rest of his companions neared. Grey yelped when he seized his arm and ripped down the sleeve, his stomach heaving at the sudden reaction, like it'd be quickly followed by the crack of a bullet leaving the chamber.

But instead, the man whistled. "What the fuck is a hemo-mancer doing up here?"

"Pl- please just let me go. I don't want to cause any troub—" He flinched as the others reached for their weapons. "I'm not threatening you, I—"

The barrel of the gun moved, tapping the back of his neck. "On your knees. Hands on your head."

His vision swayed as the gruff guy let go. That cry for Noel and Cy caught in the back of his throat as he followed their instructions with short, panicked breaths. Knees on the bricks and hands in his hair, his stomach dropped as his arms were seized again, wrists forced together, and the horrible zip of a plastic tie cut through the others' movement toward the fuel station's door. A macharomancer prisoner. Again.

"Take him to the car while we clear this building."

Pressure built in his unseeing eye, recalling that over-whelming pain inflicted over and over again. Every little stinging cut to blossoming bruises and weeping wounds. The still-face-less man who'd restrained him hauled Grey to his feet and moved to drag him forward. Every muscle in his body went taught, fear overwhelming that little voice telling him to cooperate.

A jerk of his arm, and Grey stumbled forward before digging his heels into the gabs of the street. "Please!" he cried, his voice pitching high enough this time the other macharomancers paused until soles on wood planks rang out. Guns were pulled, Grey was spun around, half-shielded by his captor.

"Whoa—" came Cy's immediate reply. Her hands flew up in the shadow of the station's doorway, followed by Noel, whose eyes went wide when they landed on Grey.

"Let him g—"

A gun flew up to point at his face. "Show us your marks. *Now.*"

Cy ripped down her sleeve. Sciomancer.

Noel's jaw set, but he tugged down the denim of his jacket's sleeve. Macharomancer.

Guns lowered slightly the second that mark was in full view. "What are you doing out here, boy?"

Cy's scowl from them not addressing her at all might as well have been a personal offense, but she kept her hands up, despite the sour look.

"What the fuck are you talking about?" Noel demanded through gritted teeth. "We're here for fucking fuel, and you're kidnapping my friend. I think the better question is what are *you* doing here?"

Cy shot him a glare. "Could you *not* get us kill—"

"Where's the station owner?"

Noel hesitated. "I'm assuming one of the dead people upstairs."

A couple of the macharomancers exchanged looks, and Grey twisted in his captor's grip.

"We didn't do it," Cy quickly jumped in. "They were like that when we got here. They look like they were poisoned or something."

"Out," the gruff guy said, motioning to the street.

They did as instructed, holding still as half the group stayed outside and the others filed in. A handful of agonizing minutes later, the gruff guy reappeared with his gun at his side.

"You can put your hands down. We hadn't heard from anyone out this way in a few days. You're lucky you didn't make it here earlier and stick around, kid." Back to only addressing Noel again.

"And I'd appreciate it if you'd let my friend go," Noel said sharply, nodding toward Grey.

The guy shook his head. "You and your sciomancer friend can go, but we're taking this one." He shook his finger in Grey's direction, and his stomach dropped.

"He didn't do anything," Noel growled. "He's with me, just let him—"

"There's a fucking curse spreading, boy. Whatever came for these people is coming for us." He stepped forward and pulled down his goggles to rest around his neck, coming face-to-face with Noel. "It eats people alive—*macharomancers* alive. And we've fucking driven out all the hemomancers because they lost their damn minds, likely to whatever this fucking thing was. So, if this one can reverse whatever's happening to us, he's staying."

Noel's lip curled in a near-snarl. "And if he can't? You'll let him go?"

The man stepped back. "I'll consider it. But I'm not making any promises." He paused, seemingly examining them for a moment. "It's going to get dark soon. If you two are in need of shelter, you can follow, but you'll be put under lockdown. No funny business like trying to take that one." He pointed at Grey again before his guard dragged him toward the gate again.

His body trembled with every step toward the beat-up cars parked just outside, even more so when his captor wrenched open a door and pushed his head down to force him into the back seat. A door slammed, and he shrank down against the ripped upholstery. More of the machoromancers approached, two zipping out on bikes to idle by the rest of the caravan.

Grey's heart almost snapped in half when more doors slammed shut with no Noel or Cy in sight. Noel had finally given up on him. Finally left him to be someone else's problem. Finally—

The appearance of Noel on his bike filled him with relief. Every tight muscle shook the second he knew he wouldn't be alone. He fell back into the seat as the car started forward, and the world blurred past, whisking him away from one looming fear to another.

37

GREY

Grey sank further down into the seat with every passing minute. Whispers from the front highlighted mentions of Grey being possibly too young or inexperienced with his abilities before the other passenger would say that was a benefit. He swallowed, fighting back the nausea that they were discussing him like a new dog they needed to train.

The squeal of the brakes and the car being thrown in park sent his pulse pounding in his ears. Doors opened, and he was yanked out onto the gravel leading to the wide mouth of a cave. Pine trees swayed around them, covering the luminescence of the LEDs running along the top of the metal fence while also concealing anything lurking in the woods that might jump out under the fast-approaching blackness of night.

Grey glanced back to Noel and Cy as they were stopped and pointed toward another gate. He suppressed that want to beg his captor to tell him where they were going in favor of cooperation the moment the guy dragged him past the rolling gate. Cables ran along the ceiling of the cave, splitting off at each intersection or running down at the caged corners through the floor to some subterranean level. Barred or solid metal doors broke up the bleak, blank corridors.

Everything looked the *same*. He might as well have been a mouse being led through a maze, never to escape. It wasn't until they turned down one final hallway and headed straight for a door sitting at the end that he was able to find a unique marking: a purple-painted machromancer symbol.

He tensed as the man leading the way stopped to unlock it, and the heavy door was pulled open to a dark, cavernous room. The only light came from a small lamp tucked into the corner, it's soft glow both soothing and depressing in the oppressive atmosphere of a space heaped with trunks, a duct-taped chair, a desk with a book propped under one leg, and a mattress laying in the center of the floor, smothered in quilts. A rattling breath from the gray-haired woman buried beneath put every one of his nerves on edge.

When the door shut, he half expected her to prop herself up and don a wicked smile like that macharomancer woman who'd sought so much joy digging tools into his skin. Grey gasped as his knees smacked into the floor beside the woman's bedside. The flick of a pocket knife sent his head spinning before the release of the zip tie—a zip tie quickly traded for a gun at his temple.

"Don't try anything stupid. Check her."

Check her? Grey didn't even know where to start. Superficial wounds? He could handle those without a problem, but *this*— whatever this was, he had so little to go on.

"I- I don't have anything to trade—"

The gun nudged his head again. "Check. Her. I didn't tell you to do anything yet."

His hands shook as he reached for her forehead. Closed eyes. Shallow breathing. Her face felt scalding hot to the touch. Grey moved his fingers down to her neck, feeling for that pulse—steady, but faint.

He swallowed. "Do you have any idea what happened to her?"

The barrel of the gun pulled away ever-so-slightly. "Found her collapsed in the storeroom a couple days ago. She was coherent until this morning."

Grey bit his lip, snagging on the memory of running into Cy. The pink-eyed fair folk. Cy's explanation they were going to a macharomancer town.

There's a fucking curse spreading, boy. Whatever came for these people is coming for us.

A curse... Grey closed his eyes and the woman's skin felt like the leather-bound tome he cradled back in that library.

Originally one of the most powerful of the mancers, hydromancers, were snuffed out during the first return of Queen Mab. Her Majesty warped the magic flowing through them to confine their power to that of blood: twisting them into beasts during the second Great Wild Hunt.

Was all of this to snuff out macharomancers? His eyes opened again, and he rocked back to sit on his feet. "I... I don't know if I can cure this," he admitted. "I don't know if it's fae madness or something else—"

His voice was swallowed by the other man on the other side of the room, who strode over to a trunk and rummaged around inside to pull out a small cloth pouch. The man stooped down next to Grey and grabbed his arm, forcing his palm to face up as he dumped the contents into his hand.

A red teardrop-shaped gem, looking shot through with black ink that pulsed in in the dim light. He knew this object—something that had been described so vividly in his Uncle Atticus's stories. "A sacrificial ruby?" Grey asked hesitantly. "Where did you get—"

"No questions," the man snapped. "Can you use it or not?"

Grey recoiled, his fingers curling around it instinctively. "I-I've never—"

"Try."

Intense dark eyes bore into his as Grey shifted and leaned forward again, his thumb tracing the buffed facets of the ruby. His other hand rested on her forehead, and he closed his eyes. Whatever dark lurked within, he could *feel*. The gentle pulse from the ruby worked through him, becoming an extension of the power thrumming under his skin—letting him push past those normal limits to tug at those binding threads dragging this woman into her nightmarish slumber.

A gasp cut through his concentration the moment he cut the final cord. His eyes flew open, the gun was lowered, and the man beside him let out a ragged breath before a relieved chuckle escaped him. The ruby was scooped from his hand as he absently stared on, unable to comprehend the blur of activity flooding into the room as he was hauled to his feet.

Grey was dragged past nameless face after nameless face until they reached another inconspicuous door. Unlocked. Lights on. A mattress in the middle of the floor with a neatly folded quilt, a pillow, and a squatty desk pushed up against the wall. His captor gave him a small shove inside.

"I'll be back with dinner and some books for you in a few minutes. Sit tight."

Then the door to his pleasant prison pulled shut. The lock clicked. And Grey was alone with his thoughts again. All while knowing what fae madness truly looked like.

38

GREY

The food sat too heavy in his stomach half-way through his meal, the taste of the seasoned chicken and diced potatoes turning sour when Grey thought about what might happen to him next.

"Not hungry?" asked the guard, who casually stood against the door to his cell to supervise him, like he might choke and die if left to his own devices.

Grey's chewing slowed as the fork clinked against the edge of the ceramic plate. He shook his head and looked away when the guard took it. "When can I leave?" he asked, swallowing the bitter remnants.

The guard's footsteps stopped before Grey glanced over to find one hand on the doorknob. "I was informed by the captain to keep you comfortable for now since there are a couple others that need tending to."

"And then you'll let me go?" Grey prodded, unable to weed the hope out of the question.

That beat of hesitation told him all he needed to know: he wasn't going anywhere.

"We'll see."

The door closed behind him, and the lock's final *click* for the night sealed his fate. Grey's head fell into his hands, his elbows bumping against the desk as he took in deep breaths. Anything to avoid breaking down in the face of another obstacle that sent him spiraling into despair. Noel wouldn't be swooping in to cradle him in a warm hug. Cy wouldn't chatter on to keep his mind off of things.

He heaved a shuddering breath as the stories of Uncle Atticus pressed into his thoughts while longing for charcoal in his hands. Something to keep himself distracted and pacified as he hit one wall after another.

A prisoner.

That was his fate in the end. A prisoner to macharomancers or fair folk, it didn't matter which when they'd both eventually throw him away or kill him. His arms folded and a sob broke free. Destruction always followed him, despite how hard he tried to be kind, gentle, and respectful, as impressed upon him by that harmonic voice that kept him anchored to the few memories he had before losing the last of any peace he'd encounter.

"I miss you," he said through tears. "I'm scared. I want to go home, but it's *gone.*"

And if we manage to break free of the Hunt, I'll be alone again.

Grey swiped at his face just before another heaving sob loosed from his chest.

I'm tired of running. I'm tired of being afraid.

He crawled over to the mattress and half-pulled the quilt around him, letting his head sink into the pillow.

I'm so tired.
I'm trying so hard.
I need help.

Noel paced down the wall of the room, ignoring Cy's eyes following him to and from with every lap he took until she finally said, "Would you fucking sit down? You're stressing me out."

"Yeah, well I'm stressing out over what the fuck they might be doing to Grey right now," he snapped. He gritted his teeth and continued down his path along the wall.

She folded her arms over her chest. "What are you two, exactly?"

He rolled his eyes. "Why do you care?"

"Well, I'm starting to think he matters a *lot* to you, or else you wouldn't be losing your damn mind like this. What makes you so attached to him, other than using him to make sure more of us escaped being captured for the Hunt?"

"We're friends," he said, the self-told lie rolling off his tongue before she even finished her question.

Her face scrunched up. "Uh huh... You know" —her arms

folded over her chest— "if I didn't know any better, my joke about you two being boyfriends holds more weight than that."

Noel didn't mean to slow, but his heart pounded a little faster in his chest when she struck that assumption. "It's not like that," he quickly snapped.

Cy's brow raised, and he felt the heat creep up his neck. "Oh." She clicked her tongue. "*You* like him, but he—"

"Stop," Noel said sharply. "You can call me a dumbass for bringing feelings into this because we're all marked for death, but I want you to know that I was fully prepared to give myself up on that bridge if the glass didn't work—if only to buy him time."

She snorted. "So you have a thing for damsels in distress?"

He sputtered. "It's not like that—"

"Yeah, *sure*. You totally don't have him following you around like you're some knight in shining armor, ready to defend him from whatever the hell fair folk decides to swoop in and spirit him away." Cy's eyes danced with amusement as he fumed.

"Yeah? And what does he talk to you about?" He jabbed a finger her direction, irritation flaring.

"*Me?*" She pointed to her own chest with shock before releasing a laugh that bordered on an unhinged cackle. "Clearly you haven't been paying attention to the fact that we've been chatting about things to *trade*—specifically, places to work on the art piece he's been telling me about. You really are a dumbass, aren't you?"

"Then why the fuck haven't you been talking to me about anything?"

"Oh, I don't know. Maybe it's because you're immediately defensive and apparently got *jealous* because your crush patched me up and decided to befriend me? Wild guess, I know." The sarcasm bled through every word, making him awkwardly shift his footing and bite down on the inside of his cheek. "Damn, you're a lovesick idiot."

"Fuck you," he muttered, his back sliding down the wall until he sat on the floor.

She watched him for a few moments, her fingers playing with her bootlaces. "You going to tell him?"

He huffed. "No."

"Why not? Don't tell me you're seriously going to pine after him for the rest of your life after we break this curse."

Noel shook his head. "No, but..." He sighed. "He's been really fucked up by macharomancers. He probably only trusts me right now because he's scared, and we're both facing that same, horrible fate. The second we're free of it, he'll leave, and I'll never see him again."

"So... you're a coward."

"I'm not a—"

"You're not even going to *ask* how he feels," she said, motioning toward the door. "What if he likes you too?"

Noel grimaced. "There's no place *for* us here, Cy. Even if he did somehow actually like me back, I can't just take him back home and say he's a hemomancer everyone in my town can trust. And if he lives in a place full of hemomancers, who's to say they're not just as weary of someone like me? What then? We live away from everything we know and try to make it work? There have been so many places that have already painted him as a monster that I..." His eyes closed as his head lulled back and thumped against the wall. "Fuck me, this is impossible. I don't know what I've been thinking."

"Sounds like you might've been thinking with your dic—"

His head snapped up to shoot her a glare, and her mouth snapped shut, lips pursed as she rocked back and forth.

"Just saying..." she said in a sing-song tone that dissolved into a thoughtful hum. "Maybe the fair folk did this on purpose to torture you? Put you alongside someone you can't help but fall for..."

Noel stared down at the blood-stained zipper track along his denim jacket. "Yeah. Maybe..."

"For what it's worth, I think he's smitten with you too," Cy said quietly. "Just something about the way he looks at you—especially back there when we were being held up."

Noel tried to suppress a snort and failed. "Yeah, I doubt that. I think he just sees me as his savior, not that I really mind that. But damn, it'll hurt if I ever work up the courage to say anything." He tugged down on the zipper pull, clicking it back into place.

That silence washed over them again for another beat until Cy shifted on the floor, scooting a little closer to him. "Hey. You want to get him out of here, right?"

He slid her a weary glance. "Yes..."

"Do you trust me?" Those dark eyes might as well have pierced his soul with the question, peeling back that layer of uncertainty to the core of his want to have Grey within reach again. When he hesitated, the question returned in a new form: "Do you trust me enough to get us out of here?"

"Yes." That single word hitched barely above a breath before her hand reached his brow, and the world tumbled into black.

⁂

When Noel opened his eyes, Cy was whispering something to a guard hovering in the doorway, food trays already set on the small table in the corner. The man's pupils were wide and dilated to the point a shiver worked through Noel, recognizing

Cy's influence being pressed onto him before the door pulled shut.

Footsteps followed, their echo trailing away from the cell with the distinct lack of a particular sound he'd anticipated that was jarringly absent: the sound of the lock. He grimaced and rubbed his head as Cy hurried over and crouched down next to him.

"Get up," she whispered. "I bought us about fifteen minutes." She helped haul him to his feet, the room swaying slightly until he shook the cobwebs from his mind.

"How long was I out?"

A partial shrug was as good of an answer he got in her shuffle toward the door. When the hinges popped open, an eerie silence greeted them—a signal that it'd been at *least* an hour, taking them into the night shift. But he didn't see any guards on their way into the corridor. No lights poured out from under the doors they passed as Cy started to backtrack a little toward the entrance to the intersection where Grey had been dragged into the opposite direction.

"Fuck," she grumbled as they crept forward, hitting a T split.

Noel's heart hammered in his chest. "They said they'd needed him for curing something, right? So, he's got to be guarded—"

"He *might* be guarded. You heard the guy, if he can't do the job—"

He gritted his teeth. "They'd kill him if he couldn't," he hissed. "But Grey *can* heal."

She eyed him wearily, her doubt starting to creep into his own mind that maybe they'd disposed of him already and hadn't bothered to give them the news just yet.

No. He refused to entertain the thought and pushed past her to a wider passage—one lined with crates and a flickering light. Something grabbed the back of his jacket and yanked him backward, just enough for him to spin around and see Cy peeking around one of the stacks of bins.

She pointed through the crack to the deeper storage recess beyond it, where a man hunched over one of the storage containers, its lid discarded on the floor. Torn paper and cheesecloth littered the empty space, tangled with crumbs and chunks of nuts, granola, dried meats and fruit. A rat slithered through the garbage and picked up the pieces left behind while the guy discarded another shred of paper and shoved a ration in his mouth, gagging.

Cy glanced back at him, her face distorted in confused horror as she mouthed, *what the actual fuck?*

He tugged on her sleeve, and they crept through to the next section. Blood ran hot in his ears, pumping harder and faster at that first sign of abnormality. Something was wrong. Something was *really* fucking wrong. Noel swallowed back the urge to call for Grey in hopes of getting a response to find him faster and blindly turned another corner in hopes of finding a sign they were headed in the right direction.

40

GREY

Warmth grazed Grey's face in the middle of the meadow, the sun's rays pooling along his canvas cloth curling around his makeshift easel resting on his knees. Every stroke of his brush nudged him closer to the end. Closer to freedom. Closer to a peaceful trek home, though he tried not to dwell on whether returning to his aunt and uncle sat right with him.

Noel dropped down into the grass next to him, those green eyes following every flick of his wrist until they slowly followed his arm to trace his face. Grey fought back the flush creeping onto his cheeks. When he drew his hand back to dab a little more paint onto his brush, the distant figure, previously hidden by his arm, gave him pause.

He'd expected a woman: a vague image of his mother as a small memorial.

Instead, Noel sat there, a blue-winged butterfly resting on his finger and a soft grin on his face while he peered back at the creature. A quiet chuckle at Grey's side made him grip his paintbrush even tighter.

"I don't think the fair folk are going to like seeing me in the painting," he whispered, his fingers brushing Grey's hair away from his blind eye. "But I'm flattered."

His neck felt hot as he turned his head to find Noel practically nose-to-nose with him. Incredibly close—a comfort he'd been craving since he reciprocated that hug. Lips brushed his, and Grey's eyes closed. Sparks bloomed in his chest and his toes curled when Noel cupped the back of his neck.

A small part of him broke, deep down, stripping away to the core of all his pain: that fear of getting too close to anyone because they'd be ripped away yet again. So it hurt worse when Noel pulled back—that sweet moment far too short for Grey's liking, even though their foreheads rested against each other.

"I knew you'd come around, little finch."

Grey's eyes flew open, and his stomach dropped. Black and blue stared back at him, piercing his soul as he tore away. His supplies tumbled to the ground, crashing into a small glass of paint-tinged water that spilled onto the canvas, drenching Noel's —no, *Reign's* painted figure.

Reign clicked their tongue and rose to their feet, brushing off their long jacket while Grey stumbled back. "I'm not sure why you insist on causing a fuss when all you need to do is surrender." They adjusted their gloves and prowled closer. Each step forward turned into another unsteady step back for Grey. "No more Hunt. No more worries. Just you and *me.*"

They reached toward him, and Grey swatted their hand away. "I'm not stupid," Grey forced out, surprised his voice didn't waver with how bad he shook. "I'll last for as long as you're amused with me, and then I'll finally be discarded. That's how the fair folk work. Twisted entertainment for you, torture for—"

A raspy chuckle cut him off, making Grey's blood run cold.

"Torture? That's what you believe I'll do to you?" They lunged forward, seizing Grey by his hoodie's collar. Grey gasped as he slammed into them, recoiling at the gloved hand sliding away from his jaw to force him to look up at them before it moved to his unseeing eye. If Grey didn't know any better, he would've thought that a glimmer of remorse bled into Reign's gaze. "I think the foul, filthy creatures scurrying around your plane have already done quite enough of that, hm?"

Grey swallowed, trying to adjust his grip on Reign's wrist while his legs turned to jelly. "You're going to hunt me," he said evenly. "And then you're going to declare me the winner, right? Just so you can fuck with me a little more and twist my feelings around before sending me back for your Grand Capital pets to euthanize me."

A sly, almost teasing smirk slid onto their face. "Oh, *Grey*," they cooed. "My dear little finch, you'll really believe all these lies they whisper, won't you?"

"Because they're no—"

Reign's sharp yank of Grey's collar made him suck in a breath.

"They. *Are*." The deadly edge overtook the usual bemused teasing, like a flipped switch similar to the one Noel had triggered by plunging a knife into their back. "If that foolish, greedy little thing hadn't noticed you so quickly, I wouldn't have been so close to freeing you from this mess before it's even begun. Stop running, little finch. Let me show you what they're keeping from you."

Bang.

Grey jolted upright on the mattress, his heart slamming

against his ribs as the gunshot rang through the halls and vibrated against the metal door. Screams and shouts turned his blood to ice as he scrambled backward. Each breath came harder and heavier than the last as he frantically searched for a place to hide—a place he wouldn't find in this cell. Certainly nowhere where Reign wouldn't be able to find him.

His body folded it on itself when he crammed himself into a corner and covered his head. The chaos beyond his little room grew louder as the seconds slipped by. He gritted his teeth and buried his face into his knees, trying to keep the tears at bay. That dream he had so many nights ago resurfaced in the back of his mind, bringing that phantom feeling of dirt crammed under his fingernails to free himself—that lost, lonely child deep within him that remained trapped in the Otherworld. A piece of himself that'd been dragged away the night his parents died, and he'd been hauled away to face the cruel reality all around him.

A sob broke through the overwhelming noise, made louder when a slam rattled the door. Grey pushed himself harder into the corner, like he might be able to make himself one with the wall and escape this inconceivable nightmare.

But there was no escape.

No hope.

No chance of happiness.

Only misery and pain, followed by an excruciating death at the hands of strangers with beautiful faces and razor-sharp smiles.

The door flew open, and Grey's head jerked up. A splotch of brown and dark blue turned to two soft circles of green through his blurred vision.

Noel.

"Come on," he said, breathless as he pulled Grey to his feet. "We have to hurry."

He stumbled alongside him, blinking away the glassy haze as Cy zipped around the corner and jogged forward, her head on a swivel. She waved behind her before sprinting down the corridor, and Noel dragged Grey with him—hand in hand. His heart squeezed with that comforting feel of their palms against each other—their fingers interlocking.

Grey swam between that strange floating sensation of dream and reality until they made a sharp turn and Cy stumbled back. A shot rang out from somewhere down the hall they'd come from, and Grey flinched. Noel grabbed Cy's shirt and shoved her behind him, letting go of Grey's hand in favor of blocking him as much as he could from the two fair folk slowing to stop in front of them.

Reign and his feminine friend with the piercing pink eyes dipped in void. Her jagged smile split her face as she prowled forward until Reign held up an arm to stop her.

"Well, well..." Reign purred, their eyes narrowing on Noel in a predatory way that made Grey's stomach twist. "If it isn't the little mutt who plunged a filthy iron dagger into my back."

Cy shuffled behind him, panting as she jiggled the door handle and cursed under her breath. Grey's throat clicked as he swallowed back that unease—that knowledge that they were trapped. Forced to face the fair folk or run head-long into an undoubtable craze of fae madness they'd sprinkled on their way inside.

Another scream made all three of them jolt, and Reign chuckled. "Would you like to join them, mutt? It's about time we did away with macharomancers. They've been a bit of a nuisance for some time, considering how difficult they can be to bend. I suppose the best way to handle them is to force them to break and start over."

A shiver slithered through Grey, the tunnel warping around him as he recalled the abandoned town surrounded by water—the mention of hydromancers being wiped out and twisted into hemomancers in that history text.

"Leave him alone," Grey blurted, pushing forward against Noel's grasp. "You want me, right? Let them both go, and you can have me—"

"*Grey*—" That horrified response from Noel ripped his heart in half, but it wasn't like they had anything else to bargain. All of their things were waiting somewhere in the depths of this maze. All of their weapons and trinkets weren't at the ready or useful to bargain for another few hours of time.

The hourglass had reached the last grains of sand, and Grey was about to be buried beneath it. But all roads led to this one, right? He'd been cursed to step into the Otherworld the day he was born because that's what the fair folk had carved into him with their magic. That's what they had mutilated him with, twisting him into something feared and outcasted with nothing to love him in return.

Except there were a couple things left for him to care for, even if they didn't reciprocate those feelings in the same way. Noel's echoing reminder of Grey being his friend was the only weight left for his feet to drag in his offered sacrifice to Reign. But Reign cocked their head, a single, pale brow arched in playful bemusement as a smirk danced onto their face.

"Oh, my dear finch," they crooned, almost like a belittling teacher. "You can't offer to trade something that already belongs to me."

His soul shattered into a million tiny pieces as the air sucked from his lungs. A shadowy creature lunged from behind the pink-eyed fair folk, straight for Noel, and Grey threw himself at it, his heart racing as he dug his fingertips into the creature's slick coat. That immediate rush to stop it from ripping Noel to pieces burst into a fiery, agonizing pain as that Otherworld energy tore through his veins.

A scream tumbled from his lips as arms wrapped around him and pulled him away from the creature—from Reign and their pink-eyed cohort as they sprang forward to grab him. Grey bucked against Noel, blood welling up in his mouth from how hard he'd bit his tongue. His arms shrieked while the barguest's lifeforce pricked under his skin, like the sensation of being stabbed over and over again—like the knife being plunged into his eye until it'd refused to fully heal.

A door slammed shut. The lock clicked. And Grey was doubled over on the floor, heaving through tears as he shakily glimpsed the blackened tips of his fingers. Another piece of his humanity gone. All hope shattered.

41

NOEL

That stunned silence that gripped Noel quickly slipped away when the barguest threw itself against the door with a vicious snarl. It'd all happened so fast—the declaration of ownership, the pink-eyed demonic fair folk sicking her hound on Noel, Grey's lunge toward it. And then that bone-chilling scream as the thing stiffened, halted in its tracks with whatever essence Grey had ripped from it. Instinct had overridden every other reaction Noel could've fathomed when he'd grabbed Grey. Tunnel vision of their sole escape became his end goal: get him somewhere safe.

But now he didn't think they had time to assess the damage. The unknowns of what Grey had done were too great, and their time was trickling down with the footsteps prowling away from the door to find another way inside. All while the feral fae beast continued to dig at the floor.

Grey's fingers curled into his palms as they tucked against his chest. The heart-shattering sobs sounded in time with the mangy mutt's rage.

"Grey," Noel whispered, gripping his shoulder. "We have to g—"

"I... can't." That small, broken gasp slid through him like a knife between his ribs.

"You can," he said, scooting closer as Cy shifted from foot to foot and glanced between the two doors to the storeroom. "We'll get out of here and fix thi—"

Grey shook his head, another violent sob spilling out. "It'll just be something else. There's always something else. There's no point," he rasped. "It's hopeless."

The hollow ring to those final words made Noel cup Grey's face and force him to look him in the eyes. Whatever spark he'd remembered seeing there back when they'd shared cookies in a quiet field had fizzled out, nowhere to be seen. He might as well have taken a punch to the gut.

He swallowed back the lump in his throat. "You promised you'd keep going for me because we're friends, Grey." Those selfish words tasted so *wrong* now—so twisted because he refused to tell him the truth like the coward he was.

"You're better off forgetting me," Grey whispered. Cold. Distant. Devoid of all hope and reason.

Cy dropped to a knee and pulled Noel's hands away, his whole body numb as she forced herself between them and hissed out a series of words that he didn't catch. The entire world was underwater, only broken by the growls and thumps of their persistent hunters. Grey's sole good eye glazed over before Cy stood and pulled him to feet.

"We'll talk this out later," she said, turning to Noel and offering Grey's hoodie-covered arm to him to take. "He'll do whatever you say for now so we can all get the fuck out of here.

We have to hurry before one of those fair folk bastards finds the other door."

She jogged over to it and released the locks, all while Noel stared down at his grip on Grey's wrist.

You're better off forgetting me.

A chill worked through him as the door squealed free, and Cy snapped for him to hurry up. He charged behind her, heartbroken by the lack of resistance in Grey keeping speed with him. A husk—a *hopeless* husk being dragged behind as they finished this gauntlet.

Other storage pods they passed were torn apart, containers toppled over, bloody bodies collapsed over crates and under lids. His head spun as they sprinted past more rooms, weaved around feral-eyed macharomancers, and ducked through doorways half-blocked by furniture used for failed blockades. When crisp night air greeted them, the pain in his chest loosened to a stifled sob of relief.

Cy kicked the corral free to their bikes, their bags still in a heap between them, completely untouched. She gently pulled Grey's bag strap over his head and helped him onto the back of Noel's bike while he revved the engine. Another sudden shot of adrenaline pumped through him with the distant sound of a howl. Cy scrambled onto her motorcycle with a curse.

The feeling of Grey's arms wrapped around him didn't have that same reassuring grip he'd desperately wanted right now, but when Cy shot forward into the dark, Noel didn't give himself another chance to dwell on it. He sent them into the void, past the wide berth of trees, and straight into the unforgiving wilds.

❦ 42 ❦

NOEL

Rushing water welcomed them after an hour of riding in the dark. The mist tickling Noel's skin sent shivers through him as they crossed a small, rickety bridge and halted in front of a run-down cabin. It was closer to a shack or a shed from its stature, but it didn't really matter when shelter was the only thing on his mind. A safe place to talk Grey down from his state of disrepair.

He followed Cy's lead as she dismounted and abandoned her bag in favor of keeping a flashlight and knife at the ready. While she braved the depths of the cabin, Noel gently guided Grey off the motorcycle, his heart squeezing with how malleable each movement was. This wasn't Grey. This was a puppet—a vessel in which Cy had suppressed the part Noel wanted to talk to so badly right now and reassure him that there was hope at the end of this journey.

But Grey's head lulled forward, his sight seemingly unfocused somewhere past Noel's shoulder to the creek.

Noel swallowed and grabbed his shoulders. "Hey," he whispered, fighting back that tightening sensation in his throat. "If you can hear me in there, I want you to know that you don't deserve any of this. I know you're in pain, but I'm not giving up on you—I refuse to let you die at their hands. You deserve happiness, even if I'm..." He glanced over to the bouncing beam of light coming from the cabin, Cy's silhouette flickering in and out of view. "Even if I'm not sure what it is you want most." His fingers dug a little deeper into Grey's sleeves.

Not knowing how much he might remember gnawed at him, pushing at the confession lingering in the back of his mind that would likely make things worse. He shoved the thought back down in favor of a hug, only to find it lackluster and heartbreaking when Grey didn't reciprocate. Something that should be comforting now felt like a violation, like he was going against every wish Grey had just to keep him alive.

Was that selfish?

Was that *wrong?*

Noel pulled away as the creaking of steps sounded from the cabin, and Cy began her trek back through the overgrown grass. "It's clear," she said, hoisting up her bag. It wasn't until he glanced over at her that he noticed the darkening circles under her eyes in the harsh glow of the flashlight's diffused haze. She grabbed Grey's arm. "Can you take his bag? I need to put him to sleep before I keel over."

"Y-yeah," Noel mumbled, quickly lifting the strap over his head before Cy led him away. The bag dipped into the grass at his feet while he stared down at where Grey had been standing. He'd saved Noel yet again, but it felt like no matter what was done to help Grey, it seemingly put him through more agony.

He squeezed the strap, biting down on his tongue until he

lifted the weight onto his shoulder and grabbed his own bag to add to the burden. Noel hauled himself inside the cabin to find Grey laying on his side, eyes closed and nestled into an old, frayed quilt folded in half along the far side of the room.

Cy blocked his view as she pulled one of the bags off his shoulder. "I can keep watch for tonight if you need—"

"We'll both keep watch," Noel said, still noting the discoloration in her face. "Are you sure you're okay?"

She nodded. "I got enough back from putting Grey to bed. I should be fine." She shuffled over to the side of the small, one-room cabin and dropped Grey's bag next to hers. The flashlight rolled back and forth along the floor next to it, falling into the dips of the boards. Its eerie dance continued as he shut the front door and started over to join her.

When he sat down next to her, the room fell unnervingly still. Noel's heartbeat threatened to drown out Grey's quiet, rhythmic breathing. How much had he fucked up by making that single choice to save him at the obelisk? Would Grey be as much of a mess right now if they'd parted ways the second they'd escaped? "Did I make a mistake?" He hadn't even realized the words had slipped out until Cy's head turned toward him.

"What the fuck are you on about?" she mumbled.

"I think you were right about us needing to split up. Grey kept pushing for that after you tore into us about it, and I kept telling him we were better off together—"

She scoffed, her head lulling back against the gutted space where a kitchen used to be. "That was before I thought there might be a chance to bribe our way out of this." Her eyes drifted over to Grey's sleeping form. "And leaving him there to die wasn't really an option."

"You say that," Noel began, a bitter tang surfacing in his mouth, "but what if we're just causing more pain in the process?"

"He's scared, Noel. He's shutting down because there's too much piled on him between that fucking fair folk and whatever the hell else people keep coming after him for. Us pulling him from that fire because he can't do it himself is the only way he can survive, even if he's struggling to fight through it all." She sighed and slid a little further down to the floor, her chin dipping into her shirt. "He's clearly fucking traumatized."

Noel slumped in on himself and picked at his boot laces. "I don't want to put him through more of this if he's breaking."

"No shit—because you're his knight."

He shot her a scowl. "I'm his friend. That's all we've agreed on. Like I said earlier, I don't even know if—"

"And you won't know if he *dies,* dumbass."

He winced and glanced away.

"Do both of yourselves a favor and consider telling him when he wakes up. If you give him more to live for than friendship, he might bounce back from whatever's eating him."

A deflated chuckle tumbled from his lips. "We don't even have anything to trade yet. We still have to find a place for Grey to paint, and—"

"A place for Grey to paint?" her brows knitted together.

"Yeah," Noel said, twisting around to rummage through Grey's bag for one of the pigments. He held it up for her, letting it shift in its glass vial. "He's going to give them a painting of nature. Something they're bound to fall in love with since it sort of immortalizes nature."

She plucked the vial from his hand and turned it around, letting the pigment dust the edges. "You're sure?"

"He came up with the idea because of it. That fair folk—the

one in black—they tried to convince him to go with them a while back when we were trying to find things to trade in some ruins. They told Grey that they could be their patron.”

Cy bit her lip and stared down at the red powder. “Do you think that maybe our keys to getting out are tied to the hunters we’re assigned to? That pink-eyed bitch talked like she’s your opponent, sort of like the other one claiming to own Grey.”

Noel paused, his gaze slipping to Grey.

Why don’t you come over and face me? A precursor to our dance on the sacred hunting grounds. Maybe I’ll even be able to convince Reign not to cut off your hands for touching their claimed prey.

He sucked in a breath. “You might be right...”

The thrum of Cy’s nails against the glass told him that her mind had started to work too. “The problem with that is that I haven’t met my hunter, which means I have no idea what they want. Wouldn’t giving something impersonal be like a slap in the face?”

“Well,” Noel mumbled, trying his best to skirt around any of the fair folk’s names and avoid summoning any more danger, “if I were up against Grey’s hunter, then I’d probably be fucked, so I can see that being a problem. They seemingly like art, and I can imagine this pink-eyed monster enjoying something like an ancient weapon that was lost on this plane.”

She tilted her head from side-to-side. “Maybe mine would be happy with something a little more mystical? I feel like there might be a bit of a pattern to it too, seeing how most of these pigments are from crushed flowers and things. It’s sort of like trading life, like how giving a weapon is trading power.”

Noel snorted, a grin tugging at the corner of his mouth. “I think you might be onto something.”

Her eyes danced as he reclaimed the vial. “I think I know of a good place for that painting. And I believe there are ruins not all that far from here either." That renewed look of hope crept onto her dirt-stained face. "We might actually have a decent fucking plan."

43

GREY

The light scent of fire clinging to the air woke Grey with a start. He propped himself up on the quilt, his heart racing until he caught sight of Cy's figure in the doorway, messing with a pan over a small fire in the early morning sunlight, right outside their lodgings—wherever they were.

Grey looked around at the torn-up walls and winced at the creaking planks of the floor as he got to his knees. The world spun when he stood, slamming him straight back to the memory of Reign's sharp, wry smile. Adrenaline pumped through him as he yanked back his sleeves. Dark spots lingered at his fingertips, grazing his nails like his hands had been dipped in ink. He quickly pulled his sleeves back down and hurried over to the bags along the wall.

Gloves. Where are Noel's gloves?

There, right at the bottom, where the worn, leather gloves he'd been searching for, and when he slipped them on, he clenched his fists a few times. No more indications that he'd done something heinous—something his mother would've considered taboo. Fae creatures were supposed to be revered and respected with a heavy dose of fear, not attacked with the magic forced on mankind.

He rubbed his gloved palms on his knees, sweating at the mere idea that he'd possibly scraped off a small portion of his soul with that transgression, and now this was his punishment—a mark to indicate he'd relinquished a piece of his humanity he'd been less and less certain he actually had in the first place.

"I'm sorry," he whispered, hoping that apology would be carried through the wind to whoever he needed to right himself with. That sudden sorrow smacked into him so hard he wobbled on the balls of his feet from where he crouched. All the emotion from the previous night washed over him until a dull numbness took its place. He jumped at the sound of soles against the planks and pitched forward to one knee when his head whipped around to the shadow in the doorframe.

"You're awake," Noel said, relief flooding his face in a way that made Grey's heart snap cleanly in two.

Grey scrambled to his feet, tugging down his sleeves over his gloves for good measure. "Y-yeah," he mumbled, his sights immediately glued to the floor. *God, you can't even look him in the eyes, can you? You basically told him you wanted to die because you're a coward. Now you're alive and you don't even have the guts to speak.*

That guilt pushed in from all around him—guilt from somehow surviving, guilt from tossing Noel aside in favor of giving up, guilt for being another burden, guilt for struggling to feel anything but guilt.

Noel started toward him, the toes of his boots stopping short of that intimate distance. "Are you okay? How are you feeling?"

Grey folded in on himself, rubbing his arms while the question rolled around in his head, unable to land on any one answer.

"I... don't know." *Like I've cheated death again and earned another badge of shame.*

The floor creaked while Grey watched Noel's stance shift. "Grey, I—" he began, his hand reaching for him until it paused, fingers curling as it retreated. A fresh stab of pain sliced through Grey, leaving an empty, throbbing ache while Noel continued. "I should've done more back there—"

Grey's head snapped up, his brows knitting together with confusion as Noel grimaced and ran a hand through his hair.

"Fuck, I shouldn't have had you sit outside when we stopped into that town to get fuel. I just thought—" He hesitated, biting his lip and glancing away. "I don't know. I don't know what I was thinking. I said I wasn't going to leave you alone again, and I fucked up."

Grey squeezed his arms, his gaze dipping down again. "I'm not your responsibility, Noel. You can't blame yourself for—"

Noel's sharp, hollow laugh cut through the rest of his thought. "I care about you, Grey. You're—"

"Your friend," Grey finished soberly. "I know. I just... can't help but feel like there isn't any more time left. You saw what happened back there—to those macharomancers—right?" He half-heartedly motioned to the doorway.

"What about it? We're talking about the fair folk getting pissy. That's nothing ne—"

"Yeah, and it started back just before we ran into Cy the first time. They're trying to twist macharomancers into something else because they're being deemed too much of a problem."

Noel scoffed. "I think you're seriously overthinkin—"

"Am I?" his voice hitched, that sadness catching in his throat. "We argued about how people look at me like I'm a monster because I'm a hemomancer. There's a reason why that is, and it's because hemomancers used to be hydromancers, Noel. That's why that ghost town protected by barriers of running water was wiped out. That's why people are always side-eyeing me when I go anywhere near any other mancer besides my own kind. The fair folk drove hydromancers mad—they warped their magic, and now they're doing the same thing to *your* people." Grey rocked back when Noel flinched and sucked in a shaky breath. "We're just *things* for them to play with. Even if we manage to make a decent trade, don't you think they'll push us to make another? And another?"

His back fell against the wall, his legs aching from how he forced himself to crookedly stand with the bags at his heels.

Noel worried his lip and glanced over at the door, a shadow disappearing with a quiet curse before he took another step closer to Grey. "What did they have you do back there?" His voice dipped into a low, dangerous tone that held a hefty dose of concern with that tiny trace of anger.

Grey readjusted his sleeves. "I think one of their leaders had fae madness," he whispered, the words coming out in a near-squeak. "They had me use a sacrificial ruby on her. I think it helped me take care of most of it, but..." He shook his head, leaving his uncertainty unsaid.

The furious pounding starting to emerge within his skull came with the question of whether or not he'd be forced to watch Noel succumb to madness as well. The most traumatic punishment Reign could think of for refusing to yield, all while knowing he'd have the capability to reverse it if he had the right tools. A slap in the face for thinking he'd be able to run from a creature that deemed themself his master.

Noel cringed, Grey barely getting a glimpse of the expression before it vanished behind a hand running down his face.

"That explains the disturbing erratic behavior from the others…"

Pressure built behind Grey's eyes as he stared down at his hands through the layers of fabric. This version of the Wild Hunt was created to appease the fair folk—to give them the sacrifices they craved in order to avoid mass bloodshed. And here Grey was, prolonging the inevitable out of the selfish fear of death. Or, rather, a slow, painful death with jeers and mocking laughter before he knew peace for the first time in so many years.

This plague could very well be the beginning of that price for disobedience.

"Maybe—" he choked out, forcing down the lump in his throat before he continued. "Maybe we should give ourselves up to the Grand Capital."

"What? What the fuck are you—Grey, *no.*"

"So we're just going to keep running while people start to die? All because we're too selfish to give up?" Tears broke free as he lifted his head to stare into those bright green eyes—like fresh clover he used to hunt through as a child to find the ones with four leaves and never could. A bitter laugh threatened to break free then, recognizing another sign of the misfortune stamped on his soul.

"Us avoiding death isn't causing this to happen, Grey," Noel said sternly. "I'd bet my ass these fucks would've done the exact same thing even if we were all corralled inside the Grand Capital the day we set our eyes on that piece of shit obelisk."

"How can you be sure?"

"Because they destroy what they can't control," he said, that green hue darkening. "Macharomancers have helped build our fortresses, so they want them to pay. And then there's us: the ones they want to hunt because we don't lay down and die—we fight.

We fight, and they hope to break us to dash the hopes of everyone else in this plane who considers standing up against them. The hydromancers were an example. They're making the macharomancers an example. They're trying to make us an example too."

Grey squeezed his eyes shut, his body trembling and forcing him to slowly slide to the floor—straight on top of the bags. He nested his arms over his knees and buried his face. "I don't have the will to fight anymore, I…" Warm tears stuck to his sleeves.

A hand cupped his elbow, and he tensed. "We're so close to the end, Grey. I'll carry you the rest of the way if you can bring yourself to give them one last thing. Just one painting, and I do everything in my power to let you finally rest."

His chest heaved as a violent sob broke free. He rubbed his forehead against his sleeve. "You shouldn't have to—"

Noel's fingers pressed a little harder. "I *want* to. You're my friend—one of the few friends I have, and I treat my friends like a second family." He shifted, rustling some of the canvas fabric around them before his voice dropped to a gentle whisper. "You remember when we first met?"

Grey forced himself to take in steady breaths while he crawled back in time to the panic he'd felt leaping from the frying pan and into a possible fire—from the Hunt to a macharomancer he didn't know. He lifted his head and sniffed, waiting for Noel to continue. He shuffled even closer, making Grey's heart flutter wildly in his chest.

"You told me I at least had a fighting chance. So I'm going to fight for us both, so we both have a chance."

"I can't ask you to—"

"You're not asking," Noel breathed. "I'm *telling* you." His other palm crested Grey's arm, so close to an embrace.

He had to resist the urge to throw himself against Noel and

melt into him. But he sat still, fighting the want to surrender—surrender to rest, to Noel, to death, to *Reign*. Grey pinched the sleeve of his hoodie to somewhat conceal his glove and swiped at his eyes.

"What do you say?" Noel asked. "Can you sacrifice one painting for these monsters before we walk away?"

Grey hesitated, warring with himself between relying too much on Noel as a potential burden or selfishly taking that offer because he so very badly wanted to *stay*. To stay protected and cared for in a way that warmed his heart and cradled his soul. He started to nod, his chest tightening at the sight of Noel's face softening.

"We'll get through this. I'll make sure of it."

44

GREY

Breakfast weighed heavy in Grey's stomach after devouring more than he'd been able to bring himself to do in days. Noel had kept pushing fresh cooked meat and crusty baked bread onto his half-broken plate until Cy stopped him with a warning that he was going to make him sick.

It was like he'd fallen into a strange new reality when they cleaned up and grabbed their things to leave, especially when Cy locked the door with a spare iron-laced lock and key. "There's not really anywhere else nearby we'll be able to get to, outside of macharomancer towns. Considering how much time we might spend out there, I don't want to take our chances. Hunkering down here for another night shouldn't hurt."

He stared back at the shack like they'd deemed it a second home, bringing a strange sense of peace that he'd laid eyes on where he would be returning to sleep. Supplies clinked together in his bag as he hopped on behind Noel and clung to him, breathing in the lingering scent of campfire smoke woven into the denim. Grey pressed his face against it, savoring the warmth on his skin from how long the fabric had soaked in the morning sunlight.

Engines revved, and they sped down the unmarked path, weaving through brush behind Cy. Every smooth turn and downward tilt made Grey's stomach flip until they reached a valley. Trees lined their view, obscuring portions of the clearing just beyond. Grey hopped off the second they stopped and jogged forward into the light piercing through the shadowy depths of the forest.

God, it looked like it'd been pulled straight from a dream. Splashes of color dotted the entirety of the meadow, greedily collecting the midday rays. Blooming riots of oranges, purples, blues, and pinks tickled that child locked within him, especially the moment he caught sight of the clover patches zigzagging through. And right in the center of it all sat a pond, smooth as a mirror with lily pads and stones staggered around the shallow rim.

"Whoa," Noel breathed, his shoulder brushing Grey's.

Grey tensed and reached into his bag when Noel glanced over, signaling he likely felt that sudden, nervous discomfort. He dug through his supplies as he started to dip into the grass, Noel shifting to survey the area before he decided to sit down next to him. Grey's heart jumped straight into his throat.

He wasn't going to watch the whole time, was he? Heat started to creep up the back of his neck as he recalled the good parts of his dream from the other night—the pieces that made him so jumpy now since they appeared to manifest right in front of him. What if the dream was a premonition? What if Noel was going to kiss him? What if Reign would show up because of that?

The questions continued to pester him until Cy tapped Noel's shoulder. "You have the map, right? Mind if we chart out the ruins for tomorrow?"

Noel's fumbled reply allowed Grey to breathe a little easier, knowing now that he was distracted. He tugged off his gloves and quickly pulled his tin of charcoal out, immediately dirtying his hands with it to obscure the lingering, magic-worn stains.

Gentle, light lines of sooty black crossed the canvas in his starting outline. Every piece had its designated place, much like how he had his. He tried to shake that thought away as he retrieved his brushes and began messing with his pigments. Each color Grey brought to life gave him hesitation before touching it to the cloth. That small fear gripped his heart that he was a single stroke or dot away from failure—denial—destruction.

But flowers bloomed along the untouched white and vibrant green he loved so much, likening it to Noel's eyes. The blue had knotted his stomach until it reached that light, powdery hue since another face came to mind and taunted the recesses of his thoughts as if this little fragment of his soul poured out onto the canvas would never be enough. That he'd be doomed to surrender to them in the end. He supposed that's why he couldn't help but paint in a woman by the mirror-like pond, flowers dotting her hair. A nameless, faceless person that might as well be one of fair folk at a distance.

The colors started to fit together seamlessly, blending like an old, blurred photograph taken before the Wild Hunt had destroyed such blasphemous, man-made creations.

"It's beautiful," came a whisper beside him.

Grey jolted and whipped his head around to find Noel leaning against his knees, completely absorbed in his creation. Those green eyes flicked up to meet Grey's, and his entire body warmed.

"Th-thank you."

Noel scooted forward a little while Cy scratched her head over the map, completely oblivious to whatever Noel had decided to do. "Do you think you'll turn to painting when this is over?"

Grey released a quiet, disbelieving laugh. "I don't see many people wanting something this elaborate on its own."

"Anyone in the Grand Capital, maybe?" Noel asked with a wry smirk. "Imagine escaping this nightmare and throwing art in their faces as the biggest fuck you of all time."

Grey ducked his head and bit his lip, trying to suppress a smile. The thought of that felt *good* though—imagining metaphorically spitting in their faces because he had more worth than a sacrifice. Did he have more worth than that? He stared down at his painted meadow and glanced up at the real thing. So much more depth and charm sprung forth in a way he could never capture in a still landscape.

He shifted, laying the canvas onto the grass to soak up the sun and melt away the still-damp spots. "What about you two? What do you plan to give?"

Noel twisted a few blades of grass in his fingers and leaned back. "Cy and I plotted out a good path to explore some ruins first thing tomorrow."

Hearing Grey's name omitted from that trek made him quietly pick at the paint flecks and charcoal on his hands. They'd decided their cabin would be their home base for now, so he supposed it wasn't out of the question. "Am I staying behind?"

Noel opened his mouth. "O-only if you want to. You can come along, but I didn't want to assume one way or another since you've already exhausted yourself. And we can try our best to ward the shack while we're gone if you—"

"I wouldn't mind going." The words fell out on their own. Trying to imagine himself sitting in there all by himself while he waited for them both to return was an impossibility. He'd either go mad from Reign's attempts to find him somewhere beyond the safety of its walls or fret over every passing noise out of fear that the wardens had finally caught up to them. And then there was the possibility that they'd be caught or die in those ruins...

"You're sure? If you're not up to it—"

Grey shook his head. "I'd rather go than be alone right now. I'll try not to cause any trouble like last time if that's what you're worried about."

Noel sputtered. "No I—No, I'm not worried about that. I just..." He readjusted his sitting position and his hand moved from tugging at the grass to pinching the stem of a flower a little closer to Grey's knee. His face heated at the stray thought of him plucking it from the ground and sliding it behind his ear—a wishful daydream that popped when Noel's arm drew back. "I'm just worried about you."

Grey's heart crumbled at the sincerity in his voice, and he had to blink away the tears starting to burn his eyes. "I appreciate it," he whispered. "I appreciate everything you've done for me, even if I kept trying to give up on you."

"Well, this isn't the easiest thing to handle on our own, and you've certainly kept me on my feet longer than I expected to be. That's what friends do, right? Look out for each other?"

Grey turned his head to take in that soft, kind expression he'd always longed to see on Noel's face. It took everything in him not to fall into another hug or try something more daring he knew he shouldn't do because it'd undoubtedly break his heart. So instead, he made himself put on a small smile in agreement, unable to use that label for what they were, not when he secretly longed for more.

Caw.

Noel pushed himself from the floor of the shack with sleep still blurring his eyes. "Fucking bird," he muttered under his breath, careful not to wake Grey or Cy on his way to the foggy glass of the door. Sure enough, the little bastard sat perched in a tree on the edge of the small clearing, its beady red eyes piercing through the dark.

But no fair folk in sight. Nothing creeping around their makeshift campsite. Nothing tampering with the bikes. Nothing but the gentle sway of grass and indents where the iron wards met the soil from various scraps they'd salvaged the night prior when he and Cy had been on high alert and decided to see what they could find under the floorboards.

Noel ran a hand through his hair and stumbled back over to the rolled-out blanket, lying back down next to Grey. The horrible urge to brush away locks of his hair from his sleeping face was quickly overridden by yet another annoying *caw*, almost like Reign was challenging him to do it so they could bust down the door and restart their battle. He sighed and stared up at the ceiling, counting each beam until he drifted back off to sleep.

When he opened his eyes again, mist clung to the cloudy, thin shack windows. The creak of Cy's footsteps told him that either something was wrong, or he'd woken up at an acceptable time. He pushed himself up to find her crouched over her bag, rifling through its contents before she glanced back at him. The dark circles under her eyes told him it was about to be a rough day, especially when he noticed Grey still sound asleep.

"Are you oka—" he started in a whisper.

"There's a bird outside that kept me up, and I wanted to make sure that you two got enough rest."

Noel grimaced and crawled over to her, careful not to make too much noise in case it might break the spell she'd put on Grey. "Are you sure you're okay to do this today then? We can—"

"I'm fine," she snapped, wincing the second the words fell out. "I'm fine. I got enough strength from you two that we should be able to manage for today. I'm pretty sure this place is burned anyway if there's something out there watching us, and *yes*, that fucker is watching us. I know a fair folk spy when I see one."

Noel bit the inside of his cheek and stole another glance at Grey's form huddled on the blanket. Hands tucked to his chest, hood up, his face the only piece of him uncovered. A small piece of him was unable to keep himself from imagining Reign's black-and-blue eyes lighting up when they fixed on Grey. They *wanted* him. Bile crept up the back of his throat, his stomach clenching at the idea that perhaps not everyone died in the Wild Hunt—at least not right away. Just because they only sent one of them back as an example doesn't mean that the others hadn't suffered in whatever way the fair folk deemed fit.

He tried to shake it from his mind as he pushed himself to his feet. "I'll wake Grey, and we'll get out of here. No point in sticking around any longer if they might already know where we're at."

Noel's steps grew heavy on his way over to gently shake Grey awake, his heart squeezing at the groggy mumbling about what was happening. He helped him up, allowing himself to hold onto one of Grey's sleeve-clad hands after they collected their bags and started out to their bikes. Cy stripped away all the iron they'd used and tucked it away for later. By the time the engines sprang to life and they rolled away, it was like they'd never been there.

He would be lying if he'd said he hadn't noticed the raven following above them through the fog, or when it perched on a tree branch during their quick break to eat. Clearly Cy had noticed it too from the way she wolfed down her ration and knocked back a long drink of water before saying they needed to get a move-on.

It wasn't until they arrived that Noel felt more uneasy than he had the entire morning. They hadn't passed a single source of running water on the way here, and when he reached for Grey after they dismounted, he found he was wearing gloves. Despite how hard he tried not to think about the latter, he clung onto that horrible sensation biting at his nerves that said there was a lack of trust there—a lack of trust, or something far worse that drove Grey to putting those on after being so adamant not to borrow Noel's when they'd first met. A way of snuffing out one of his lines of direct defense in favor of his wild, somewhat unpredictable radial grasp onto anything and everything.

But Noel kept a firm hold on Grey's gloved hand as they started into the crumbling structures with Cy leading the way. The obscuring mist and spindly trees made him jump in his skin and half-shield Grey out of fear that spriggans were pulling themselves out of the facets of the stone and wood to reach for something to capture at the order of their fae masters. Grey kept close on his heels when they entered the sanctum: a smaller, more dilapidated shrine with cobwebs around the sacrificial altar.

Cy's flashlight beam roamed around the recesses of the boxy hall, running it over moth-eaten mats laid out like the rows of benches set up in his hometown's meeting house. Grey grabbed onto his arm as Noel started into one of the back rooms, where stacks upon stacks of locked crates remained untouched. She jiggled one of the locks and ran her thumb over the dust-coated, green-tinted metal with a hum. The metal bands binding the things together matched that sheen, reminding him of the blade he'd held back in the looters' crate when they'd tried to sell him his freedom at such a steep price.

"Need a key," Cy whispered, jerking the beam toward another corner of the room.

Grey tugged on Noel's arm to get his attention and pointed over to the small set of stairs through a broken-open door. He swallowed. The decision to leave him here with Cy or bring him up into the unknown second story of the building made him queasy, but he gently pried Grey's hands, as well as his own, away. "Stick close to her, okay? I'll be right back."

The hesitant nod that answered didn't instill much confidence in him, especially with that raven fluttering around nearby, but Grey started for Cy, and Noel headed for the steps. He slid the iron dagger from his boot and kept it at his side during the upward creep to a single doorway around the corner. A desk sat inside, facing an ornate, stained-glass window, where dirt and grime covered every panel.

Filtered, multicolored remnants of dim light through the fog illuminated the entire shelf of trinkets behind the worn, wooden chair. He picked up a glass bauble, turning it around until a sudden sharp *caw* ripped through the silence. Noel jumped. The orb fell from his hands and shattered on impact as he spun on his heel to find the dreaded creature perched on the ledge outside the window.

"You fucking—" he started, cut off by two pairs of footfalls clamering up the stairs.

"Noel, are you—" Grey stumbled into the room, Cy on his heels.

Caw.

Their heads snapped toward the fair folk's little alarm bell, and Grey tensed.

Cy gritted her teeth and moved past him. "This little mother-fucker," she hissed, slamming her fist against the window.

The raven fluttered back as Grey shot forward. "You shouldn't—"

"This damn bird is going to tattle and sick the fair folk on us again."

"That doesn't mean you should do *that*," Grey argued. "It'll just make them more aggressive."

She scoffed. "I'm pretty sure they're already plenty aggressive." She stepped back and glanced over to Noel. "What'd you break?"

He grimaced and looked down to the shards of glass at his feet. "Just some trinket, I think. Looked man-made. I think if there are still keys around to the chests downstairs, my bet is that they'll be up here."

"Then let's be quick about it," she said, striding over to the other side of the bookcase. "If that flying rat comes back, we might be fucked. Not to mention the fact that everything is relatively untouched makes me feel like there's something lurking nearby that no one wants to mess with."

Grey jogged over and started pulling open desk drawers while Noel and Cy scanned shelf after shelf before crouching down and opening up the lower cabinets. That sudden spike of adrenaline sharpened every sense—every part of him acutely aware of Grey's presence before they bumped shoulders and Noel's neck heated from Grey's mumbled apology.

Another set of cabinets flung open and Noel stilled. Tucked inside were several ornate boxes, their lids carved in intricate, whimsical designs that screamed fae-made. He lifted one out and ran his thumb over the inset lock, hissing and ripping his hand away at the sharp sting. When he turned up his palm, a bead of blood welled up on the pad of the offending finger. A second later though, the lock clicked. The entire room halted activity. Cy and Grey's neck craned as they tried to peer at what he was hunched over. Noel lifted the lid and gaped.

A dagger—one with an embellished handle of twisting faux-thorns and roses blooming around the hand-guard—sat on the plush, crimson cushion within. The blade itself gleamed with that greenish sheen like he'd noted from the other one he'd held all those days ago, but this one... This one was a pristine instrument in comparison.

"Holy shit," Noel breathed.

Grey reached for his hand, his glove peeled back from his palm to rest against his wrist until the dot of blood receded. The light outside the window shifted, some of the ivy drooping in his trade.

A wonderstruck grin pulled at Cy's lips as she dropped down next to them and grasped the box lid for a better look. "Damn that's beautiful too..."

"Yeah," Noel echoed, slowly closing it again. "Let's see if we can open a few more of these and find you something just as good."

Grey took the box, cradling it while Noel and Cy started retrieving leather-covered, wood, and stone containers, each etched with striking faerie designs. Some opened to coins, priceless gems, and vials of mysterious liquids while others refused to yield to their force.

Cy picked up a vial, the midnight-black contents oozing to the top when she tilted it and thousands of glittering specks shone like stars. "I don't know what the hell this is, but it'll have to do."

"You sure?" Noel asked with a frown. "We can find something else."

She shook her head. "There's... some sort of feeling with this one I can't quite explain. Something that my magic keeps drawing me to. If I'm going to bet my life on any single item, I feel like this one is as good as any." Cy shoved herself to her feet. "Let's go."

46

GREY

Grey kept close behind Noel and Cy on the way back out through the ruins, clutching the fae-dagger box close to his chest. Noel's ticket to freedom. In his arms. He worried the inside of his cheek and gripped it tighter when he noted Noel's blade still held at the ready. At least that explained why he wasn't trying to hold his hand again, even though Grey's heart had sank when he hadn't even tried on the way out.

The box, the iron dagger, Noel being on high alert—they were all rationales for Grey chew on and tell himself there was an explanation for every intimate action that inevitably resulted in *nothing*. After all, they were just trying to keep each other alive, right? His chin dipped against the side of the box, his gaze downcast until he bumped into Noel and stumbled backward with his heart pounding in his chest.

"S-sorry," he said. "I wasn't looking ahead."

"You're fine," Noel said over his shoulder, hoisting up Grey's bag to pass off to him. "If you could toss the box in yours for now, that would be ideal."

He nodded, despite Noel still being turned and hopping on the bike. Grey quickly crammed the box inside and climbed on at the rev of the engine, wrapping his arms around Noel and closing his eyes. Focusing on his breathing to eliminate the pulse pounding in his ears turned impossible. The wind tickled his hair as he rested his cheek against Noel's back and listened to the rush of the world falling away behind them.

No raven cries or ravenous faerie wolves. No pink-eyed fair folk with her razor-sharp grin nipping at their heels. No Reign and their taunting temptations for him to give up. For once, he could feel the freedom creeping ever-closer, but even that left him with so many more questions than when he began the trek for his Calling.

When the bikes pulled off of the main trail, Grey opened his eyes to the foggy cover of trees while Cy asked Noel for the map again.

"Why?" Noel's face scrunched up in confusion as he handed it off.

"Because I saw a spot on it yesterday that I'm pretty sure is the only fair folk shrine left in-tact since it's used by the Grand Capital. If we're going to sacrifice anything, I promise you it'll have to be there."

Noel scoffed. "There's no way in hell they'll let us near that thing. We're better off facing the two that are after us now and handing everything over."

"Yeah, and what about me?" Cy scowled. "Look, Noel, I know you might want to just throw everything at them and be done with it, but there's a *reason* why these places were erected. If we don't do this right, they might spit in our faces. We need to make these deals as formal as fucking possible or else they'll find a loophole to get us and the things we're trading for free." She waved the map at him before unfolding it on the handlebars.

Noel shifted and drummed on his knees. "So where is it? If it's *in* the Grand Capital, we're pretty much fucked."

She shook her head. "It's underground. That's where they tend to dwell in our realm, so it's dug into the other side of the mountain, facing the city. There's a pilgrimage for it and everything."

"And how do you know so much about this?"

Grey glanced up to Noel's weary look.

She forced a heavy, begrudging sigh through her nose. "Because," she said evenly, "I used to live in the slums outside of the Grand Capital. You hear a lot of shit over there, especially with all the fae-worshiping zealots..." Her fingertip landed on a point on the map right as she tilted it for Noel to see.

Noel raised his shoulders and bit his lip. "Do you happen to know how often it's occupied?"

Cy pushed away some of her hair and folded the map back up. "They only use it weekly I think. Outside of that, it might be lightly guarded, but if we distract them or disguise ourselves as spoiled Grand Capital brats, we should be able to get in. No problem." She half shrugged as she passed the map back.

"How the fuck are we going to get Grand Capital clothing without stepping foot in the city?" he asked, tugging the map from her hands. "I think our only option is to distract the guards, but even that's risky."

She sat a little straighter, her eyes lighting up. "*But* they wouldn't bother guarding it at night. No one goes out at night unless they have a death wish right? That's why we've been braving it. There's no point in guarding the shrine if no one would be crazy enough to head straight into the single place most influenced by the fair folk in the dark."

Hope welled up in Grey's chest, even before Noel started to nod. "That... could work."

"*And*," Cy said, grinning, "we have someone that's able to see in the dark." She winked, and Noel huffed out a short breath of a laugh. "So, think we can make it by nightfall to end this?"

47

NOEL

Noel tried not to rock back and forth as he and Cy refilled the bikes. Every passing second turned into agony, especially knowing that they were right at the finish line. He stole a glance over at Grey, hunched over on the steps of the same cursed fuel depot he'd been taken from mere night ago, a glove on his lap as he examined his hand. Whatever had been there, he quickly covered up by the time Noel discarded the fuel can by the door. Going inside with the growing stench of decay didn't sound like an experience he wanted to endure yet again.

"Are you okay?" Noel asked as Grey got up and dusted himself off.

"Y-yeah." He wrung his gloved hands, worry creasing his features. "Why?"

"You just seem... A little distracted." Like when he'd smacked into his back when they left the shrine. Noel tried to remind himself that Grey was wishing for death not all that long ago, but his recurring periods of silence put every part of him on edge. "It's okay if you're worried about this. I think we're all stressed about trying to get this done and over with but remember that you're not alone."

Grey hesitantly nodded and rubbed his arms, almost like he was staving off a chill in the lingering, eerie mist.

Cy dropped her fuel canister next to Noel's. "I think we're good for the final stretch. You two ready?"

Noel's eyes flicked to Grey, who bit his lip.

He cleared his throat. "Nervous, but I'm ready to be done with this."

"You planning to go back home, or...?" she asked, tilting her head while her arms folded over her chest.

It took everything in him not to steal another look at Grey. He felt Cy's scrutiny, like she was nudging him to let him spill his guts here and now, but he'd be lucky to get a squeak out with how badly his heart started to race. So he opted for a, "Maybe."

She rolled her eyes—the most subtle way to call him a coward before setting her sights on Grey. "And what about you?"

Grey stiffened, looking like a deer caught in a city guard's spotlight. "Um..." He squeezed his arms a little tighter. "I don't know. Probably home. Don't really have many options."

Noel's heart sank, but Cy patted Grey's shoulder and reassured him he'd figure it out. This was undoubtedly another way for Cy to needle at him, but she didn't direct any further jabs in his direction before climbing onto her bike.

Noel stepped in front of Grey. "Hey," he whispered, fighting back that urge to pull him into a hug and tell him he'd take him anywhere he wanted when this was over—a promise he wanted to make, despite wanting nothing more than to take him back to his parents and lie about every horror they'd encountered. A scenario in which he'd paint them this wonderful picture of the two of them meeting and becoming so intertwined in each other's lives that they'd have to accept him as another son. The easiest way to give Grey a family he deserved, but one he'd likely recoil from since they were macharomancers that watched hemomancers with hostile stares.

Grey's eyes met his, seemingly searching for the words Noel was trying to pull forth.

He held his tongue while he scavenged his mind for the right thing to say—the right sentiment for the moment that said just enough, but not too much to shatter everything between them. "If you don't want to go home after this, I can help you in finding somewhere else."

God, that sounds so needy. You don't really think he'll take you up on that, do you?

Grey looked away, his shoulders dropping ever-so-slightly with Noel's heart. "I don't want to trouble you anymore. I think if this has taught me anything, it's that I'm better off staying with other hemomancers. I'm... I'm glad I met you though."

The way his face lifted again made Noel's chest tighten. Here he was, so close to letting it all spill out, and he'd fumbled it. His throat closed when he tried to ready a question and another—all of them related to something closer to his true feelings, skirting that fine line he didn't want to cross until this curse was broken, at the very least. So he settled for the one thing he could bring himself to say: "I'm glad I met you too."

*C*oward.

That was the sole thought looping through Noel's mind during the winding paths cutting through the woods. Every other sound of rustling or eyes glinting somewhere in the depths of the darkness rolled off his back with that single damn word. And it crushed his heart when Grey held on even tighter, like their world might erupt into one last fury of fair folk trying to stop them from escaping their twisted snare.

But it wasn't dark yet. Whatever lurked just beyond their vision was waiting for the next couple hours to slip by to when they were plunged into the cover of night. Not that the time of day really mattered when they were heading straight toward a den of vipers dressed in finery calling for their blood. Or people like Cavan seeking to use them for selfish gains—a trade in which he would've lost nothing, only to gain something in return.

His hands tightened on the handles, his body leaning forward to match Cy's increasing speed. The world flew past in a flurry of greens and grays, the mist dispersing in their wake, as if it were finally bending to their will.

Across a bridge, down another winding path, following the bend that sloped down and around the mountainside, the Grand Capital's hulking, white-stone walls came into view during the descent. He could crush it with his thumb, but the sheer sight of it from this height made his stomach twist. It grew smaller during the downward hurtle until it was enveloped by foliage stretching between them.

Cy rolled to a stop along the widened dirt path, glancing back at Noel as he glided forward to catch up.

"Something wrong?" he asked, feeling Grey shift at his back.

Her eyes flicked skyward in her brief pause. "We should find a place nearby where we can watch the entrance. I don't think it's going to be dark enough by the time we get there."

Noel took in the cascading, orange-tinted hue of twilight, biting down on his tongue. "You don't happen to know of a good stake-out spot, do you?"

Cy grimaced. "Not really... Skirting the edge of the woods might be our best option, even though it's a risky one."

Grey's arms squeezed a little tighter around him again, that fear cascading into Noel until he willed it back.

"Take us as far out as you can while keeping it in view, and then I guess we'll work our way through the woods from there."

She nodded, her engine revved again, and her bike cut in front of him. Cy's head-first dive into the unknown made Grey suck in a sharp breath, but Noel reached to give one of his arms a reassuring squeeze before shooting after her.

The claustrophobic mess of this untraveled path made Noel's vision tunnel to the next turn and the next until Cy slowed again at the edge of the tree line. Orange began to dip into that pinkish hue, still too bright for last-minute stragglers not to be on the road. The evidence of that was clear when the rumble of another vehicle sounded ahead. They rolled further back into the trees and behind the cover of leaves as a polished black car rolled past, windows rolled down for them to take in the clean-cut Grand Capital members lounging inside.

Cy muttered something under her breath Noel didn't quite catch, outside of a couple choice words like *motherfuckers* and *bastards* before they vanished from view again. Noel began his slow countdown, his heart pounding wildly as he strained to listen for any other signs of remaining travelers heading for shelter.

"I think we're clear," he breathed after a prolonged, uneasy silence.

Cy nodded in agreement and nudged forward again, turning sharply to run parallel with the road while keeping concealed by the trees. The pinkish hue dipped to a lilac during the crawl, only to be interrupted by one more rumble.

He peered out ahead of them as Grey sat up straighter, his body twisting behind him before he breathed Noel's name and a tug on his jacket. Noel whipped his head around to the silver van tearing through, the Grand Capital emblem painted on the doors and hood.

"Fuck me," Noel hissed, zipping behind cover before they reached them.

Grey's trembling offset the idle vibrations of the bike, turning Noel into another shaking mess until the van fell out of sight. He shot forward until he found Cy glancing around just up ahead.

"What the hell?" he hissed. "What was—"

She shook her head. "I don't know."

Her bike lurched forward, rocketing ahead with far less

subterfuge than before. Every scrap of caution quickly abandoned in favor of satiating curiosity. Grey winced at the hurtle of Noel's pursuit, but all he could focus on now was another variable potentially throwing one final wrench into their plans.

The rounded entry drive leading to the metallic-green gates barring the mouth of the stone-arched entrance to the mountain was cluttered with people in stark white uniforms and crimson Grand Capital emblems on their sleeves.

"Shit," Cy hissed as the uniformed individuals passed by each other—the set by the doors heading for the van while the one by the van strode toward the doors.

"What?" Grey asked, his breathy question tickling Noel's ear as he craned his neck to peer past him. Instead of the good shivers of him being so incredibly close, the panicked, bone-chilling kind replaced it.

"Guard change," she said. "They're swapping out macharomancers. Are you fucking kidding me? Why bother putting anyone out here when—"

The van's engine turning over solidified that horrible realization that they'd have to fight their way in or prolong this curse to find another solution. Gravel crunched under tires as the previous shift left, right as the sky's lilac deepened into a velvety shade that called forth the night.

Cy turned off her motorcycle and dropped her bag in the grass. "Leave your shit here," she ordered. "Only take your trades and haul ass inside the second I lead them away."

"*What?*" Grey's distressed snap of a reply practically slashed through Noel as he turned to face her, donning a mask of horror.

"Cy, you *can't*," Noel ground out.

"I can, and I fucking *will*." She hopped off and crouched down to pluck out the black, glittering vial. "I'll circle back when

I lose them and duck inside then. Be quick. The altar's bound to be in the far back. Drop your shit, pray, and get the hell out once you're done. Don't agree to anything else outside of that trade because whatever fair folk creature greets you in there will absolutely try to do that."

Noel fumbled with his keys and scrambled off his motorcycle to stop her. "How are you so sure? What if—"

"The dark shit the Grand Capital gets up to spreads quickly the second it leaks from the wall. Trust me on this. Whatever greets you, play nice with it and *run.*"

He didn't even get the chance to seize her arm before she sprinted out of the woods and onto the gravel. His blood ran cold as she jogged up toward them and one of the guards loudly demanded her identification. Grey's boots hit the grass behind him, his bag dropping next to Noel while he rifled through it for a wooden box and a rolled swatch of canvas.

Cy's voice rose, curses spilled out, and the guards advanced on her. Grey's whispered pleadings for her to run fell on the wrong ears, but she bolted the opposite direction. Noel's legs locked up for the briefest moment, unable to convince himself to move until Grey started past and grabbed a fist-full of his jacket sleeve.

She'd done this for them—for Noel to play the part of the hero that he'd already fumbled at the starting line. He pushed down that piece of him that revolted at treading inside a Grand Capital monument and grabbed Grey's hand. Soon, this would be nothing but a bad dream. Because it had to be.

49
GREY

Grey's heart hammered in his chest when he tugged on the gate. It clanged in protest against its catch. *No, no, no—*

Noel reached past him and gasped where the lock was holding it until a *click* flooded Grey with another fresh shot of adrenaline. He tore it open and ushered Grey inside.

Dim light bounced off the domed, metal-plated ceiling of the entryway, diffusing the circular hall in an eerie, green ethereal glow. Each mancer symbol glimmered at his feet from silver tiles set into a large hexagon—a mimicry of the obelisk they'd stood face-to-face with so many nights ago. Heavy curtains framed the door up ahead, its darkened room beyond making Grey clutch his and Noel's sacrifices a little tighter. Noel led the way, iron dagger kept at his hip. Grey fell in step behind.

The inner sanctum stopped him dead in his tracks once his eye adjusted to the dim lighting. Rows upon rows of benches spread out like waves from the dais at the far side, their cushions upholstered with crushed velvet and armrests carved with woodland creatures. Everything had a freshly polished or cleaned sheen to it, not a single speck of dust in sight. How could he walk out of here and live his life again after knowing that so much time was poured into *this?* An overembellished, empty monument while people like Cy scavenged for scraps.

"Grey?"

The echoing whisper of his name made every muscle grow taut. He fixed his gaze on Noel's eyes and hurried forward. "Sorry," he mumbled. "I just got... a little distracted by—"

"All this?" Noel asked, half motioning to the tapestries hanging from the dark wooden ceiling beams. "It's a little fucking over the top. We just need to hurry it up and get the hell out of here."

Grey forced himself to nod and kept up the pace on Noel's way to the dais, hesitantly climbing up the steps after him. No altar. Just a raised platform with heavy curtains around the half-circular recess it notched into the wall. Noel frowned and slowly spun around, taking it all in, but Grey's sights narrowed on a slight part in the two curtains in the dead center. He crept forward and pulled one of the curtain panels back.

Two round door pulls. A curved door, split in two. Noel was already at his side, peeling back the other panel and taking the wooden box from under Grey's arm. "Ready?"

The urge to say no and bolt out the doors slammed into Grey like a wall. There was a possibility that Reign was lounging on the other side, reclining in a chair with a pleased smile that Grey had walked straight into their domain. So he pushed down his instinctive answer and shoved his side open, Noel quickly mirroring the action.

A flat, wooden slab, looking stripped straight from the largest trees he'd ever seen, sat cradled by chiseled stone. Behind it, a pitch-black form sat in a chair with its back reaching out on either side like a pair of antlers. Glowing gold eyes fixed on them as the shadow settled in the seat and leaned forward with seemingly corporeal elbows against the wooden altar—almost like an office desk.

The rumbling purr thrummed through Grey with a deeper cadence than Reign, sending an uneasy shiver through him. "Step inside. We have sacrifices to discuss, do we not?"

Noel exchanged a short glance with Grey before they walked in. Cy's reminders thundered in his thoughts until the doors slammed shut. He yelped and spun around, panic seizing him in a split second with every alarm bell ringing uncontrollably in his head.

"*Quiet.*" The command echoed off the walls, clamping Grey's mouth shut. "Face me, hemomancer."

Grey trembled as he turned around, watching the shadow's fingers drum against the altar before their gold irises slid over to Noel.

"You there—macharomancer, have you come to make me a deal?"

Noel started forward, the box in his hands scraping against the stand as he set it down and lifted the lid for the creature to peer inside. "I'm offering this in exchange for my exclusion from the Wild Hunt."

A velvety, bemused chuckle filled the chamber, making Grey's hair stand on end. "A clever little iron-wielder, aren't you?" The box snapped shut on its own and darkness consumed it in a heart-beat. "You are hereby released from the Wild Hunt, little one."

Grey's head spun as Noel looked back at him with wide eyes and a growing smile on his face. They'd done it. They were going to walk away from this. He quickly stepped back as Grey rushed forward to unroll his canvas on the altar, his heart racing as the shadow hummed.

"I'm also offering in exchange to be released from the Wild Hunt," Grey said as evenly as he could, trying to tamp down his growing nerves with each passing second.

"I see..." The creature's hand traced the tree line, the mirror-like pond, and then it stopped on the woman peering into it. "A shame, really."

Grey swallowed, fighting back the urge to ask what was a shame while he fidgeted with his gloved fingers.

"Such talent for a human. Truly a waste." The creature snapped its fingers, and the canvas erupted into a flurry of blooming flowers and grass eating up every inch of it, spilling out onto the floor.

Grey and Noel danced back as the shadow stood from the chair. "Anything created from human hands isn't worthy of trade, dear boy."

His stomach dropped, and the room began to stretch in his vision. "What?" he breathed, unable to comprehend what this fae creature had just said.

A cruel laugh bubbled up from the shadow's form. "Foolish thing, you offered a scrap of yourself. Do you truly think that's something worthy?"

Noel stepped forward. "Then free him from the Hunt and take me instead."

Grey's heart caught in his throat. "No!" He grabbed Noel's arm, his entire body shaking. "Please don't—"

The shadow sneered. "Didn't I just say nothing human was

worthy? You can either take the offer, or you can face the hunting grounds, macharomancer."

Grey let go, stumbling back as tears filled his eyes. How foolish to think anything he could create would be taken as an offering. Reign had planted that false hope and idea in his mind to trap him.

"There's still time," Noel said. "We can go back to—"

Shouts rang out in the inner sanctum, and the shadow cackled. "I'm afraid your time is up, so what will you choose? I can pardon you when I open those doors, or..."

Grey buried his face in his hands, gritting his teeth and blocking out everything crumbling around him. Of course it'd come to this—of course the Wild Hunt would still drag him in.

Something clamped around his wrists, pulling them away to take in Noel's green eyes peering back at him. "I'm going with you."

"Don't—" Grey cried, the rest of his pleading cut off by a sudden, world-shattering kiss.

Everything dulled as he squeezed his eyes shut and reached for Noel's hands now cupping his face. He wasn't sure if he'd tumbled into a dream or nightmare anymore until his senses finally gripped him and pushed Noel away, panting.

"Take it back!" he screamed, his vision glossing over. "Please take it back. I can't lose you too—"

The door vibrated with a heavy *thump* as the shadow cackled again. "It's no wonder Reign hisses when they speak of you, little iron-wielder. You're playing a very dangerous game even before the Hunt with that sort of affection toward their object of desire."

Noel's head whipped around, and his dagger slid from under his jacket. He lunged at the shadow, slicing at it right after it dissolved into a cauldron of ravens shooting outward. Grey ducked and dropped into a crouch, his body shaking uncontrollably, even as Noel covered him and tangled a hand in his hair.

"I'm not leaving you. I don't care if you hate me, but I can't let them drag you away by yourself."

A tortured, hopeless sob erupted from Grey, and then the doors flew open.

❦ 50 ❦

GREY

Noel's scream of fury when he was pried away pierced him like a knife to the heart. The clatter of Noel's dagger against the floor was the second blow. All the fight had left Grey by the time the guards ripped him to his feet and tied his arms behind his back. He tamped down a twisted, morbid giggle that he'd been so generous as to wear gloves for them this time around.

"Grey—Grey, look at me," Noel demanded, trying to struggle free as he was hauled through the door to the dais.

"Shut the fuck up," one of the guards spat.

Grey's head spun too wildly for him to focus on anything but the flurry of black birds zipping across the ceiling and out an opened, stained-glass window at the top of the altar room's tower. A cruel thing sent by Reign or not, that creature had broken the last thread holding on for the possibility of a different future. Now, whatever waited in the Otherworld would decide his fate.

He didn't resist when the guards dragged him after Noel, stopping occasionally due to a couple outbursts and strings of choice words before they made it outside. The cover of night greeted them, enveloping Grey in its cold embrace. They shoved Noel in the back of the van and held him down while they chained his ankles to one of the two long, grated metal benches inside. Grey's guards helped him up instead, working around the two still pinning Noel down across from him, like he was some sort of wild animal.

Two resounding *clicks*, and Noel's guards hopped out. The doors slammed shut behind them, dropping them into darkness.

"Grey," Noel panted, the bench creaking as he leaned forward like he wanted to reach out and touch him if it weren't for his arms at his back. "Please say something—*anything*."

"I'm so stupid," Grey whispered, warm tears sliding down his face. "I don't know why I thought that would be enough."

"You couldn't have known. We weren't even sure if—"

"You should've let that thing pardon you," Grey blurted. "I'm not fucking worth it, Noel. I'm not fucking worth *anything*."

"Shhh..."

Another heaving sob tumbled out through Noel's cooing and consoling whispers.

"You are the gentlest person I've ever met. I *wanted* to protect you after we escaped, and you offered me something for my trade. I started to fall for every little kind gesture and rare smile—"

Grey's tears slipped out faster with another wracking sob as he shook his head and the words tumbled out with increasing malice. "You deserve someone who isn't a useless, deformed, blood-rending—"

Chains clinked, as if Noel was teetering on the edge of his seat. "An adorable, brilliant, multi-talented healer that I'd love nothing more than to give my love to because you deserve it."

Grey sniffed and bowed his head, letting whatever tears he had left fall free.

"I understand if you don't feel the same way about me, but—"

A quiet, bitter laugh interrupted his sulking, accompanied by another sniffle. "You probably had every macharomancer flocking to you back home. There's not much about you *not* to like."

"But do you?" Noel asked, that careful, prodding question needling at Grey.

"Why do you care so much?" he rasped. "I just said you could practically have anyone you want."

"But I want *you*."

Grey clamped his mouth shut, tensing as the doors swung closed at the front of the van while orders were belted out. The vehicle shook and the back overhead light flicked on with the start of the engine.

He couldn't stop himself from staring into the green radiating out from his pupils in the shock of sudden brightness. Noel's brow creased with worry like Grey was about to punch him in the chest.

"I'm afraid," Grey finally choked out. "I don't want to lose someone else I love."

Noel's face crumpled. "If I'm doomed to die, I want to be with the person I love in my final hours because I'll be far less afraid. Then neither of us will lose each other. We'll go together to whatever waits for us at the end."

The van lurched forward, and Grey swayed with Noel from the force.

"I love you, Grey," he whispered, ripping Grey's heart in two. "I've loved you for a while, but I was too much of a coward to say it. I've wanted more than your friendship, even when I declared it. So, do you love me too?"

Grey's mouth quivered, his vision blurring again as he nodded, wishing more than anything he could curl up in Noel's arms. "I love you."

Noel's soft, kind smile felt like a warm blanket being wrapped around him as he uttered the last words of their ride: "Then we'll see the end together."

MORE BY CARA NOX

For an up-to-date list of all of Cara Nox's books visit their website:

caranox.com/books

ACKNOWLEDGMENTS

Oh boy, this page always seems like the most intimidating one to write in the entire book because it feels impossible to express my gratitude toward so many people that helped me bring this story to life.

Melli, thank you for helping me realize I accidentally wrote a romantasy—the one thing I never imagined writing in my entire career. Cybil, I owe you my life with your feedback and support. Menoa, please don't eat glass because of this book! I promise I'll make it up in the next two! Jake, I've absolutely loved reading your reactions to all the tropes, twists, and turns that gave me a confidence boost. Freddie, it was wonderful to have you sit and chat with me during edits, as well as giving me the extra push of motivation I needed this time around. Dominique, thank for you encouraging me to keep writing this book (and simping over Reign).

Thank you to all my friends who allowed me to slowly open up to my queer identity over the past decade. This is the first of many with characters that don't fit the binary, much like myself.

And finally, as always, thank you, the reader of this book. Without you, I wouldn't be making my childhood dream a reality: to introduce others to weird and wonderful worlds.

ABOUT THE AUTHOR

Cara Nox is an urban and science fantasy writer, combining their love of magically-inclined chaotic idiots and modern/futuristic tech. They also love mysteries, thrillers, and anything that draws inspiration from stars. Cara works as a web developer by day, holds BA in Japanese Language and Literature they occasionally use to read video game announcements, and resides in Ohio with their younger sister and two black cats.

For more information on all of their books, visit **caranox.com**.

To find some of their newest works-in-progress, bonus content, serialized stories, where they're at on social media, how to get deals on their current and upcoming works, and where to preview the first few chapters of their other books, visit **caranox.com/ links**.